WHEN STARS ALIGN

WHEN STARS ALIGN

A Novel

MELISSA
DE LA CRUZ

MINDY'S BOOK STUDIO

Text copyright © 2025 by Melissa de la Cruz
All rights reserved.

Published by Mindy's Book Studio, New York

www.apub.com

Amazon, the Amazon logo, and Mindy's Book Studio are trademarks of Amazon.com, Inc., or its affiliates.

ISBN-13: 9781662526541 (hardcover)
ISBN-13: 9781662526534 (paperback)
ISBN-13: 9781662525353 (digital)

Cover design Alicia Tatone
Cover images: © XiXinXing / Getty; © ProfessionalTextures / Adobe Stock;
© wendy laurel, © Liliya Rodnikova / Stocksy

Printed in the United States of America
First edition

For Mike and Mattie, always

A NOTE FROM MINDY KALING

I have a soft spot for those peak celebrity culture years of the early 2000s. The pop music, the paparazzi shots, the fake tans, the teen magazines . . . all before social media took over completely.

And now I've found the perfect book to capture that time. Melissa de La Cruz's *When Stars Align* is an entertaining and poignant coming-of-age story about three young celebrity friends (a singer, an actress, and a daughter of a billionaire) who go through the ups and downs of fame in the glaring eye of the media spotlight. Over the course of three decades, they live their lives to the fullest, while fighting their inner demons, and finally find redemption later in life.

The story grabbed me from the beginning with the amazing portrayal of young women who are learning life's lessons in the public eye. I love the novel's fresh take on how these stories are told—with more empathy and understanding—and I'm so excited to be publishing it as part of Mindy's Book Studio.

PROLOGUE

2004

At the peak of it all, when the money came easily and the crowds were fawning and their bodies were young and naturally stunning, it all felt possible. Those heady, sultry nights in West Hollywood felt like ascending to the height of a Ferris wheel in a blur of noise, color, and mystery cocktails that made your heart fly and your body feel as though you were barely hanging on to the quickly spinning Earth.

Tonight was one of those nights.

It was midnight. The three girls were on their way to the party; everyone knew it. The sudden onslaught of paparazzi signaled their imminent arrival, like pilot fish preceding sharks. Cars and motorcycles swarmed the street in front of the midcentury modern house in the Hollywood Hills, some photographers even being so bold as to sneak past the gate and enter the yard on foot. But security was lax that night—the sprawling, angular house was ablaze with color and strings of lights that adorned every inch of its gable roof. The walls of glass showed off the expensive interior, a floor littered with balloons and packed with partygoers, and a DJ at turntables that boomed bass across the teeming water of the pool in the backyard. This was a place that wanted to be seen. Ogled, even.

A final wave of paparazzi screamed around the corner, parking haphazardly on the curb and tumbling out with car doors left open.

They had driven at top speed to beat the limo they'd overtaken from a private club on Sunset, and now they knelt on the pavement with cameras raised and shuttering as it pulled up.

The limo moved almost silently amid their clamor, but one of the back windows cracked open to reveal shrieking laughter and a rich interior.

The photographers followed it up the drive, pushing forward in a crush as it finally came to a stop. The doors swung wide.

One by one, three young women climbed out of the limo, teetering on sky-high heels and shimmering in minidresses that caught every flash of the cameras.

"3AM Girls!" one man bellowed. "This way! Over here!"

The girls grinned as they surveyed the crowd, slightly unfocused, too many men shouting for a single one to hold their attention for long. In three short years, they'd come a long way from their days together on the Blast Off! Network's *Kidz Klub* show, acting in silly comic sketches, dancing in matching T-shirts, and belting out cheesy Broadway-style songs to a live studio audience.

They learned an important lesson from a young age: attention gets you love, gets you roaring applause, gets you adoration and money and fame. So they didn't mind the suggestive tabloid nickname, *3AM Girls*, the kind of girls you meet in humid back rooms of parties, the nocturnal kind who come alive only at night, whom you'd never bring home to your mother—much less mention in polite conversation. They flashed the crowd as they wriggled from limos, sans underwear in barely there dresses, ready to slip behind the velvet rope of a VIP room or strut around the pool of some hotshot's mansion.

The youngest flipped her long auburn hair over a bare shoulder and showed off her gold-lamé clutch to the photographers.

"Miranda! Look at me, sweetheart! Let's have a pose!"

And Miranda Montana did as she was told. Tall and striking at only seventeen years old, she'd garnered attention with her exuberant acting and sharp timing on the Blast Off! channel. She'd already become a fan favorite in a number of family and comedy films since then and, armed with a smattering of awards, was poised to break out at the box office. With the fame came her easy transformation into a wild child, never too far from a bottle of champagne and the arm of a handsome young actor or trust-fund boy, and ready to unleash her "spicy" temper on whichever of them wronged her.

Tonight, that boy was eighteen-year-old Zane Blue, son of a retired rock musician and his *much* younger Venezuelan wife. Zane tumbled from the limo, ran a hand through his mop of hair, and tugged at his oversize T-shirt as he draped an arm around Miranda. He was a somebody because of his money alone, which he spent on premium weed and the latest video games.

Miranda and Zane made such a cute couple, everyone said. The tabloids were plastered with high-contrast images of their baby faces, gazing at each other or smiling for the cameras.

Everyone also said they wouldn't last a week.

Less eager to smile was Germaine St. Germaine-Chang as she frowned at her Motorola next to Zane, acting as though she hardly noticed the paps. Unlike the minuscule clutches the other girls carried, she had slung around her shoulder a chunky, bright-pink bag, from which a tiny pointed snout stuck out.

"Hush, Milano," she cooed, kissing the nose of the Yorkie. At twenty years old, the daughter of international hotel moguls was rich enough to have shod Milano and his many siblings in Louboutins if she wanted to. Germaine was the best dancer on the *Kidz Klub* crew, lithe and acrobatic. Nowadays, however, she did more shopping than dancing, and her tastes—and whims—could make or break a hotel, club, store, designer, or restaurant. Everyone knew the story of the five-star chophouse that had mixed up her tomato bisque with another customer's french onion soup: they had shuttered within the month.

A fresh wave of shutter clicks sounded as another person emerged—Sicily Bell, nineteen and smiling sweetly, always the last out of the limo, always tugging at her dress and laughing. Her thick blond hair curtained her face for a moment as she struggled with her heel, but she straightened and blew kisses to the photographers, ducking shyly behind the others. In her glittery pink dress and choker with the heart-shaped pendant, Sicily looked the very picture of the petite girl next door. The tabloids had been trying for quite some time to unearth dirt on her personal life, hinting at forthcoming exposés about her all-controlling, restrictive family and how they strove to rebrand her hot-child-in-the-city image.

But that family didn't seem to mind it when she was onstage, transforming into the world's sexiest singer. And they didn't seem to mind that she was in tonight's spotlight.

The girls and Zane made their way to the door of the mansion, laughing as they skirted the crowd, high on life—or maybe something else.

As if on cue, the three women stopped and threw backward glances to the cameras that surrounded them, pouting and twisting their bodies to display the right angle. That night, everyone wanted to see them. Everyone wanted to know every single detail of their lives, from the line of flared yoga pants they wore to their hair products to the brand of designer water they drank.

They were starlets, on the brink of becoming stars.

"Miranda!" one man bellowed. "Is Zane the love of your life? What do you think?"

"Wouldn't you like to know!" she yelled back, and the three dissolved into a fit of giggles. *The love of your life*—TLOYL—they would splash that acronym over the front pages of all their tabloids. Zane only blinked into the flashing lights, smiling a lazy, wide grin, response slow from uncertainty or whatever substance he was on.

With one last pose, the women waved goodbye with manicured fingers and disappeared into the house. It didn't matter how late they stayed out or what day of the week it was. That night was like all other nights for the 3AM Girls, riding the momentum of one party and waiting until the next started.

After all, girls just wanted to have fun.

4

But when you reached the top of the Ferris wheel, the only way to go was down.

Gradually, the paparazzi retreated from the yard, through the gate, and back into the steaming, shadowed streets. They had their photos. Tonight it was the 3AM Girls; last year it was someone else. Next year would bring fresh blood. This wasn't Neverland, after all; it was Hollywood—where nothing lasts. Not fame, not youth, not friendship, not fun. Even the Hollywood sign was looking shabby lately.

No one knew it then, but that night would be the last time the three girls ever rode in a limo together to a party.

The clock was ticking . . .

PART I

ONE

MIRANDA

2006

Miranda does not want to be here.

The chairs are hard plastic, no cushions. They're set up in a circle, for "equality," and she hates that everyone can see her face and she can see theirs. If the chairs were in rows like a regular classroom, Miranda could focus on the back of someone else's head instead of the fact that she *knows* everyone is looking at her. She doesn't want to be looked at. It's one of the main reasons she's taken to wearing hooded sweatshirts and large sunglasses, Anna Wintour–style. They have the added benefit of curbing the headaches brought on by the oppressive, fluorescent lights of Horizons, the expensive Miami rehab center where she's been sent "for her own good." Plus, they hide the red eyes and the puffiness brought on by tears and long sleepless nights.

Everything makes Miranda irritable here. She hates the politeness of the staff. Hates the way they enunciate, like they're talking to children. Hates how loud the clock ticks and how the silverware in the cafeteria is all bent and beat up and the way her skin feels itchy all the time. She has a permanent headache.

"We don't inquire about people's personal lives unless they freely share it." Deirdre, the facilitator with the build of a linebacker and the demeanor of a librarian, has raised her voice. With a start, Miranda realizes that Deirdre is casting a concerned look at her.

"What?" Miranda says.

But it's Henry, another inpatient with a Jersey accent, who had apparently spoken. "I said, weren't you Miranda Montana? Back in the day? I'm just saying." He rubs his nose, fixes her with a squinting look. "If not, you're a dead ringer for her."

There's a silence that stretches thin and taut. They're not supposed to ask each other direct questions during group share time, but Henry's one for pushing the envelope. And Miranda knows the others have been giving her sideways glances, surely wondering the same thing.

Fine. So what if they know it's her? They're idiots if they haven't figured out her identity by now. Miranda's fall from grace was as public as they get, and there were paparazzi in the parking lot the day she arrived at Horizons, no matter how confidential her stay was.

"Yes, Henry," she snaps. A familiar ache flares at the base of her neck, near her skull. "I still *am* Miranda Montana."

Henry snorts. "Yeah. Okay. In the legal sense, I guess."

The room's tension works its way into Miranda's muscles, making her body feel warm and tightly wound. The anger comes even easier these days. "What the hell is that supposed to mean?"

"Miranda," Deirdre cautions.

Henry holds up both his hands. "Don't mean anything by it. I was just saying how I'm a businessman. Even when my using brought my whole business down, I still wasn't at rock bottom. Your name is Miranda Montana, sure, but the *brand* Miranda Montana was your business. I'm trying to make a point. Both of us shot our businesses in the foot. Our reputations."

Miranda stares at him. "You can't say that to me." She turns to Deirdre. "He can't say that to me, right?"

"Henry, let's try to keep a constructive dialogue—" Deirdre begins.
"I can say whatever I want," Henry interrupts. "Look, I'm trying
to help you here."

"I don't need your help!" Miranda says. Her leg has been bouncing
without her realizing it, and now the energy of it propels her to stand.

"This is such bullshit—"

"That's your problem, you know?" Henry says, starting to sound
short himself. "That's everyone's problem here. You think you don't
need help, that it's someone else's fault that you're in Miami, that it's
not *your* fault you collapsed on the boardwalk with no underwear on
and your dress over your head in the middle of the Santa Monica—"

Two things happen at once, and he never finishes his sentence.
First, Miranda crosses the circle in one step and slaps her hand hard
across Henry's face. Second, Deirdre leaps out of her chair and pins
Miranda's arms to her side in one swift movement.

"HEY!" Deirdre barks. "That is *not* what we do here!"

Miranda feels Deirdre's fingers dig into her biceps and tries to shove
the facilitator off. Deirdre lets go but places herself between Miranda
and Henry as he groans. She fixes Miranda with a frightening glare that
is very unlike a librarian.

"You know this, Montana. This is meant to be a safe, constructive
space, and you have *got* to get that temper under control if you're going
to do any healing. You're going to go to your room and think about
what you did. You want to act like a child and throw a tantrum? You
get treated like a child, too. Go."

The heat coursing through Miranda's body rises to her face,
coloring her earlobes and round cheeks in the same way it did when she
was younger. As if anyone's taught her how to be anything but a child.
Aware of every eye on her back, Miranda turns for the door, making
sure to slam it as hard as she can on her way out.

∽

In her room, Miranda lies face down on her cot with the sheet like a paper towel, trying to ride out the wave of rage overtaking her. But Henry and his stupid face swim before her eyes, exaggerated and mean. *Weren't you Miranda Montana? Back in the day?* Miranda could spit. How could there be a "back in the day" when she was still a teenager, only a few months shy of her nineteenth birthday?

She wonders how many people end up in rehab before their twenty-first.

Henry's wrong. Miranda *can't* be blamed for ending up here. She's barely an adult in society's eyes, and didn't this shit start years ago? Well, whose fault is that? Would they drag a thirteen-year-old into Horizons and demand that she take responsibility for her actions?

In her twisted position on the bed, Miranda's ankle begins to ache. It's an old injury she'd gotten on set, a short fall from a prop balcony that wasn't built to regulation. She should have sued. She knew that now, and her mother would have done it if she'd been paying any attention to reality, but no one looked out for Miranda back then. No one seemed to think anything else was important except that she ice it and get back on it as quickly as possible, or production schedules would run behind. And she didn't want that, did she?

Can I give her some Advil? the producer had asked Miranda's mother.

For some reason, Miranda remembers that her mother was wearing a swishy black corset top that day. It was something new she was trying—something to make her look younger. Miranda thought she looked like Ursula the sea witch.

Sure, whatever you think will help, Bobbie had said, shrugging, uncertainly tugging at the top's laces.

Whatever it was that she was given, Miranda is pretty sure in hindsight that it hadn't been Advil. Advil doesn't make you feel floaty, like your head is a balloon. But in the moment, it was a quick, effective fix.

So no one cared when Miranda's injury turned out to be a bone fracture that needed surgery, and her mother didn't scrutinize what she was taking on set. From there it was a short step to self-medicating and figuring out where to get more painkillers after her prescription ran out. All anyone cared about was the production schedule. And why shouldn't Miranda take what made her feel better? She knew her body best.

Besides, how did they expect her to sing, dance, jump through every hoop since the age of five without that stuff? It was exhausting work. Meds to numb physical pain, champagne to keep things positive—not to mention cocaine to wind down after twelve hours on set, doing the same emotionally taxing scene over and over again, and then to wind up again when you had to be back at it the next day. It was basically standard practice in the industry. Everyone mixed their own cocktails to get through a job. And weren't you supposed to have a little fun when you were a teenager and had plenty of money to splash around?

Now, for some reason, they were telling her she'd done it all wrong. Misstepped, overstepped, didn't hide it well enough. Miranda was just one of the weak ones, apparently, who started letting the facade slip to the public. It was a trickle that turned into a deluge once the supposed TLOYL, Zane, came on the scene, ramping up her partying and acting like a big shot, having her on his arm. A little fun became chaos real quick. Name-calling and screaming matches in clubs, the public humiliations that Henry had so kindly mentioned, Miranda crashing her beloved Porsche on Lincoln Boulevard. And the paparazzi were there to capture every bad decision and wrong move. They ate it up like dogs.

So no, it wasn't her fault. Not at all.

Miranda takes a deep breath and fishes her phone out from under her pillow, flipping it open. She finds the most recent message that Bobbie sent over two weeks ago, when Miranda realized she was being taken to rehab. Only three words: Sorry. Luv u.

Miranda glares at it, sucks her teeth, and types: Im bettr now. Want 2 come home

She hits "Send," waits. But five minutes pass, then more, and her phone remains silent. Bobbie is in tough-love mode right now, mandated by her own therapist, and is probably discussing the text in a session this very moment.

And Miranda can't text the love of her life, because he's in prison for dealing weed—small-time stuff, but some judge wanted to make an example of rich kids like Zane, and his parents weren't *quite* rich or powerful enough to hire the right lawyer.

Miranda cringes at the memory; she'd barely made it to his court appearance, overslept, and showed up hungover in a rumpled blouse. She slipped in the back door just as the judge was reading the sentence, and saw Zane's shoulders slump in disbelief as he realized he'd be incarcerated. He'd never had great posture, but the movement made Miranda's heart go a little cold. It was like Zane was getting the wind knocked out of him.

She hurried over to him once the court adjourned, ignoring the dirty look from his parents.

"Babe, I'm so sorry," Miranda said, throwing her arms around him. "I'll visit you every day, okay? We'll figure this out."

But his body was unyielding, his face dazed. "I'm going to jail, Miranda."

She pursed her lips, unsure how to answer. His suit jacket, she noticed, was a little too big in the shoulders. He was looking somewhere beyond her.

"How did we end up like this?" he asked. "What were we even doing?"

That rubbed Miranda the wrong way. "Just trying to live our lives. Have fun. Sometimes life likes to take a shit on your fun."

He frowned, ran his hand through his mess of hair, poorly combed for the occasion. "I don't know. I need to think. I think you need to think, too."

Miranda narrowed her eyes at him. "About *what?*"

"That . . . we're better than this." He rubbed his hands over his face. "Or—we could be, someday. You're more than just some 3AM Girl, and I'm more than a pothead."

"What are you even talking about?"

Miranda half glared at him; of course she was a 3AM Girl, that was her *thing*. That was why everyone loved her. She would be boring without it.

But his mother had appeared at his side and shut them both up.

So TLOYL is a no for now. Miranda scrolls through her contacts, looking for someone—anyone—who cares about her. In the *F* section, Miranda comes upon Sam Free and takes a chance.

Ready 2 rejoin human race, she texts the agent, the first man who signed her. Any projects?

She waits another stretch of eternity, listening to a wheelchair roll by and the nurse's telephone ring out in the hall. Sam's probably blocked her number, even though it was her, Miranda, who helped him make it big over the past ten years.

Ten—the number hits her and she slumps back against the wall. Has it really been ten years since she got her actual big break? She started in pageants back in Indiana. Bobbie loved dressing her up, doing her makeup just so, getting involved with the other pageant moms and the whole drama of the thing. Miranda got excited by her mom's excitement. And it didn't hurt when they started winning a little money.

Then there were local TV commercials, and people around town started to recognize her; then there were kids' choirs and musicals in Chicago—Bobbie started homeschooling at that point, and she'd quiz Miranda on her times tables as they made the three-hour drive from South Bend for rehearsals multiple times each week.

And then one day it seemed to Miranda that they just *kept* driving, all the way to Los Angeles with hardly enough room for Miranda herself among the suitcases and trash bags of clothes that filled the old Chevy.

After a brief interview and audition, Miranda signed with Sam's agency and was cast in the TV comedy / variety show *Kidz Klub*. Miranda was the youngest cast member and the best at everything— that's what they told her at least. And with a screen test and the stroke of a pen—boom, she was a star. The surreal feeling of seeing her own face on lunch boxes, posters, movie trailers that aired between the evening news, became normal. And then necessary.

A knock jars Miranda from her thoughts. Her door opens directly after the warning knock; there's very little privacy here.

"Montana?" calls the voice of Rick, the facilities manager, a tired-looking guy in his forties with an equally tired dirty-blond goatee. The staff tend to call patients by their last names here, a weird quirk Miranda hates; it makes her feel like they're trying to be hip high school teachers. Not that she knows what real high school teachers are like—but the staff seem to be ripping off the eighties movies she grew up with.

He even pulls her desk chair out and turns it around when he sits, elbows resting on its back, and Miranda knows he's about to Get Real with her about Her Behavior.

"What was that in group?" Rick starts out.

What was what? It's a stupid question, so Miranda stays quiet. He doesn't seem like he's expecting an answer, anyway.

"Listen." Rick pinches the bridge of his nose. "I hate having these conversations. But you know how this works. You don't want to be here any more than I want you to have to be here. But as a court-mandated patient, you're required to complete this program as a condition of bail, yada yada. We know this. Don't we?"

His short hair is spiked up and Miranda sneers, inwardly, at how obvious it is that he's trying to look younger. Everyone always tries to be younger but punishes her when she acts her age. She can smell the faint chemical scent of his hair gel.

"I *want* you to complete this program and go out to live a healthy life. *You* should want to complete it so you don't face probation. But, Montana—"

"What about Henry?" Miranda snaps. "Did you go have this little talk with him, too?"

"Deirdre is reviewing community guidelines with him. But the only person you should be worrying about is—"

"I'm just trying to figure out where *my* safe space is. What are the consequences when someone belittles *me*, comes at *my* career?"

"You're on your second infraction, Montana." Rick looks her in the eyes, and his expression is not optimistic. "Three strikes, you're out."

Out in the cold. And into tabloid infamy, it goes without saying.

Miranda looks away, at a spot in the very corner of the otherwise sterile room where a tiny dust bunny is drifting back and forth in the current of the vents. All she wants is to be left alone, in this obscenely overpriced place that's more Motel 6 than Ritz-Carlton. She realizes, suddenly, that the people she should have texted are the people who were once her only friends in the world: Germaine and Sicily. They never judge her. They're always there for her. Even if they hardly see each other these days—and while Miranda called to tell them about Horizons when she realized that Bobbie was shipping her off, she realizes she talked about herself the whole time. So she isn't even sure where her best friends are now or what's going on in their lives.

Germaine's parents dragged her back to New York while she studied for some business qualification, but is that where she stayed? Sicily's parents have her touring a different city practically every week of the year.

Miranda hasn't been a very good friend.

But Rick is holding out his hand. For a confused moment, she thinks he wants her to shake.

"The phone," he says. "You've lost privileges for a week."

"Rick, no." She could cry. And nothing she's experienced at Horizons so far would be more humiliating than crying in front of this Backstreet Boy wannabe.

"We have to get through to you somehow. No phones for a week, no TV, meals in your room."

When she still doesn't make a move, he plucks it right out of her hand and pockets it.

"You—" she starts.

"You can have your recovery journal," he offers, like he's being incredibly generous. "And one book a day from the library cart. I'd highly recommend *Lose Your Ego, Gain the World*. It really turned my life around."

He has the audacity to smile at her.

And then Miranda is left alone in her room, on her bed, with nothing to do and no one to talk to.

A kid in time-out, yet again.

TWO

GERMAINE

2006

Germaine very carefully adjusts the edge of her pink lapel with her thumb and frowns, again.

The presenter is still going on, directing the boardroom's attention to a list of bullet points, but all Germaine can focus on is the bold serif title at the top of the slide.

"I'm sorry," she interrupts, and she feels all eyes turn to her. The presenter pauses midsentence, a bland smile frozen on his face. "But what exactly is the issue with the original brand proposal?"

The title should say *Scent Germaine*, referring to Germaine's brainchild, her million-dollar idea to launch a new line of signature room scents at the most upmarket of her family's hotels all over the world. She's devoted a lot of time to it, many long hours in her office thinking aloud to Milano and Tivoli. So why does the proprietary font read *Saint Scents*, and why is everyone in the room acting like this was the name all along?

"No issue at all!" the presenter replies. "You'll see we have a robust brand strategy that aligns with your proposal, and—"

"The name," Germaine clarifies, a little sharply. "I meant, what is wrong with Scent Germaine?"

The tension that began to hum at her interruption intensifies by a margin. Germaine squares her shoulders and keeps her gaze steady on the presenter, though she knows what they all think of her. Spoiled brat. Princess. Hit with the lucky stick. A former child star who's still just an attention-seeking kid, desperate for her parents' approval, with no actual business acumen or knowledge of the real world. No credentials besides a degree that she didn't really earn—and a whole heap of nepotism.

"Ah." The syllable comes out like a cough, and the man glances at the VP of marketing, who gives the slightest of shrugs as if to say, *You're on your own.* The presenter looks back at Germaine and smiles again. "Just a bit of a pivot, at the request of the seventh floor."

The seventh floor is company slang for Germaine's father's office, situated at the top of the oldest, most historic St. Germaine hotel in Manhattan.

"Did the seventh floor provide a reason for the pivot?" Germaine presses, keeping her voice as level as possible.

The presenter is still smiling, but a slight slick of perspiration forms on his brow. "Just to—well, they wanted to remove a direct tie to any one person, or personality, to give it more of a timeless feeling, you know?"

Germaine continues to stare him down.

"Just to avoid"—he licks his lips and presses his palms together—"if there was to be a scenario where public images of a certain person or persons may be—well, tarnished. They knew that could undermine the brand's integrity."

Undermine the brand. Germaine knows those words came directly from her father; it's a phrase both he and her mother have repeated ever since Germaine began having a little more fun in LA. The St. Germaine-Chang reputation—and international brand—was meant to be highly sophisticated, classic, refined, intellectual, blah blah blah, Germaine could rattle off a thousand adjectives like a thesaurus with the number of times one of her parents has given her a lecture. Essentially, the point was always brought home: the brand should be everything that Germaine *isn't*.

And yet it is they who are undermining Germaine, and not for the first time. It's a pattern of theirs: give her a responsibility or encourage one of her initiatives, only to devalue—or completely torpedo—it. They've never done this with her brothers. But with Germaine, their only daughter? Oh, you'd better believe it.

Germaine gives a frosty smile and a very small nod. "I understand," she says, lacing her fingers together and feeling the boardroom hesitantly relax.

~

Germaine wishes her parents did not have doormen so she could slam the thick oaken panels when she arrives for dinner that night. She tosses her Chanel clutch onto the Hepplewhite table in the foyer, hoping the latch will snag the weaving of the Raphael tapestry hanging above it.

Gregoire and Giles are already seated at the wide mahogany table in the dining room, deep in discussion about some rugby player they're both obsessed with. They don't even glance at Germaine when she comes into the room. Her father, Terence, is reclining in after-work mode at the head of the table, suit jacket removed and tailored shirtsleeves rolled up as he sips bourbon from a crystal rocks glass. He's watching the boys with only the slightest look of disdain on his face, hand under his chin. When he sees Germaine arrive, he smiles at her.

Germaine does not smile back. She drops gracelessly into her chair as her mother, Céline, enters the room in tailored navy slacks and a cashmere sweater, a glass of claret already in her hand, the soft light of the dining room making her high cheekbones only more dramatic. She is the only one whose gaze immediately rests on Germaine—and, as always, it's calculating. Germaine looks sullenly back, knowing her mother is noticing her posture, the smudge of mascara in the corner of her left eye, the millimeters of space between her nail beds and nail polish, where she's let her manicure grow out just a bit too long.

"Sit up straight, darling," Céline chirps as she takes a seat. "What's that look for?"

Germaine doesn't waste time with small talk. "Why didn't you tell me we were changing Scent Germaine?"

Terence makes a sympathetic face as the house staff bring the salads, frisée with fennel, pear, and dates. "We thought you might be unhappy. But unfortunately it's necessary."

Germaine picks up her salad fork and sets it back down, worried she'll be tempted to do something violent with it.

"What's the point?" she asks. "I got this degree, I did what you wanted, I came up with a great idea—but if you're not going to trust me to actually *participate* in the business, why am I even here?"

Céline rolls her eyes. "For god's sake, Germaine, it's just a name."

"It was *my* name. Mine. That you didn't want. And if you don't want me here, I don't see why I shouldn't just go back to LA, where I was actually happy. Where people do want me."

"Oh, don't kid yourself." Céline waves her hand. "It's not talent they want you for. It's the sleazy paparazzi shots and brand sponsorships. There's more to life than that, Gigi."

Germaine picks the fork back up.

"Sweetheart, we want to see you mature a little, prove that you've grown up," says Terence. "You're not going back to LA. Stay here and do what we need you to do. LA doesn't have the bachelors New York does. Start thinking about picking one of them out, eh? A beautiful wedding, a few grandchildren—*that's* grown up, all right."

Germaine stabs at the airy greens, hitting all the way down to the fine china plate. "I'm not going to have this conversation again. I'm way too young to get married."

Céline snorts into her wine, a most refined, delicate noise that somehow makes her appear even more charming. "Well, you're not getting any younger."

Céline was a nineteen-year-old French-Vietnamese model when she married Terence, a Taiwanese-born self-made billionaire with a massive property empire. She's always held that over Germaine, cracking down on her only daughter. Miranda Montana had the acting talent, Céline told her, and Sicily Bell was the one who could sing. Germaine was lucky to get on *Kidz Klub* at all, perhaps only because of the influence of her father, who wanted to give his sweet little pet the chance to be on her favorite show. And because the studio needed a cute Asian face for a diversity hire. Terence had friends in high places, and they did favors for each other.

Germaine has always scoffed at this. *I was the best dancer!* she says each time they start the same tired routine. *I won Audience Favorite for the hand jive!*

But somewhere, deep inside herself, she's terrified that everything Terence and Céline say is true. Miranda got movie roles after their Blast Off! contract was up. Sicily got a record deal. What did Germaine get, apart from publicity?

She'd been excited by the prospect of going to business school, one mandate of her parents' that Germaine surprisingly didn't hate. Cornell, nonetheless. Sure, the family name opened doors, but people who went to Cornell *did* things.

And yet, just when Germaine was beginning to see herself as Ivy League material, her parents sabotaged that, too. She should have realized the Dyson School program was meant to be superficial. Just another little token to adorn her with. When Germaine wanted to study, Terence and Céline insisted she travel overseas for ski trips and hotel launches instead of taking finals. And after a generous donation to Cornell's Nestlé Library from the St. Germaine-Changs, the degree was conferred upon Germaine anyway. It demonstrated, once again, that whatever she did mattered very little.

She can have more clothes than she can wear, as many Yorkies as can fit into cute purses, as many face-whitening treatments and mani-pedis and massages as she wants. She can vacation in Hawaii and Ibiza and Mauritius whenever she likes.

But work? She apparently doesn't need to do that. Her role in life, as far as Germaine can see, is to look perfect and marry well. Which means someone else rich and Asian, preferably in the hotel business so the conglomerate can keep on growing.

Her family is still eating their salads as if nothing is wrong. Her brothers have picked up their conversation again—whether Jonah Lomu or Richie McCaw is the greatest rugby player of all time. Céline is signaling to the porter to bring more wine.

"I need to have some purpose in my life!" Germaine bursts out, throwing her fork onto her plate a little harder than she means to.

But her family doesn't miss a beat.

"Like the 'purpose' you had in LA, falling out of limos?" Terence asks with a smirk. Céline and the boys laugh, and Germaine looks in disgust at the half-chewed mouthfuls of salad that Gregoire and Giles don't bother to hide. Soon the entrées of pheasant paillard will be brought out, and they'll be able to inhale it without scrutiny. They've never had their weight monitored or their choices criticized, even when they were drunk frat boys about to fail out of school. They both got into Dartmouth after Terence and Céline paid for a business-school annex there. To them, Germaine is just an airhead who used to jump around on TV.

And then she made a fool of herself jumping around bars and clubs.

"Heard your alkie friend was in trouble again," Giles says.

Gregoire snorts. "Yeah, Joe had a copy of *Star*, and she was right on the front page. She is looking *loco*, man. Big sunglasses, middle finger to the paps as she's walking into rehab . . ."

"What was the headline again?" Giles asks him. "It was something hilarious. 'Miranda Made'—no—"

"'Miranda's Mandated Miami'—" starts Gregoire.

"'Miranda's Mandated Miami Meltdown.'"

They both fall over themselves laughing.

"Hell *yes*, dude!" Giles howls. "So stupid, I love it."

Germaine feels heat boiling at her collarbone, her temple, just like it did in the boardroom. This is nothing new; her family has always disparaged her friends.

"Some people *have* to work in entertainment," Terence says pityingly, wiping his mouth as the salad plates are cleared and the staff set dishes of tender roast pheasant with shallot-lemon cream sauce before them. "Their families need the money."

This is nothing new. But Germaine is dead sick of it.

With her two slender hands, she lifts the heavy, hot plate in front of her. She makes a ninety-degree turn to her right and lets it go, antique Royal Copenhagen porcelain shattering over the Tibetan rug. Butter and oil seep into the handwoven fibers.

"Germaine!" Terence bellows.

Germaine grasps the end of the French-linen tablecloth, taking handfuls of the fabric in her fists and pulling.

"What the hell!" Gregoire shouts. He grabs at his plate, but Giles is too slow; so is Céline. The dishes, the silverware, the Kangxi porcelain vase of lilies, everything is clattering and crashing and spilling to the floor. Terence and Gregoire are roaring at her; Giles has flung himself on the tablecloth to try to stop her, toppling the stemware into Céline's lap.

But Germaine has the upper hand, and she doesn't care. If they think she's nothing but a spoiled brat, she'll act like one. If they expect her to make a scene anyway, she'll do it. They don't see a grown woman when they look at her. They see a child.

So she'll throw a tantrum.

Céline is the only one who doesn't react. She stares straight ahead, stonily, crossing her arms and ignoring the dark stain of wine spreading across her trousers.

"Just ignore her," Céline says, almost casually. "She's acting out, as usual. Probably premenstrual—no wonder she looks so bloated tonight. I have Midol, Gigi, if you need it."

With a cry of frustration, Germaine throws her hands in the air and storms out of the room, breathing so hard she imagines palpitations in her chest.

She may have all the money in the world, but what's the point if her family treats her like an accessory? The message is loud and clear.

You're lucky we tolerate you. You're nothing without us.

That's the part that hurts the most—because Germaine knows it's true.

THREE

SICILY

2006

Sicily allows herself a sip from her water bottle, but she doesn't let her speed lag as her feet beat down on the treadmill. She's covered in a sheen of sweat and her calf is beginning to cramp, but at least the view is nice.

The treadmill has been placed before a wall of floor-to-ceiling windows that look out over Hyde Park from the top floor of her favorite boutique-hotel penthouse suite, where she can see the snow blanketing the forested paths beneath her. The quiet monochrome landscape is a welcome sight after the glitzy sprint of twelve sold-out concert dates across Europe. And her respite here in London is brief—there are only a few more shows to come.

A beep sounds from the treadmill: she's been running for sixty minutes. The machine is a top-of-the-line model that keeps track of miles, speed, heart rate, calories burned, you name it. Sicily has it shipped around with her whenever she spends more than three days in one place. That way she can maintain her strict training regimen: running for at least an hour, training with one of her backup dancers—who's also a certified Pilates instructor—and sticking to a high-protein, low-carb diet. Toned, taut, and tanned—that's her mantra. Although it's hard to stay tanned in Northern Europe, which is why she'll be visiting an exclusive salon on Bond Street before dinner.

Coincidentally, that mantra is the same for her team: Mom, Dad, Uncle Henry (who really is her uncle as well as her booking agent), and her cousin Jim, who manages security. Even Emmylou, her makeup and hair artist, and Kendra, her personal assistant, are family members, all from the same small town in northern Arkansas. Sicily's father, Day, is her manager, and her mother, Carole, is director of communications, which means she puts her former telemarketer voice to use working with promoters and record-company publicists.

It really is a family affair. It surprised, and then gratified, and then alarmed Sicily—just a little—to see how they all rallied around her, adjusting to her stage name without missing a beat. When Sicily had auditioned for *Kidz Klub*, her real name was Cecilia. But her parents were more than on board when the casting agent suggested a change. Actually, the casting agent's assistant didn't know how to spell "Cecilia" and wrote "Sicily" instead. So Sicily's new name was just a mistake.

But Sicily has always rolled with the punches, and the path of least resistance is to be easygoing with her family members. Fortunately, it comes naturally to her. It feels good to be a good daughter, cousin, niece. And Sicily knows better than to complain. It wasn't as though they were dirt poor before *Kidz Klub*, but there was plenty of coupon clipping, passing around of hand-me-downs from one cousin to the next, buying shoes at the Salvation Army. Cracking open the swear jar for Dairy Queen on birthdays and holidays was the pinnacle of luxury. The family has come a long way from Boone County, now having more than they know what to do with. Sicily is happy to provide. The operation is a finely tuned machine—and she's the engine.

When poor Miranda got her injury near the end of *Kidz Klub*, Sicily saw how hard she leaned on the pills and where that eventually led her: rock bottom. So when Sicily twisted her ankle onstage one night, all she took was Tylenol and an ice pack. A little overnight elevation. The show must go on.

In the Bell family, everyone is there to support you with love and prayer. You don't need a shrink or drugs or a fancy doctor telling you to take time off and laze around. They traveled as a pack and would always be there to protect Sicily.

Sicily thinks this is sweet and nice for the most part, except that they want to protect her from Miranda and Germaine, too. Bad influences, they say.

"You need to keep your eye on the prize," Day had told her, and Sicily knows what that means. Go from starlet to star and take the whole family with you, spreading the wealth around. They deserve it, after all, for everything they've done to help her.

Another beep sounds. But this is from Sicily's phone, not the treadmill. Her heart skips forward as she reads the text, the same way it does at the end of every show when she's waving goodbye to an arena of screaming fans.

Outside, it says.

A wide grin spreads across her face. The message is from Hugo, the tall, cute one with loads of thick locks from the boy band No Exit. They opened for her in Paris—could that have been only two weeks ago? It feels like she's known Hugo forever, memorized his floppy hair, his British accent, his dimples, his biceps tattoo of Lord Byron—*The bad-boy poet of his generation,* Hugo had said—by heart. He makes her swoon. He wears velvet jackets with ripped jeans and custom Doc Martens studded with mini skulls. He makes her want to run away with him to some remote place and leave their lives behind.

Sicily towels off and rushes around the suite, yanking a brush through her hair, grabbing a hoodie, and spritzing herself with perfume—Victoria's Secret Love Spell, which feels a little too on the nose, but she's been wearing it since 1999 whenever she's needed a boost of good luck. Who says you can't keep wearing the same perfume you wore at fourteen years old? If it ain't broke . . .

She pulls the hood tightly around her head and grabs her key card from the bathroom counter. She has ninety minutes before the tanning appointment; everyone knows she's running and then taking a shower, so they won't be looking for her.

And honestly, she *is* still running—down the back stairwell, where no one will see her; not the front desk, not the paparazzi, not her entourage. Sicily is breathless by the time she reaches the alley where Hugo is parked in his Audi TT. If she was still hooked up to the treadmill, her heart rate would be even higher than normal at the thought of touching him.

Sicily knows what Germaine would say: *Not another crush, Sis!* Sicily talks to her every week or so, but she's conveniently forgotten to mention Hugo so far. Germaine's interests are more aloof, focused on big projects and new ideas, and Sicily knows G thinks she always falls too hard and fast for any pretty-boy charmer who manages to break through the family barricades. G would remind her, if she were here right now, that Sicily has managed to get her heart broken by two backup dancers, a tour physio, her cousin's college roommate, a record-company exec in Nashville, and Lenny G, another former cast member in *Kidz Klub*, despite being one of the biggest pop stars in the world at the tender age of twenty-one.

There was someone else, too, someone who Sicily thought was her first love until he got too forward with her at the age of fourteen and dumped her like she was nothing when she said she didn't feel ready. But Germaine didn't know that, and Sicily wouldn't allow herself to think of his name anymore.

It is Miranda who would have been sympathetic to Sicily's falling in and out of love, even though it was mostly the guy doing the falling out and Sicily who was always left devastated. But Miranda is hard to get ahold of at the moment. And she doesn't know what it's like to be unlucky in love, having been as hot and heavy with TLOYL as she has for over two years. The only reason they're not together right now is because—well, their respective vices got them in trouble.

But inwardly, Sicily's been worried about Miranda. She was just as outraged, just as sympathetic as Germaine when Miranda called them with the news about Horizons, joined in with *God, that sucks* and *It's totally unfair* and half-joking promises to go on a rescue mission with G to bail Miranda out.

And yet Sicily saw how easily she could have spiraled down the same path with one small injury. She can't imagine having a break from the world like Miranda's been forced to do. Sicily feels guilty for thinking so, but in some ways six weeks of quiet time and limited contact with the outside world sounds like a luxury.

But Sicily would never let the machine stop like that.

The Audi is there where he said it would be, idling in the alley with the lights off. Though she wants to look cool and collected like Germaine does, Sicily can hardly help herself from grinning from ear to ear and scrambling into the passenger seat.

Miranda might be going through a tough spot. But still, she doesn't know what it's like to be rejected the way Sicily has. *So pretty! So talented! She writes all her own songs!* everyone raves about her. But she hasn't been pretty and talented enough that any guy stays interested in her for more than three months, max.

"You're in love with love," her mother likes to say. "Focus on your career first, and the rest will follow."

Sicily *has* been focusing on her career, and now she's in love with Hugo. And everything will change—she knows it. She's already writing a song about him: "So Bad, So Good." What's more career focused than that?

But she's sneaking around because she just needs a little more time with Hugo before doing the whole meet-the-parents thing.

The wicked smile on Hugo's face when she climbs into the car is irresistible. He kisses her immediately, slowly, deeply, before she can even shut the door.

"We have an hour," she murmurs into his lips.

He clucks his tongue, pouting. "I wanted to take you up to Hampstead Heath and seduce you under the trees."

Sicily wants to tell him to just go, then, take her there; who cares what happens? The way he speaks and looks at her makes her ache, makes her want to commit to wildly irresponsible decisions. She's used to adoring fans, but the earnestness in Hugo's face makes her feel like the most special, most loved girl in the world. The two of them may be skyrocketing to fame, but his sensual, quiet demeanor gives her the distinct feeling that they would have found each other in other lives, too. They might have met on the street and spent the rest of their days together. Their time now is always unbearably short.

But Sicily will not let the machine stop.

"Let's see what else you can do in an hour," she makes herself say, savoring the way this intensifies the desire in his gaze. He steps on the gas without even taking his eyes off her, and they fly into the frozen streets.

~

Hugo has just moved into a tiny mews house not too far from Hyde Park. He parks in the street, and they nearly run through the courtyard, Sicily shrieking as he scoops her up and carries her through the door, over boxes and around furniture covered in sheets. He starts up the stairs and then stops on the landing as she kisses his neck, pressing her back against the wall as she buries her hands in his hair.

"I forgot," he murmurs into her ear. "The bed's not set up yet."

"Not a problem," Sicily whispers back, and then he's unzipping her hoodie, pulling his shirt over his head and kicking off his jeans and boxers while Sicily yanks off her yoga pants. He pins her to the wall with his hips while she wraps around him, breathing him in, responding to the rhythms of his body.

"I think I just might be in love with you," she sighs as she clings to his broad shoulders. It spills out of her even though she hadn't meant to say it—not yet.

32

As he slows, he kisses the hollow just above her clavicle and runs his thumb along her cheek. "You're something very special, Sicily Bell."

She looks into his eyes and wants to say it again, wants to ask him to run away with her, to tell her his darkest secrets.

But he grabs her hand before she can. "Come on. I want to show you something."

Sicily moves for her clothes, but Hugo pulls her away.

"You won't be needing those," he says in a low, playful voice.

He leads her the rest of the way up the stairs, and then up another flight, until they're on the threshold of the rooftop terrace. It's going on evening now, getting dark, getting late—but Sicily doesn't want to mention this.

He steps out onto the roof, still naked as a jaybird.

"Hugo!" Sicily hisses.

He grins at her, daring. "No one can see us. C'mere."

She'll do anything he tells her. So she follows, wrapping her arms around herself due to the cold wind until Hugo presses warmth against her, taking her in his arms.

"It's my second-favorite view," he says, nodding out at the neighborhood of twinkling lights and parlor windows that emit a soft glow. The bustle of the city sounds far away. Down the street, a few people emerge from a café, laughing.

Hugo rests his chin on the top of her head, then pulls back and looks at her. "You want to know what my first-favorite view is?"

Sicily smiles and rolls her eyes, though she loves it. She could listen to him say things like that all day. He kisses her once, twice, and then she's melting again. Feverish and hot even in the winter air.

Hugo lowers her onto the floor of the terrace and envelops her again, right there in the open. Sicily thinks absently that the pattern of the tiles will be printed onto her back. She'll need to keep her robe right up until she gets into the tanning booth—her mother notices everything.

But right now Sicily is helpless to Hugo's advances, absolute putty in his hands. She can't think of anything more romantic, more thrilling, more wrong than what they're doing right now.

~

As the Audi slips back through the darkening streets to the hotel, Sicily knows she has to say it. Even though she doesn't want to.

"I'm only in London two more days." It comes out quiet in the luxury interior of the car, both a statement and a question.

When he only looks regretfully at her and pulls into the alley next to the hotel, she adds, "The next leg of my tour is in Canada. I hear it's beautiful this time of year."

Hugo parks. He lifts her hand and brings it to his lips, running his thumb over her knuckles.

"You know I'll go anywhere with you," he says.

Joy blooms inside her. She knew it would be different this time. She knew.

Hugo gives her hand one more kiss, then guides it down to the zipper of his jeans.

"Something to remember you by?" he asks, a mock pout on his face.

"You are insatiable," she says, shaking her head, but she does it, even though she needs to go. She'll do anything for him.

~

When Sicily arrives in Canada and texts Hugo, he texts back that he's sorry, so sorry, love, but No Exit picked up gigs in Italy and Spain; it wasn't his decision. They're about to begin recording a new album. Their manager thinks it could be really major this time.

Sicily understands. She rolls with the punches. She's easygoing.

They'll meet up in the spring, they decide, when Sicily will be taking a short break in LA before the summer tour launches.

It will be on this short break that Sicily will miss a period, suddenly become fatigued when working on dance routines she could do in her sleep. The 3AM Girls will be the first to know; Kendra can't be trusted with something this big.

Sicily will hide it from her parents as long as she can. But soon the truth will come out even to Hugo: she's pregnant.

FOUR

MIRANDA

2007

Six months before Sicily's due date, Miranda drops yogurt, peanut butter, bananas, blackberries, milk, and a whole heap of spinach into her Hamilton Beach blender and hits the switch. She's been starting her day with these green smoothies, a recipe that someone in rehab posted on a beat-up bulletin board next to the counselor's office.

She does her gratitude exercises as the contents spin hypnotically in the plastic pitcher. *I am grateful to be alive. I am grateful to have friends. I am grateful to have a home. I am grateful to be working toward health.*

Picking up the mantra—and saying it out loud where the counselors could hear—was what allowed her to finally graduate from rehab. When she was kicked out of Miami, she went to Taos, and then to a mind-numbing stint in Bemidji, Minnesota, where she almost lost the will to live. But it had worked. Miranda's now off painkillers for the first time since she was thirteen, and her drinking is under control. She's back in LA and about to start work after almost two years, a point that felt impossible to reach over the past few months.

The doorbell rings through the Malibu beach house, a light-and-airy tone that Miranda picked out herself. There was still plenty in her savings after the rehab bills were paid, so why not celebrate? Miranda feels she's earned it.

"Knock knock!" Miranda's mother squeals, even though Miranda has already opened the door, green smoothie in hand. "Oh, it's so good to see you back where you belong!"

Bobbie bursts forth and hugs her daughter, squeezing a little too tightly for Miranda's liking. "Hey, Mom," Miranda says. "Thanks for coming by."

Bobbie steps back and smooths her box-blond hair. "*Absolutely.* You are my only child, and I want to make sure you're healthy as a horse."

Miranda lifts the tall glass of green liquid in a toast and takes a sip. "So far so good."

"Sleeping well?"

"Well enough." The sleep of the dead, actually, now that her brain has been unplugged from electronics and substances long enough. It was in Bemidji that Miranda, for the first time in a long time, slept through the night without waking.

"Staying out of trouble?" Bobbie arches an eyebrow as they head back through the house.

Miranda feels a twitch of annoyance. "Mother, I have been out of rehab for all of seventy-two hours."

"I know, I know." Her mother waves her hand vaguely.

They settle into the living room, where wide bay windows let in the sea breeze. There's a black leather sectional that Miranda loves—she had it shipped over from Italy, and now she eases back into its plush cushions and puts her feet on the glass coffee table while Bobbie perches on the other edge.

"What?" Miranda says when she sees the way her mother's hands are folded and her lips are pressed in a line.

"I've been talking to Joan, and she thinks it's a good idea for me to voice some things to you," Bobbie says, referring to her therapist.

Miranda nearly rolls her eyes—it's what she would have done pre-rehab—but resists. "Oh, Mom, please."

"No. Now listen—"

And Miranda does, because she has no other choice, and her mother's eyes are welling up with tears.

"The place you were two years ago—you can't go there again. You can't backslide. It was so hard to see my baby girl struggling like that, and—"

She wipes impatiently at her eyes.

"Mom," Miranda says, more quietly now.

Bobbie puts her hands up and shakes her head. "And now you're healthy. You're going back to work. Nothing could make me happier. So think of this as a pre-intervention: you need to stay clean this time. No drugs, no drinking, and especially no bad-boy relationships." She leans forward more intently as Miranda opens her mouth to protest. "In fact, how about no good boys, either? There's too much on the line; take some time to yourself, time to get your head on straight. Sure, it's easy to fall for someone, but that feeling makes others think they can—well, control you, influence you . . ."

"Are we talking about me, or you?" Miranda says flatly.

Bobbie is just as bad as Miranda with relationships. Miranda knows that Doug, Bobbie's second boyfriend of that year, is home right now in Bobbie's condo watching World Series of Poker tapes to "hone his craft." He's been trying to hone it for over sixteen years, apparently. But Doug has told Bobbie that what he's been missing is a good woman by his side to help him win—and to fund his lifestyle—and Bobbie seems to be more than obliging.

"We're talking about you." Bobbie frowns. "Because we both know that you-know-who is supposed to be coming back from Venezuela soon."

Miranda is still holding her smoothie glass, and she looks into the dregs. Zane. He got out of jail before she emerged from rehab, and his parents sent him to the family hacienda outside of Barquisimeto to work on the land, take care of the horses, and make a clean break with his old life. Which meant a break with Miranda, too—permanently.

Zane's family's dislike for Miranda is clear; in fact, his parents seem to think it's *her* who's the bad influence. And despite what Bobbie is saying now, Miranda has gotten the distinct impression that her mother, in her heart of hearts, feels the same way.

Every time Miranda got her phone back from confiscation, she was sure she'd have a message from Zane. It seemed like an impossibility that he wouldn't reach out after his release from prison. But time and time again, she powered up her cell, just to be disappointed.

At last, Miranda had composed her own text to Zane when she got out—just one. She still had some pride.

Finally made it out. U 2?

He hasn't responded yet.

"Just—no distractions, okay?" Bobbie continues. "*The Bennington Bookshop* will be a good step to building a career. It's wholesome, it's low stakes, it's cute—"

"Mom, I know. I *have* a career. I just need to get back into it."

What Miranda doesn't want to say is that she knows her mother is right. A low-budget film for the Holiday Heartwarmers channel does not an Emmy nominee make. She will not be walking the red carpet at the Golden Globes or the People's Choice Awards this year. She'll be lucky if she gets a photo in *TV Guide*, much less the cover. Maybe if she really sells the performance. Her audience will not be high-profile critics and loyal fans, but retirees and parents with young children.

But it's a step. A step forward.

"No." Bobbie looks grim. "No. You do not have a career. You are building back from square one, do you understand, Miranda? You need to start over. The move here is to behave, put your head down, and produce good work. Show people you've matured. Turn this slump into life experience that you can use, because the career that *Kidz Klub* alumna Miranda Montana had is gone. Forgotten. And I'm waiting to see what kind of career post-rehab Miranda Montana will *make*."

Bobbie would have gotten along with Henry at Horizons, Miranda thinks, as her grip on her glass tightens.

It's not exactly a pep talk, and it's a hard truth that Miranda isn't interested in hearing, but there's no stopping Bobbie. As her lecture intensifies, Miranda swears to herself that she'll do so well that her mother will be embarrassed to think she ever needed a pre-intervention.

And she does do well, at first. The next morning, Miranda wakes up early, showers, and even fits in a half hour of yoga before pouring her green smoothie into a stainless-steel coffee thermos and heading out the door.

She drives herself—in a Porsche, to be sure—but drives herself, alone, to set. She used to be important enough for someone else to do that job. It used to be the three of them—Miranda, Sicily, and Germaine—piling into whatever car their agents had arranged for them, tearing off down the Hollywood strip. They rarely even knew their drivers as more than silhouettes behind privacy glass. They didn't need to worry about where they were going—it was a given that they would reach whatever destination they were meant to, and that the press and people there would be thrilled to see them.

How things have changed. As Miranda grips the steering wheel and inches impatiently down the 110, she does her gratitude exercises and swears she'll get back to that place again. She'll claw her way back if she needs to.

She arrives on time and breathes deeply, caught off guard by the electric ripple of nerves that hit when she finds herself back on a soundstage for the first time in what feels like forever. It even smells the same—sawdust, hydraulic oil, the buttery scent of stale croissants on the craft services table. She's back. She's ready.

The set has been built to look like some Anytown, USA, Main Street, with a wrought-iron lamppost and tiny boutique storefronts, including the pastel-pink one with the white trim like a gingerbread house that will serve as her character's shop. Miranda has been cast as Genevieve, a young woman who takes over her ailing grandfather's beloved bookshop and organizes the town to prevent a big-shot investment banker from developing the historic street.

Miranda knows it's not real. But the glass of the streetlight is frosted just so; there are actual vintage books in the window of the shop, and the snow that pools in banks along the curb of the cobblestone street looks as though she could reach out and feel the cold on her fingertips. It's beautiful. She wants to be part of it all again, and just for a moment she remembers feeling the same magic when she stepped onto the *Kidz Klub* set for the first time.

And then a tall man with blond hair and a trimmed beard opens the door of the bookshop and strolls out.

Miranda laughs. "Tyler? What the hell?"

Tyler grins sheepishly. "Hey, Miranda. Surprise."

Tyler Xavier—now known as Tyler X—is another one of the *Kidz Klub* alums. He was the funny one back then, always cracking jokes and playing pranks on the cast and crew, but he got away with it as a cutie with a gorgeous smile. He's still cute now, Miranda notices, although alcohol and steroids have bloated him a bit. She knows he's also recently out of rehab, but she didn't know he was ready to work again.

"What is this?" she asks, giving him a hug. "You weren't at the table read! I had no idea."

The only person who'd been missing from the table read was Jacob Sullivan, an up-and-coming character actor who was playing Chris, the New York banker. The director and coproducer, George, had stepped in to read for him, saying he was recovering from strep.

"Yeah, it was pretty last minute." He scratches his nose and leans in close. "Jacob got poached for a better project. Don't tell anyone."

Miranda opens her eyes in mock scandal, though she *is* surprised. "Juicy."

"Yeah. George was furious. It was a right-place-right-time kind of deal, and my agent got me in."

"Well, hey, congrats! It'll be great to work together again."

"I think so, too. We'll show these losers what Blast Off! Network kids can do, huh?" Tyler winks at her.

Miranda flicks her long hair over her shoulder. She can't help it; it's instinct. "You ready to get your ass handed to you by a small-town gal who'll do anything to save her family's bookshop?"

Tyler puts on a very serious expression. "Young lady, I'll have you know that in the cutthroat world of investment banking, we have entire departments devoted to the business of handling asses. Dear me, I mean assets. Your shop has large assets, and I'd like to handle them." He narrows his eyes. "Those are my lines, right? I've been practicing since the crack of dawn."

Miranda snorts and then succumbs to full-on laughter. He's still got it.

The way he breaks, relaxes, and then laughs with her makes something in Miranda flutter.

"Okay, shut up about my assets," she says. "I have to get to costumes."

"Not a chance." He winks again.

~

The first few scenes are gold. George begins production about a third of the way through the film, starting Miranda and Tyler with the scene in which the two main characters meet. They bring the same energy that came naturally an hour before, combative yet playful, easing into their characters and developing the tenuous chemistry of a man and a woman who are hopelessly at odds. Tyler has been outfitted in a tailored camel coat and starched white shirt with a few of the top buttons carelessly left open. He wears a cashmere scarf around the lapel of his jacket, and his blond hair is combed rakishly to one side.

Holiday Heartwarmers may tout themselves as a wholesome, family-friendly channel, but there's no question that they go for bodice ripper in their male leads.

Miranda's auburn hair flows in elegant—if slightly stiff—curls, and she wears a navy-and-white polka-dotted dress with a Peter Pan collar under a soft cream coat. And a scarf. Everybody wears scarves. They shoot one full scene and then move to another, George seeming happy with the pace. He wants to shoot all the Genevieve and Chris scenes early on, then add characters as production continues until they finally fly to Vermont to shoot on location with a hundred or so extras.

By the end of the day, a small pocket of confidence is glowing inside Miranda. It only intensifies when Tyler walks into the parking lot with her, touches her shoulder lightly, and says, "Hey, great job today. See you tomorrow, Genevieve."

This time she's the one who winks. "Wouldn't miss it, Chris."

~

The first few days of shooting sail by. Miranda feels invincible. Then, on Friday, they're scheduled to do the scene in which Genevieve and Chris have an argument and end up kissing.

She knew it was in the script. It shouldn't have surprised her.

But Miranda hasn't kissed anyone in a while. Like, since before rehab. And no one since Zane, who has—frustratingly—still not responded to her text. So Friday morning is the first time in four months, two weeks, and six days that she suddenly, unexpectedly, craves Oxy.

She wakes up with it like a low burn in her mouth. Oxy, a bump of coke, even a shot of cheap vodka—anything to blunt her nerves would feel like a cool, refreshing drink of water right now.

Bobbie has emptied the beach house of all substances and alcohol. In rehab, Miranda sat with a sponsor and texted or called anyone in her phone who enabled her use, including her dealers.

She drinks her green smoothie, and it tastes like sand.

She drives to set and notices every liquor store, every alleyway, every gas station. By the time she gets on the 110, it's too late to stop anywhere. Why didn't she pick up a pack of cigarettes? Cigarettes would be good. They're allowed. She should be keeping a carton in her purse, in her glove compartment, under her pillow at night.

Miranda grips the steering wheel and stares at the license plate of the car in front of her. She reads it over and over: 9JRI205. She feels sweat damping the underarms of her shirt. She tries to do her gratitude exercises but is so distracted she can't think of anything she has ever been grateful for.

If she gets through this day, she tells herself she will buy out Mobil's entire stock of Kools.

~

"Cut!" George yells. "Come on, Montana."

She's flubbed the line again. She's supposed to say, *Well, you're not so innocent either!* And shove Tyler; then, after a beat, they of course fall into each other's arms. But Miranda can't get it straight in her head—it keeps coming out as *Well, you're not so great yourself!* which, of course, has a slightly different connotation and doesn't make as much sense in context.

"Sorry, sorry." Miranda rubs her hand over her face, a habit she got into in rehab, and too late remembers her makeup.

George gives her a hard stare, then sighs with exasperation. "Let's just take five. Miranda, have makeup touch you up, and then get your head in the game, yeah?"

Tyler looks like he's about to say something, but Miranda hurries away before he can. She feels a familiar shame, like she can't do this and doesn't remember why she ever tried. But as the makeup artist reapplies powder, it turns into something worse. Miranda knows she's letting Tyler down, too. The two of them really have to prove themselves here, turn *The Bennington Bookshop* into a launchpad for the bigger, better projects they used to score in the past. She's embarrassed that he's seen her stumble.

So when makeup is done with her, Miranda slips out the stage door and goes to Tyler's trailer. She wants to apologize to him; as costars, she wants them to be real with each other. She wants to lay out what she's been through, what this project means for her, and promise to be a better coworker.

But all these thoughts vanish from her mind when Tyler opens the door with a bottle of Don Julio in hand.

"Hey," he says. "You okay?"

Miranda looks from the bottle to him. It's hard to tear her eyes away. "What are you doing?" she asks.

"What?"

"You're sober, aren't you? You're out of rehab?"

Tyler blinks at the tequila as if he's surprised to find it in his hand. "Oh, this? I mean, I'm California sober. No drugs, but I still drink here and there."

She wants to chastise him, to tell him it's not even 11:00 a.m. But she also wants him to share.

He squints at her, trying to figure out her silence. "You better come in," he says.

"Sorry." Miranda shakes her head. "I'm not here to judge you. I just wanted to apologize."

Tyler frowns, waves his hand like it's nothing.

"No, really," Miranda protests. "I need to get it together. I was just nervous this morning, and I let that affect my performance."

He smirks. "Nervous? About kissing me?"

Miranda sucks her teeth. "Oh, come on, don't make it sound like we're in middle school. Listen, it's just . . . been a while since I've kissed someone."

She expects him to make a joke, but instead he rubs his nose and becomes solemn. "No, I get it. You're—you're not the only one who's been through that," he says. "Not a lot of dating opportunities in rehab."

She gives a short laugh, shakes her head.

"Here." He hands her the bottle of tequila. "Just take a sip, reactivate your acting muscles. I mean, we never used to do this shit completely sober, right? Why would everyone expect us to now?"

It hits her like down-home common sense, because of course not—from her injury forward, Miranda always took something to help her on set. This past week has been the first time in her adult life that she's been doing her job completely on her own.

In a perfect world she would protest. She would call her accountability partner. She would at least take a moment to weigh her options and consider the gravity of what she's about to do.

But Miranda simply takes the bottle from him and drinks without hesitation.

The effect is immediate. The familiar taste gives her a deep comfort, and suddenly everything about the world seems a little warmer, kinder. Tyler is smiling at her. She realizes he's a shot or two ahead of her.

"There we go," he says.

"Maybe we should practice." The idea just occurred to her.

"Practice what?"

"You know . . ."

"Oh." He raises his eyebrows. "Listen—I'm going to confess. I always had a little crush on you at *Kidz Klub*. Let's face it, all you girls were hot. So maybe that's what's making this harder."

The tequila is leaving a gentle burn through her throat, her abdomen. She takes another sip, just a tiny one, and moves closer to Tyler.

He takes a moment, brushing his nose against hers. Then he kisses her. The feeling is electric; Miranda leans into it and so does he, not pulling away but going in for another and another. She brings her arms around his neck, and he wraps his around her waist, gently at first, then pulling her tightly in against his hips.

Back on set, they nail it.

"Whew!" George exclaims, pretending to fan himself. "Whatever you did to turn things around, don't stop!"

~

So they don't. Miranda and Tyler steal time in their trailers between scenes to undress each other as much as possible and later get scolded by makeup, who can tell exactly what's going on, seeing their blotchy skin and mussed hair.

So proud of U, honey, Bobbie texts, one phrase in a series of motivational messages she's been peppering Miranda's phone with for the past two weeks. U got this!

Miranda just texts back <3.

At the top of the bell curve, it's good. Miranda feels sharp and relaxed, acting with an ease she feels she never could have achieved without the tequila. And Tyler.

But somewhere in the second week, things start to slip. She hasn't been feeling well—the lights on set are starting to give her a headache. She's in a red satin evening dress—sans scarf, for once—and kitten heels, dressed up for the town benefit that Genevieve organizes to raise money for the Main Street Business Association. There's a group of extras with them now, gathered on the interior set of the historic library. Genevieve is supposed to give a speech about how the town came together to save their shops, but she can't remember how it starts out.

Tyler comes up in a sharply pressed suit, heading to his place.

"I'd like to rip that thing off you," he murmurs in her ear as he passes.

She giggles, heart racing at the thought. They haven't gotten much further than second base, but she wishes the two of them could spend some time alone. Maybe this weekend. Maybe she could take him to her beach house, or they could drive up the coast, or find a secluded spot in Franklin Canyon under the stars . . .

She realizes everyone is staring at her.

"Sorry?" Miranda says.

"Goddammit, Montana, I said action!" George shouts. "Can we *focus*, please?"

"Sorry, sorry." She finds her prop champagne glass and steps up on her podium.

George runs a hand over his face. "Top of scene. Action!"

Miranda stares into the bright lights. The extras look up at her, faces expectant.

"People of Bennington," she begins after a moment of silence that lasts a little too long. "My friends and neighbors. I could not be more proud to call you my—no, sorry. My friends. I could not be more proud to call you my neighbors—"

CRASH.

Everyone jumps. George has thrown his clipboard like a Frisbee onto the set.

"My neighbors!" he yells, clapping his hands to emphasize every word. "I—could—not—be—more—"

"Proud to call you my *friends*," Miranda recites along with him, face burning.

"What's going on?" He lifts his shoulders, hands open, like he's genuinely asking.

"I'm sorry." Miranda tries to shake the feeling that she's underwater, one step behind. "Sorry, I have it now. I won't mess it up."

"You better not." George points a finger at her. "Again!"

~

At the end of the day, Miranda gathers her things without speaking to anyone and hurries to her car. She's fumbling with her keys when she feels a hand on her waist in the twilight and recognizes Tyler's scent—musky, a little sweaty, spearmint from the chewing gum he uses to curb his cravings—before she sees him. Miranda turns instinctively into his arms and buries her face in his shoulder.

"Hey," he says, enveloping her. "Hey. You okay?"

"No." It's muffled.

"Let's get out of here, huh?"

She nods, not caring where they go, not wanting to be in charge.

~

He buckles her into the passenger seat of his car and drives to his house in Santa Monica as she pretends she isn't crying. Tyler leads her into a cavernous living room and sits her on a sectional in front of a gas fireplace. He flicks a switch on the mantel, and it roars to life.

"Pretty cool, huh?" he says, wiggling his eyebrows.

Miranda laughs and nods, rubbing her nose. He leaves her alone for a moment to stare into the flames, and then returns with two cut-crystal rocks glasses and a bottle of Jameson, setting them on the coffee table and sitting on the couch opposite her. He pours two fingers in each and then folds his hands.

Miranda shakes her head. "I'm not supposed to . . ."

He sighs. "You've been acting your ass off, stone-cold sober. Even before the tequila. I see how hard you're trying with recovery. You know that, right? I see you. I know how it is, too."

God, it feels so good to hear someone say that.

"So now cut yourself some slack," Tyler continues. "Let yourself take a break."

Somewhere in her more rational mind, she wishes it took more convincing. If Tyler had simply said, *Drink the whiskey, Miranda,* she would have. But it's nice to have someone rationalize things for you.

And he's in rehab, too. He seems to know what he's doing. So Miranda feels good, almost eager, and much more like her old self when she reaches for the glass and touches it to his in a toast.

One glass turns into three.

Three turns into four.

Four turns into Miranda crawling across the table, the two of them grappling with each other, finding bare skin as quickly as possible, hands in each other's hair and around each other's necks and backs.

"You're so good," Tyler murmurs.

"But a bad actress," Miranda teases, sighing into his ear.

"Mmm. No." He shakes his head. "You're the best actress, better than all of those *Kidz Klub* girls, better than Sicily . . ."

She giggles, confused; he's slurring a little. "What? Am not."

"Are too. Just look at you."

Miranda knows it isn't true, but the comparison to her international pop star best friend does wonders for her insecurity. She straddles Tyler, guiding him into her, and then they've somehow ended up on the floor, with him on top and holding her as close to his chest as possible.

She loses track of everything, able to focus only on how he makes her feel until it's as though she's about to tumble off the edge of the earth.

They fall asleep right there in front of the fireplace, wrapped in each other's arms on the floor.

~

Sometime in the night Miranda wakes up, body stiff and mouth dry. Her head is pounding as though she's been hitting it against a brick wall.

She somehow makes it back up to the couch, shivering in bare skin, but Tyler is nowhere to be found.

Miranda sits up and tries to get a bearing on her surroundings; the room is completely dark. Where did she leave her phone?

There, on the island in the kitchen. She digs in her purse, finding the cell and flipping it open: 1:37. She's going to be dead tomorrow.

There's also a text from Bobbie: Howd it go 2day?

By force of habit, she checks for a text from Zane, but there are none.

"Hey." Tyler's voice comes from behind her.

"Hey," she says quietly. "What are you doing up?"

He gives her a crooked smile, and where it would normally trigger butterflies, Miranda now feels a foreboding. It's too formal. He's found a pair of sweatpants and has his hands in his pockets, like he doesn't know where else to put them.

He shrugs. "I could ask you the same thing."

"Well . . . ," she starts. "Maybe we should get to bed."

"Maybe."

She waits for him to make a move, to invite her to his room; he doesn't. Instead, he says, "You want me to . . . Should I call you a cab?"

Miranda is aware of her heart beating. Its pulse is fast in her throat. "You don't want me to stay?" Her voice sounds embarrassingly small when she says it.

"I just think we'd both get better sleep in our own beds. We have to be fresh tomorrow, you know."

"You sure?" She's trying to sound coy, but she doesn't know why she's pushing it. It's over. "We could get some breakfast . . . ride to set together . . ."

He does that smile again. She hates it.

"Eh." Tyler shakes his head. "I think it's better this way."

～

Miranda is late to set in the morning. She was out of spinach for her green smoothie. It didn't matter; she didn't feel like she could keep anything down, anyway. George glares at her when she arrives, but she just walks past him and finds her place next to Tyler in the scene. He smiles politely at her, then stares straight ahead.

That day proves to be the worst day of shooting she has.

Miranda misses cues, mixes up her lines, and has trouble focusing on anything that's going on. Trying, at one point, to understand where lighting wants her to walk, she catches Tyler rolling his eyes at a few of the extras and shaking his head. They snicker, trying to hide their laughter from Miranda.

But she sees it. She knows that Tyler didn't want to be seen with her this morning, doesn't want anyone to know that the two addicts are sleeping together. She's bad for his image. Or maybe good, if he uses her correctly: *Look how much better Tyler is doing than Miranda! If anyone can make a comeback, it's him.*

She can see the headlines now.

When the day is nearly over, there's a knock at the door of Miranda's trailer, and she hates her heart for leaping in the hopes that it's Tyler.

But she opens the door to find George, brow sweaty and shirtsleeves rolled up.

"We have to talk," he says.

Miranda sighs. "I know."

"This isn't working. Production is behind. You and Tyler were hot stuff at the beginning of shooting, but your chemistry's gone, *poof.* I don't know what to do here."

"I'm sorry. I'll do better, I promise."

George wipes his mouth. "I've heard that before. Promises don't get movies made. Montana . . . we may be looking at a pinch hitter."

The world tilts around Miranda for a moment, but she should have seen it coming.

"George, I hear you, but please—don't replace me," she says. "I'll do whatever you need. I'll stay later, I'll get a coach. Tyler and I will make it work."

Miranda had been seeing a future again when she started this project, just a pinhole light at the end of a long tunnel, but one that would allow her to get back to the old life she used to love. Without that life, what is she? She has no degree, no education. She has no transferable skills and has never been part of "regular" society an adult day in her life. She would be reduced to nothing but a savings account, slowly dwindling over the years.

"It's not Tyler that's the problem." George shakes his head, stares into the middle distance. Then he passes a hand over his forehead. "All right, look. We'll see how tomorrow goes, and we'll have a production meeting about the whole thing tomorrow night, all right? I can't make any promises, though."

"Okay." Miranda could hug him, but she just nods very quickly. "Thank you. I won't let you down."

~

That night Miranda lies in bed and dials Germaine's number.

She'd made a quick call to the girls right when she got out of rehab, but quickly turned the conversation to Sicily's pregnancy and Germaine's parental woes. Beyond that, they've exchanged texts, but they haven't had a real conversation in forever.

Miranda still feels a little embarrassed. Germaine and Sicily have their lives together—thriving in a global business, going on a world tour and becoming a mom. She's the only one that's a mess. And although G and Sicily would never care about that, she hasn't really figured out how to talk about herself again. But she feels like nothing could make her feel lower than this week has.

There's a loud shriek on the other end of the line when Germaine picks up; Miranda smiles and holds the phone an inch away from her ear.

"MIRANDA!" G hollers. "Babes, how *are* you?"

And in that moment Miranda knows she was being silly. As if a conversation with Germaine could ever be awkward or stuffy.

"Hey," Miranda says. "I know, I know. I've been bad at reaching out."

"Listen, it's my fault, too," Germaine says. "I think about you every day, bitch."

Miranda feels a hard lump in her throat. "You too. How have things been?"

"Tragic. Greg and Giles are as nightmarish as ever—Dad has them out for something in the Maldives right now. But am I invited? No. I'm stuck at home with Queen Maleficent."

"Shh, she'll hear you," Miranda says. She hears G scoff on the other end and imagines her rolling her eyes.

"Yeah," says Germaine. "And come and prick my finger on a spindle of Botox."

"You should get out of there," Miranda says, only half joking. "Why don't you go somewhere? You could go anywhere you want."

Like here, she means, but she doesn't say it.

"I don't know. Maybe I will. But M&M, you've been too quiet! Now tell me *everything* that's been going on with you."

So Miranda does. She talks about the high hopes she had for this movie, how well it was going at first, how great it was working with Tyler again. How new it felt to have feelings for someone other than Zane. Then she curls under her covers as she recounts the past few days and how much of a downward spiral everything has become. Germaine listens to every word.

"Oh, babes," Germaine says when Miranda finally takes a deep breath. "I'm really sorry. And I'm sorry you've being going through this shit alone."

Miranda sighs. "It's okay." It does feel more okay, letting it all out.

"I'd like to get my hands on Tyler. No one would recognize him after I beat the crap out of him."

Miranda allows herself to giggle, just a little. "He's going through his own shit, too, I guess."

"Maybe so. But I never liked him on *Kidz Klub*—he always joked about me being taller than him like I was some freak, remember? And he kept making comments about Sicily's boobs and stuff when she was so self-conscious about developing. Such an immature perv." She clucks her tongue on the other end of the line. "I've seen the tabloids; it drives me insane how they paint him as the picture of reform, turning his life around, doing think pieces about him on celebrities and recovery. But they don't do anything except slander you, dissect your looks, post awful pictures of you leaving rehab . . ."

"I know, G." Miranda doesn't need to be reminded of that. Part of her recovery plan was a strict and total ban on reading anything that's been reported about her, at least until after her first project has wrapped.

Germaine sighs. "I wish I could come out there right now. I wish I could steal the family jet and be there before you can snap your fingers."

Then do it! Miranda wants to say. She would give anything to have a sleepover with Germaine and Sicily right now, just like they used to back in their *Kidz Klub* days, crimping each other's hair and watching *George of the Jungle* and talking about how they would rule the world someday—where they would live, what they would do with their lives, whom they would marry.

But Miranda already knows why Germaine can't. She may be richer than all of them, even Sicily with all her international success, but it's family money. And her family doesn't like Miranda. They wouldn't even let her come to the opening of one of their fancy hotels on the beach in Santa Monica, even though she was less than fifteen minutes away.

"We'll find some time," Miranda says, which is what they've been saying and texting for two years. "We'll see each other soon enough."

Germaine sighs. "I love you, M&M."

"You too, G."

~

Things are not exactly better. But talking to Germaine has given Miranda resolve. She feels marginally more confident the next day on set, and by the time she's driving to the address George gave her for the production meeting, she feels certain that she'll be able to convince the producers to keep her on. She'll be honest about the backsliding she's done with Tyler, straightforward about how she plans to stick to her recovery plan. She'll show them the number of her accountability partner, Margie. She's identified an AA group in LA that will help her stay on track.

She needs this job.

Miranda pulls up to the house in Westwood and takes a deep breath. It's a more modest one than the mansions she's seen—a short driveway and a bungalow style—but still smacks of money. She squares her shoulders and rings the doorbell.

George answers. "Miranda. Come in."

He's wearing a quarter zip and khakis. She steps inside and finds herself in a well-furnished living room with a Chesterfield sofa and framed posters of Holiday Heartwarmers movies on the wall, among other made-for-TV hits.

This is George's house. And the room is empty.

"Am I the first to get here?" she asks, her mind beginning to catch up with her observations. She already knows the answer. But she wants to hear him say it.

"You're the only one," he says without missing a beat. "I thought we could do some one-on-one coaching."

"Oh." There is no question about what that means. She is here, alone, and she is being offered a choice. But part of her is still hoping that the other producers are on their way, that Tyler is here somewhere, that they're going to talk about performance goals and strategies and other cut-and-dried things. She suddenly misses her mom. So, so badly.

"Because, you know," George says, wiping his nose on his sleeve. "Without some coaching, I don't know if we're going to be able to keep you on."

She needs this job.

Miranda shifts her weight. She tosses her hair over one shoulder and smiles.

"What did you have in mind?"

~

On the drive back to Malibu, Miranda pulls the car over on San Vicente Boulevard and throws up beneath a coral tree, vomit spattering the rotting fruit that has fallen on the curb below. She will not tell anybody about this—not even Germaine or Sicily. She will not let anyone know how low she's sinking.

FIVE

GERMAINE

2007

Germaine stands before her closet in the Park Avenue apartment, which is roughly the size of a standard bedroom. Built-in oak shelves line its walls, holding clothes folded carefully on hangers and in drawers that light automatically when opened. There is a separate walk-in closet within the closet for shoes, her favorites of which are displayed on fabric plinths and others are kept in their tissue paper and original boxes. Some have never been opened.

There are three gilded floor-length mirrors, each of which are equipped with several light settings—natural daylight, standard indoor light, intimate low light—so Germaine can evaluate how her outfits perform in each. Because when you are a woman with as much money as Germaine, every outfit is, indeed, a performance of the highest caliber.

That may be well and good. But talking to Miranda drove home a point that Germaine has felt at many different times in her life: she is so goddamn lonely. She can have all of this—the entire world if she wants it, really—but it's worth nothing if she just sits around cooped up in it all day.

All Germaine's work feels fake. She kept thinking about how much fun she had with the two of them in *Kidz Klub*—and how she hasn't had any fun since. No sense of fulfillment or purpose, just getting moved around by her parents like a piece on a chessboard.

Germaine goes to the athleisure section and rifles through the Lycra sweatshirts, the quarter zips, the long-sleeved shirts with the holes cut out for her thumbs. She chooses a light-blue three-quarter-length sleeve that comes down to her forearms and feels buttery soft but as breathable as though she's wearing nothing at all. Germaine puts on skintight black leggings and Air Jordans, tucking Italian-leather jazz shoes into her Chanel bag before heading down to meet her driver.

She would walk the blocks to Studio Rochelle if she could, to warm up. But her parents would have even more of a fit about that than they're already having about her decision to take dance classes again.

When *Kidz Klub* wrapped, Germaine had an offer to join Unlimited, the premier studio in Los Angeles, home to the most talented dancers who performed in hip-hop routines and for top artists all around the world. She'd already signed the contract when her parents found out and voided it, threatening to cut off her finances. Not wanting to get involved with the St. Germaine-Changs' powerful legal team, the studio had backed off. Germaine had still been a minor, after all. Only just.

Germaine managed to stay in LA for the three years after that before her parents' patience ran out and they dragged her back to New York. She never got offers from any other studios out west, and she wondered if Terence had gotten her blacklisted.

But they hadn't thought about New York studios.

Céline, at least, doesn't seem to mind.

"It would do your figure good to finally get some exercise," she quipped when Germaine announced her plan at the family dinner. "As long as you don't develop big muscles in your legs. You'll look like a weight lifter. No one will want to marry a weight lifter."

"I don't care about looking like a weight lifter," Germaine said. "And I don't care about getting married."

Her mother had sighed, rubbing the bridge of her nose with her slender fingers as though Germaine was the most obstinate girl she'd ever met.

"Do you really think that's a valuable use of your time?" Terence had asked, seeming baffled. "Wriggling around in skimpy clothes—for what? Surely you're not thinking of performing."

It was Germaine's turn to sigh. Everything had to be a means to some end for her father. "It's just for fun, Dad. I need something. Don't you ever do anything just for fun?"

He frowned, did a little confused twitch of his head. "Are there even any reputable studios in this city?"

"I was thinking the YMCA," she said, just to see him choke on his foie gras.

In the end, Germaine had managed to make her parents feel like they'd won something by agreeing to go to Studio Rochelle, a place with a reputation for working with Broadway stars, visiting Bolshevik ballerinas, and backup dancers for the likes of Beyoncé and Christina Aguilera. And Sicily, but Germaine conveniently left that part out.

She takes a deep breath and tightens her ponytail as the car pulls up to the curb. She has her water bottle; she has an extra scrunchie. It's an advanced class, and she hasn't really danced in years, but she'll pick it back up, right?

After a short drive, Germaine hops out of the Audi and ascends to the studio in the elevator. A handful of dancers are already there, stretching and warming up—the class has already been running for three weeks, and she joined late.

A man with curly black hair in a black tank top and matching sweatpants greets her. "Germaine! Welcome," he says. "I'm Sam; I believe I spoke to your people on the phone."

"Yes," Germaine says. "Hi." She's more nervous than she thought she'd be.

"So I know you have some experience. Feel free to stretch however you'd like; we'll do a full class warm-up once everyone's here, and then we'll get into the routine. We have some folks here working on *Rent*, so we've decided to incorporate some of that for fun."

Germaine nods. "Great. Yeah."

"You're welcome to just jump in and pick up whatever you can. We'll work together after class to get you caught up, if that sounds good."

"Sure." Germaine nods again. "Thank you."

"Of course."

Germaine's parents make a point of never saying *Thank you*, but she really appreciates how Sam is treating her like she's a regular person. Most people are intimidated by Germaine and keep so much distance that she can never have a normal conversation with any of them.

Germaine sets her purse on a shelf at one end of the room and hangs her jacket on a hook. When she turns, she catches a few of the other dancers looking quickly away.

Germaine sucks her teeth, trying to ignore them. She begins the stretching routine she used to do so long ago. It's as bad as she feared— her body is stiff and unyielding to the contortions she used to fall into easily as a teenager. She used to love being able to show off how she could drop into the splits without even warming up.

More than anything, though, she loved just hanging out and goofing off with Miranda and Sicily on set. The dancing and music are the only other thing she misses from *Kidz Klub*, and she's hoping that this class will unlock some muscle memory of what all that feels like, being young and happy.

She sits and brings the bottoms of her feet together, dropping her head as low to the ground as she can get. Germaine is still young.

But happy? No. More like numb.

When the room is more full and Germaine finally straightens up, she sees that there's an eight-foot circle around her. The others are giving her a wide berth, being careful to avoid looking at her.

Germaine purses her lips. People fall into two camps: the ones who fear her and the ones who have contempt for her. Actually, she's pretty sure that Venn diagram is a circle. The family staff acts the same way toward her as these dancers do, ever since she got the housekeeper fired for tripping over Milano.

Whatever. Germaine's parents have created a monster—an unhappy, raging, bored monster.

Miranda may be a mess, but at least she's back making movies. Soon she'll be acting in even better films with better costars, and later on she'll probably write some pedantic *Don't drink, kids* book that she'll be interviewed by Oprah about.

And Sicily will keep on recording and singing, appearing on every TV set and radio around the world, performing sold-out shows and writhing and strutting onstage to disguise her—let's face it—pretty average dancing.

Two-thirds of the 3AM Girls are going to be huge stars. And what's Germaine? Some eye candy that shows up at galas, charity dinners, and launches for new magazines and fashion lines, there to be photographed and sign big checks. Serving no greater purpose than some confetti or a decorative tablecloth.

That's her mother's life, and Germaine doesn't want it.

So what *does* she want?

The studio assistant turns on the soundtrack, and Germaine feels the music vibrate into her bones. Studio Rochelle uses a built-in surround-sound system, better than the tinny CD players Germaine is sure are typical for lesser dance classes. The bass is electric and warm and makes Germaine want to move.

Sam and the dancers take positions and begin their routine. It *is* advanced, and it involves more than a little athleticism and strenuous training.

But after watching a few times and moving through the motions, she starts to pick it up. It feels good to move her body again, to hit the right positions on the same beat as the music and see the artistic, almost sculptural angles her body creates in the mirror.

With it floods back a long-lost self-assurance. Dancing had been her thing. Miranda could light up the stage with her acting, Sicily could turn heads with her singing. Neither of those had been Germaine's strong suits. She didn't like the feeling of overperforming, and her voice was on the weaker side. But even so, the urge to dance to the music was like a natural reflex. She could still be her serious self that way, smiling when the occasion called for it but devoting more attention to what the music was doing than engaging with costars or the audience. She found the choreography more easily than anyone, so much so that the Blast Off! studio coach always put her at the front so she could lead the others.

Germaine has spent too many years listening to her parents tell her this doesn't matter; it doesn't constitute any sort of valuable skill. But Germaine forgot how much it had mattered to *her*.

She watches herself in the mirror, a few steps behind the others but by no means an amateur. Beneath the rush of endorphins and relief that she hasn't lost the muscle memory, there's a little curdle of resentment that starts in Germaine's stomach. What if she had been allowed to stay in Los Angeles, building a post-show career like Miranda and Sicily had?

Germaine would never begrudge Miranda and Sicily their success. Much. But she could have had it, too.

She could have, if her parents had given her the chance. People danced for a living—did plenty of things with music that didn't involve singing—and with the connections that *Kidz Klub* had allowed the girls to build, Germaine is sure in this moment that she would have found a path to a career she loved.

Is it too late? Could she buy her way back? But she's done no relevant industry work since *Kidz Klub*; now she's just like the other schmucks who went back to their regular lives and now have no claim to Hollywood fame except to say that they used to be on the show. And Germaine has a feeling that if she were to try to break back into a show business career, it would mean a break with her family. And her entire way of life.

That's a hard sell.

By the time the class is over, Germaine is nearly able to keep up with the rest of the dancers. She's caught more than a few surprised glances her way, and even Sam seems impressed.

"Looks like we might not have to catch you up too much, after all!" he says.

~

All day, Germaine feels better than she has in months. Years, maybe. She fills the rest of it with the various pointless tasks she always does: getting brunch with the daughter of one of her father's business associates who's supposed to be her friend, tipping off paparazzi to their location. But humming in the back of her mind is the music, the movement. She brushes Milano and Shibuya and Tivoli and Monaco, trying to corral them so she can dress them in new outfits she ordered special from Paris. She watches *Desperate Housewives* on the big screen in the home theater.

And when her mother finally gets home for dinner from a women's benefit, Germaine is excited enough about the class to tell her about it.

"Hello, Maman," Germaine says, kissing her mother on the cheek and taking a seat at the dinner table.

Céline looks at Germaine as though she's been slapped.

"Are you drunk?" her mother asks.

Germaine frowns. "No. I'm in a good mood."

"What on earth about?"

"I had my first dance class this morning."

"Your what?"

Germaine shakes her head. "The dance class? At Studio Rochelle?"

"Oh." Her mother blinks a few times. "Right. Well, the benefit was a success. But I heard from your father today, and—"

"You're not even going to ask how it went?" She feels her good mood begin to deflate in the stale air of the dining room. The curdle of resentment rises to a low burn.

Céline looks at her like she's an idiot. "Apparently it went well. I thought we covered that. Anyway, there are more important things we need to go over. Gregoire's on his way back; you two need to go to Aspen this weekend. Your father's friend Asgerdur—do you remember Asgerdur?—he has a table at the Silver Ball benefit and wants to fill it with 'beautiful people.' You know how he is."

Asgerdur was a hotel investor friend of Terence's who placed high importance on public appearance. The two of them often traded favors.

"What if I don't want to?" Germaine says. "I hate Aspen."

Céline waves her hand. "It's already settled. The stylist is coming tonight so we can select wardrobe."

Germaine decides on the cold shoulder. She says nothing for the rest of dinner, but her mother doesn't seem to notice. She says nothing as they relocate to her mother's bedroom with the stylist, Marie, or as she tries on a large selection of dresses—Chanel, Dior, Louis Vuitton, Armani, and the even higher-end nameless brands of each of those houses—parading them around the carpeted suite.

"C'est très jolie, non?" Marie says of each outfit.

But every time, Céline shakes her head. "Non."

Finally, Céline gets up, casts a beleaguered glance at the poor stylist, and disappears into her closet.

"If you want something done right, you have to do it yourself," she says, reemerging with a large dress box. From the tissue paper, she pulls out a midnight-blue vintage Yves Saint Laurent evening gown.

"You need something slimming," she says.

"Mama, this isn't going to be slimming," Germaine says. She recognizes the gown. It's a hammered silk piece with a slight cowl neck, creating a wraithlike silhouette and cut on a bias to drape at the bottom. "It's going to be tight."

"It was my favorite back in the day. Try it on."

Germaine does as she is told, but she's right. Germaine is not large by any means, but her shoulders are broader than her mother's, and she's taller than Céline was when she originally wore this dress. The garment is tight at the arms and hips, falling slightly above where it's supposed to on her body.

But Céline thinks it's perfect. "That's the one," she says. "Just stunning."

"No, it's not," Germaine says, emboldened, perhaps, by the way she felt this morning and the way her mother ruined her mood. "It looks ugly on me. In fact, it's just an ugly dress."

Céline doesn't say anything, so Germaine keeps going. "I have an entire room full of clothes. Why don't you ever let me wear something of *mine*? What are those clothes even *for*? I haven't worn half of them. I don't want to look like you. I want to look like *me*, wear things that fit *my* body and *my* personal style." She's yelling now, but she can't stop. "I'm a human being, do you realize that? I'm not some doll you can dress up! I'm not your property!"

Céline stares at her levelly, but Germaine sees a muscle in her jaw jump and knows her mother is clenching her teeth. In some ways Germaine hates how calm Céline is when she's angry. She wishes she would scream, throw things at her, anything. She wants them to fight. She wants them to break through this cool veneer and tell each other everything the other has done that's hurt them, everything they've hated about each other, get down to the real shit, the grit. Céline never says how she feels. She never seems to have real emotion. If only there was something she could do to provoke her mother enough to break her out of this inhuman, unfeeling exterior.

But Céline speaks softly. "These little outbursts are getting very boring."

She stands and heads for the door, signaling that the conversation is over. Germaine would throw something at her mother if she could, but she has nothing.

"There's nothing worse than an ungrateful child," Céline says, and then she is gone.

~

It's 3:00 p.m. and Gregoire has already been drinking. His voice is loud in the limo as they head from their mountain-view hotel to the Silver Ball banquet, talking about some girl he was hitting on in the Maldives.

Germaine has not been drinking, but she already has a headache. She isn't listening to anything Greg—or Gross, as she likes to call him—is saying. She's staring at the bleak gray sky over the mountains, the insufferable Colorado streets, and trying not to breathe too hard for fear that the delicate structure of her mother's YSL won't take well to it. She's promising herself that she'll get through this weekend, she'll do the stupid events, she'll do whatever they want if she can just keep going to dance classes each week and figure out how to build a hobby or secret side gig around that enveloping music. Maybe that could get her through the rest of her life. Maybe she could even teach alongside Sam someday, if she worked hard at it. And didn't tell her parents.

". . . and then when I told her my last name, you should've seen the way her eyes popped out of her head, G." Greg laughs way too loudly. "I thought she was going to drop her panties right there in the middle of Oishii!"

"Greg!" Germaine snaps. The limo pulls into the drive. She speaks to him as though she's talking to a misbehaving kindergartner. "Why. Would you think. I would care. About *any* of this?"

He looks at her, seeming genuinely confused. "I thought you'd want to hear what you missed out on in Malé," he says.

Germaine gives as exasperated a sigh as she can possibly muster and steps gingerly out of the car as the driver opens the door. A flurry of photographers rush to the edge of the velvet ropes, and she tucks a piece of hair behind her ear that's fallen loose from her french twist, smiling as widely as she can. She knows her mother will be reviewing the press from the event.

Greg catches up with her.

"Joke," he says, and they laugh merrily at each other, positively sparkling with ease and sophistication. It's the shorthand they use for public appearances, placeholders for actual conversation to keep up their image of a close-knit but intimidatingly intellectual and wealthy family.

She leans into him and speaks low into his ear. "Serious."

He raises his eyebrows thoughtfully at her, as though he's mildly surprised but intrigued by her comment, and she lifts her chin in response, displaying another, more formal, side of themselves to the paparazzi.

Then they're inside and can drop the act, just marginally.

Asgerdur would be pleased, because the event is, indeed, filled with beautiful people. The collective net worth gathered in the grand banquet hall is far, far more than the Silver Ball could ever hope to raise. It's primarily older men in sharply pressed suits who haven't bothered to do much else with their appearance, and very young women who have likely had entire teams of staff working for hours to make their impossible goddess-like beauty look effortless.

Germaine and Gregoire mingle, detached but never far from each other, Greg talking about sports and acquisitions and mergers with men who all look the same, and Germaine mostly laughing along at their jokes—bland at best and offensive at worst—and smiling wide. There are photographers inside as well. She allows herself a glass of champagne, then another, to take the edge off, and sips slowly, although she'd like to down them both in one gulp.

Then the lights dim in the hall and come up on the stage, prompting everyone to take their seats. They find Asgerdur's table, filled with other titans of industry and A-list celebrities.

Gregoire sits. As Germaine lowers herself, a little too quickly, into the chair next to him, the strain at last proves to be too much for the vintage YSL.

A seam at her rib cage splits just as an event photographer snaps their picture.

Germaine freezes. Many things become apparent to her all at once. The photographers here are hired professionals, but selling a photo of Germaine St. Germaine-Chang's dress splitting open with a minuscule glimpse of her lacy black bra would be a temptation too great and a product too priceless for even the most scrupulous photog.

She could demand he delete the photo in front of her, but then she would be drawing even more attention to what just happened.

She could find the event organizers and make them deal with it, but by then he'd have backed up the photo. And anyway, he's already moved to another table; all the photographers are dressed in black, and now she's not even sure which one it was.

And maybe, just maybe, if she tries not to move her arm too much, no one will even notice.

Except for the fact that Greg is pointing at her and laughing.

"Excuse my sister," he snorts, getting the rest of the table in on it. "She's taking dance classes to lose weight."

There's a wraithlike young woman to Germaine's right, someone who's been in a few movies but whose name Germaine can't remember. She leans in conspiratorially, and Germaine feels dizzy by the amount of perfume she's wearing.

"I have a good lipo surgeon, if you're looking for someone," she says.

Germaine could spit. She could reenact her tantrum with the tablecloth, not caring about the reactions of any of these people she doesn't know or like.

But she will be good.

"I guess I *won't* be having dessert," she says, to the great mirth of the rest of the table, laughing lightly along with them.

The banquet goes on, and Germaine picks at her food. All the women are picking at their food.

But her reluctance to eat is because she feels sick, dreading what she'll say to her mother when they get home.

She hates Aspen.

～

But the apartment is empty when Germaine returns on Sunday night—alone, because Greg decided to stay out in Aspen a few more days to schmooze with Asgerdur's friends.

A new housekeeper is there.

"Is my mother here?" Germaine asks, afraid to go into the parlor and find out for herself.

"No, Miss St. Germaine-Chang," the woman says, looking as terrified of her as every other staff member. Germaine is starting to get a little tired of it. "Your mother has gone to East Hampton for a long weekend, and your father was meeting her there."

Germaine lets out a long breath, relieved. Maybe her mother hasn't seen the photo. Maybe she can get the dress repaired before they get back, and Céline will never have to know.

"Good," Germaine says. "I'm going to bed, then."

"Miss St. Germaine-Chang," the housekeeper says quickly, a tremor in her voice.

Germaine waves her hand. "Listen, you don't have to be afraid of me, okay? I'm not my mother."

The housekeeper looks like she wants to say something else, but she shuts her mouth and nods very quickly.

Germaine sighs and heads for her room. She's more than ready to put on something comfortable and sink into bed. Maybe by morning she'll have dreamed up a plan to destroy that photo of the split dress and do some damage control.

But then she flicks on the light to her suite and nearly screams.

It's empty.

Her bed is still there, its flurry of throw pillows and fluffy quilts replaced with plain cotton sheets. Her antique boudoir has been cleared of all her jewelry boxes and hair accessories and scarves; a plastic hairbrush and an unopened package of Goody hair bands from Walgreens have been placed next to the mirror.

Germaine runs to her closet and turns on the recessed lights. On the ottoman in the center of the room, there is a folded pair of leggings, a sweatshirt, some socks, and a pair of underwear. The racks of clothes are gone; the shelves are empty. Her shoes, her dresses, everything—vanished.

She whirls around to find the housekeeper peeking through the door, visibly terrified.

"Miss St. Germaine-Chang," she says again.

"What is this?" Germaine barks.

"I'm very sorry. Miss, your mother—she asked me to tell you that she's stopped your credit cards. Your accounts have been frozen. She says that the situation will be reviewed next week."

Germaine opens her mouth, closes it again. "Did she say anything else?"

"Just—she asked me to take the dress from you, miss. And send it out for repair."

Germaine stands still, stunned. Then she says, "It's in my luggage. They're bringing it up now."

"Yes, miss." The housekeeper gives a curt bow and hurries out of the room.

Germaine slumps to the floor. Something like this happened once before, during the last season of *Kidz Klub*. She earned more than a decent income on the show—by normal-person standards, at least— but since she was a minor when she started, her parents were cosigners on all her accounts. That fact never changed. Germaine's never had a reason to understand any of her own finances. She doesn't have the slightest idea how to set up her own accounts, and there's no one she can trust to help her. In fact, to this day, she hasn't ever set foot in a bank or met with her parents' financial adviser. Why would she? Money flows as freely as air or water for the St. Germaine-Changs, a seemingly inexhaustible resource.

Except for the time Germaine's parents thought she was getting too arrogant, too cocky. She was, probably. She was high on the freedom of LA, the independence she had there, and the friends who made her feel like anything was possible.

When she arrived back in New York for the holiday break, home from filming, all her childhood things were gone. Her dolls and picture books, her Legos and stuffed animals, even the raggedy bunny that her first and most favorite nanny, who was later replaced and then replaced again, had given her as a tearful goodbye gift. Germaine had slept with it every night and would have continued to, even into adulthood, if they hadn't thrown it away.

"If you don't respect us," her mother had said, "then we will take away the things we've given you. You depend on us for all of this. You would have nothing without your father's hard work. You would *be* nothing."

The message is the same tonight.

So here Germaine is: nothing, once again.

SIX

SICILY

2007

Sicily places her hands on her belly and stares up at the popcorn drop ceiling, doing her breathing exercises. Her mother told her she should be praying extra hard right now, but she can't seem to find the words. A boxy TV mounted in the corner plays the Atlanta weather report: fifty-one degrees, humid, chance of scattered showers overnight. She tries to remember whether she's ever been in Atlanta before. Officially speaking, she still isn't. Her family have pulled out all the stops to ensure that the location of the hospital where Sicily is going to give birth remains private. There's a bodyguard at the door, another down the hall, and a security team on the ground, keeping watch over the hospital campus. Everyone was sworn to secrecy, and, in fact, one of her cousins was responsible for leaking a few other locations to the press as decoys. It's not quite Beyoncé-level security, but almost.

Sicily knows it's not about protecting her privacy—it's about keeping the pregnancy hush-hush. Which is ridiculous. Everyone in the world knows she's having a baby; she's been asked about it in interviews for months. Press statements have circulated, both from her people and from Hugo's.

Sicily's statement was a vague announcement about beginning a new chapter in her life and requests for privacy. But the headlines on Hugo's articles are splashed with phrases like Excited for fatherhood! and paired with flattering, high-contrast images of Hugo smiling wide.

But Sicily knows the truth.

"That's not possible," he'd said, horrified, when she told him back in LA. "Are you sure it's mine?"

That hurt. "Of course it is," Sicily said. "I thought—God, I feel so stupid. I thought you'd be excited."

She was excited. Or had been. She was half-terrified when the pregnancy test came back positive, of course, but the other half was thrilled. A little baby of her own that she could love? A baby of hers and Hugo's, a man she adored? Sure, the timing wasn't great, but it never would have been. Sicily had even thought for a moment that maybe this was God's special plan for her, an unexpected little miracle that might never have happened had she waited until retirement to finally settle down. She certainly wouldn't have let the machine stop for something as selfish as *intentionally* wanting to get pregnant and begin a family. Babies and strict tour schedules didn't mesh well.

But with every dismal reaction, her initial joy faltered.

Hugo had brought his hands to his face, rubbed it hard. "Sicily, you're a lovely girl, but—"

Her heart began to sink. It couldn't be happening again. They loved each other, didn't they? They'd made love and she confessed how she felt, they held each other that night in London—

But he hadn't said it back.

"It was just a bit of fun. I'm not ready—this isn't where I'm at in my life right now. In my career."

Sicily fought hard to hold back tears. "Well, maybe I'm not either! But I already love this child, *our* child, and sometimes things don't go the way you expect them to, but you just have to make the best—"

He'd put his hand up then. "I'm sorry. I'm sorry. Just—I have to think. I have to call my manager."

She'd opened and closed her mouth like a fish. She racked her brain for something, anything, she could say to turn this conversation around. But Hugo was done talking.

They'd spoken only via representatives since then. The various managers and handlers agreed on a party line: *Although, sadly, Hugo and Sicily are no longer together as a couple, they remain close friends and look forward to coparenting their child.*

Lies, lies, lies. Sicily's not sure when or if Hugo will meet the baby, although the child's last name will be his: Smythe. It's a win for Hugo, since his management team insisted on it and wouldn't agree to hyphenation. Sicily's parents take this as a personal affront. But Sicily doesn't care. She doesn't need his child support—her net worth far outweighs his, anyway. The baby will want for nothing.

Except a father who's around all the time, who's in love with the baby's mother, building a happy little family. Sicily never imagined things would turn out this way. Judging by all the weeping and prayer circles her family keeps holding, neither did they. Her parents went through at least four stages of grief when she confessed to them, and Sicily is sure they haven't reached acceptance yet. They've been oscillating between anger and depression over this last trimester, their agitation growing in tandem with her belly.

You know better than to act this way, her father had said.

We gave you the tools you needed, expectations on how to conduct yourself, and you just cast it all aside, her mother had said. *And you cast us, and the family reputation, with it. It was incredibly selfish of you.*

They didn't directly say *slut,* but they didn't need to—all the harping on about running around behind their backs for her own filthy desires got the point across pretty well. Day, especially, even managed to turn the whole situation into a tirade about international relations, saying that at least a good American man would have had enough decency to marry Sicily. Better to be with some boisterous, boozy down-home man than a smug, uncaring English pop star—as bad as anyone in that backward country.

She's not thinking right, Uncle Henry had said. They did a lot of that these days, talking about her like she wasn't in the room with them. *Her behavior isn't only wanton, it's a sign that there's too much stress on her. She's breaking down. Can we trust her to know what's best?* Tour dates need to stay on some sort of schedule. So Sicily is having a voluntary cesarean in order to control the due date. This is her parents' idea, not hers, although she appreciates the fact that she'll have time to fully recover before the South America tour. She'll need to pump milk every day, and yet another cousin will join the entourage as a nanny, but nothing will derail the Bell Express, Day says.

Sicily has rewritten the lyrics to "So Bad, So Good" now that it no longer has a happy ending. Uncle Henry thinks the angst in it will sell well. No one knows it's about Hugo.

"There she is!" The door opens and Kendra walks in, dressed as usual in a leather blazer with her signature planner in hand.

"Hey, cuz." Sicily smiles weakly. Kendra hasn't had as much to do, personal assisting–wise, for about a month. Sicily has been lying very low from any and all press and social engagements; in the interim, Kendra has turned to reputation and public relations management and taken to it with a little too much relish, Sicily thinks.

"How we holding up?" she asks, pulling up a chair and resting her kitten-heeled feet on the bed.

"Okay. Just nervous."

"Don't be. You don't even have to do anything—you'll be asleep the whole time."

"Yeah, well." Sicily sighs. "I'm nervous for everything afterward, too."

Kendra smirks at her. "Well, don't worry about that, either. If you can sell out world tours like you do, I'm sure you're capable of anything."

"Thanks, Kends." Sicily closes her eyes for just a moment, trying to believe it.

"Okay, daily roundup," Kendra announces, pulling out her iPhone and ignoring Sicily's groan. The entire entourage has splurged on the brand-new smartphones and full data plans so they can stay plugged in to email and media at all times. Sicily likes it less and less. Why would she need even more devices that tell her all the terrible things people are saying? She wanted to keep her old phone, with its familiar buttons and little screen, but Carole insisted.

"Hush—I know it's not fun, but we need to stay on top of it, especially now." Kendra's eyes are glued to her screen. She's two years older than Sicily and has always been someone Sicily looks up to. Being close in age—and spending so much time together in Sicily's career—she feels closer to Kendra than most of the others in the entourage. Kendra accepted the news about the pregnancy with a sigh, a shrug, and a *Well, what do you want to do about it?* Which was the reason why Sicily told her first. She's felt, sometimes, that Kendra is a buffer between Sicily and her parents, scheduling fake appointments when Sicily just needs a break, and taking her out for pedicures and sushi when she needs it.

But Sicily hates Kendra's practice of the "daily roundup": a rundown of the gossip highlights about Sicily. They used to laugh through it, with Kendra roasting poorly written and absurdly inaccurate headlines to cheer her up.

But it stopped being fun a long time ago.

More and more, Sicily is worried that there's a rift beginning to open in the way her family perceives her. There should be two Sicilys: the stage presence, the brand they all manage, the product that allows them to sign their checks. And then the daughter, cousin, niece, actual person that they know and love in real life.

She doesn't want them to forget about the second Sicily.

"'Irresponsible: How Sicily Bell's Fall from Grace Signals a Moral Deficit in Today's Youth.' Oof," Kendra says. "Weird how they forget that yesterday's youth all smoked pot at Woodstock . . . Let's see . . . ooh, this one links to a personal blog: the *Church Crusader.* 'Agents of Satan Posing as False Idol Pop Stars.' You made the list!"

Sicily lies back and looks at the ceiling. "It's not funny, Kendra."

"Oh come on, it is a *little*. No one really thinks you're a demon."

But Kendra's wrong about that, Sicily knows. Some of her own extended family may be harboring the same thoughts. And a lot of people take the ramblings of bad press at face value.

"Let's see . . . blah blah blah, 'How Not to Do Pregnancy Fashion' . . . shoot, they got pictures from your checkup in Sedona. I thought we were really buckled down there. I hope we don't have a snitch . . ."

Sicily closes her eyes again and places her hands on her belly, as if to cover the ears of the baby inside. She hopes the child can't hear what they're saying about her. She knows that she looked like a mess at that appointment—hair in a topknot, oversize sweatshirt, flip-flops, eyes puffy and red from crying. She'd been thirty-two weeks pregnant and incredibly hormonal, for god's sake.

But they would not forgive her for corrupting the sexy, girly fantasy image they held of her with something as sexless and bland as motherhood. The two sides could not be reconciled. And everyone who resented her fame and power for one reason or another could now dogpile in self-righteous moral panic. She's a terrible role model for the young girls who looked up to her. She'll be an absent mother who's too focused on a selfish career. She needs to either give up the baby or give up performing. Her sales will plummet because no one will want to pay to see a woman dancing around with stretch marks. She'll have a weak pelvic floor for the rest of her life. It's over for her.

So why do the little movements that ripple under her palms feel like a beginning? She is, despite everything, looking forward to meeting the baby. No one has allowed her to be excited. She wants to gush about how she already knows the child will be so smart, so beautiful, so talented and perfect. She wants to show the little fists and head in the ultrasound to everyone she meets. She imagines buying adorable outfits, bringing her baby outside to see the sun for the first time, and playing lullabies on the old acoustic that she got for her birthday when she turned ten. Sicily's guitar skills aren't polished enough to perform, and acoustic sound doesn't fit her brand. But she can play just fine to sing her baby to sleep.

"Listen to this one," Kendra says, interrupting her thoughts. "'Disco Daddy: British Rogue Hugo Smythe Spotted in Ibiza Days before the Birth of His Child.'"

"'Rogue,'" Sicily spits, disgusted. They paint him as a sexy cad, as James Bond. What would they say if they saw *her* in Ibiza this week? The outrage would be so intense that it would put her safety at risk.

A nurse walks briskly into the room. "Almost time," she tells Sicily. "The anesthesiologist is on her way. Are you ready?"

Sicily nods, even though she isn't, even though it doesn't matter whether or not she's ready. She didn't choose the cesarean or the general anesthetic. She didn't choose the hospital.

As she lies back and allows the anesthesiologist to fit a mask over her mouth and nose, Sicily presses her hands tight to her abdomen, fighting paranoia that her family will snatch the baby while she's knocked out, fast asleep, and send the child to be raised in a convent.

She closes her eyes and tells herself—as she has told herself many times—that this is ridiculous. She is safe and everything is going to be fine.

Still: becoming pregnant has made her realize how few decisions she's actually allowed to make for herself.

~

There's something wailing like a siren on steroids, and Sicily is suddenly awake. She's seized with a panic she doesn't understand, her whole body focused on the source and pitch of the sound.

Then all at once the bleary room around her comes into sharp focus as she sees Kendra holding a wrinkled pink thing wrapped in a blanket, screaming like the world's about to end.

In spite of herself, Kendra smiles. "Here he is," she says. "He wants you."

And Sicily sees the little arms struggling to break free from the blanket, to reach for her.

"Hey, you," she says breathlessly, like she's saying a prayer. "Hey, Noah. Come here."

He fits like a puzzle piece in her arms, calming immediately and staring slightly open-mouthed at her with big blue eyes.

Noah: for the Bible story, for the rainbow and God's promise to never flood the world again. Carole and Day had picked it out. There was some subtext meant for Sicily, perhaps—a reminder that *she* should never flood their world again with her poor decisions. Sicily wanted Noah's name to be James, and gazing at him now, she thinks he looks like one. But her parents never would have agreed to something so English sounding as James Smythe.

It doesn't matter now. Nothing matters but him.

Sicily cradles the baby, slowly coming back awake to the sights and sounds of the hospital around her. There's a big bouquet of flowers—white spray of lilies, indigo violets, periwinkle lupines—on the table at the foot of her bed.

"Who are those from?" she asks Kendra, nodding at the arrangement. Kendra hands the card to Sicily. It's crammed with printed text.

> From both of us! G's parents cut up her credit cards
> again LOL. Long story. So one bouquet from two of
> us, but all our love. Don't make us godmothers; we
> would suck.

Sicily smiles and presses the card to her heart, right next to little Noah's head.

~

Kendra is Sicily's only visitor, even after Noah's birth. None of the family want to have their photos taken coming in and out of the hospital. Emmylou would have come—"Just because she's giving birth doesn't mean she shouldn't have her hair and makeup done!" she'd said—but

Day and Uncle Henry had forbidden it. Carole told Sicily that they'd all celebrate after the fact.

"Are you sure?" Sicily had asked her mother in a small voice. She felt like she was five years old again, asking whether Carole could check under the bed for monsters.

They had spoken on the phone before Sicily left for Atlanta, and she had almost heard the frown on her mother's face.

"Sorry, honey," Carole had said. "It won't be like a regular birth, though. You won't need to squeeze my hand through the labor pains, lucky you!"

Sicily had not felt lucky. She would have given a lot for a hand to hold during the anesthesia, but she'd felt too embarrassed to ask Kendra.

The rest of the Bells plan to meet Noah back in Arkansas, where they've retreated to the family ranch.

"You going to be okay here for a few days?" Kendra asks after they've been sitting in relative silence, apart from Noah's cooing, for most of the afternoon. "My cab will be here soon."

Sicily feels a flare of alarm; she'd momentarily forgotten that Kendra had taken advantage of the stay to book a quick flight over to Nashville and conference with some music execs.

"Of course," Sicily says lightly.

"All right. Good job today." Kendra gives her a kiss on the top of her head and is gone.

Sicily shifts Noah to the other arm. "Just you and me now, bud," she says.

Someone had turned the TV off, and Sicily can't reach the remote; it's just as well. The hospital is growing quiet apart from an announcement here and there over the PA and a phone ringing in the distance. Sicily would sleep, but she feels wired and wide awake.

Noah has closed his eyes, and she watches as his head begins to loll back over her elbow. Is it supposed to do that? She nudges his belly with her finger, and he doesn't respond.

Fear prickles at the back of her neck.

"Noah?" she says. She jostles him—still nothing.

"Noah!" Sicily nearly yells it this time, and his eyes fly open and his face screws up. "Oh, there you are," she says with relief. "There we go, you're okay."

But he's not. He balls his tiny hands into fists and starts to fuss, then cry.

"Oh no," Sicily says. "No, it's okay."

The cry is shrill and insistent, and Sicily doesn't know what to do.

"Hey," she says, trying to bounce him, but she can't do that and support his head at the same time. She can't reach the call button for the nurse while she's holding him. "Hello?" she calls, feeling a bitter lump forming in her throat. "Could someone help me?"

After what feels like an eternity, a different nurse comes in. "What happened?" she asks.

"I don't know," Sicily says. "He started crying—I don't know why—"

"He's probably just hungry. Has anyone shown you how to latch?"

She says it so matter-of-factly that Sicily feels like an idiot. Of course he's hungry—he hasn't eaten anything at all.

"Oh. Yeah. That's probably it. No, no one's been in here."

"Okay. Do you mind?" The nurse puts her fingers on the snaps of Sicily's hospital gown and looks at her. Sicily shakes her head as Noah continues to wail.

"So what you'll want to do," the nurse says, folding back the front of the gown, "is prop him in the crook of your elbow there. Yep. Then line up his mouth—"

It's hard to focus on what she's saying while Noah is still screaming. Sicily presses his face against her, but he turns his head and tries to wriggle away, suddenly stronger than he looks.

"Why won't he drink?" she asks.

"That's okay," the nurse says. "Some babies don't at first. Try again."

But Noah won't have it. Sicily feels her pulse racing—she's almost glad her family isn't here to see how badly she's struggling to do something that should be natural.

The nurse dangles her badge above Noah's head and trills. "Hey! Hey, little guy! It's okay, look at me."

He quiets abruptly and stares at the badge and the woman above it, mesmerized. Sicily immediately wishes she had the power this woman has.

"You can keep trying for a little while, but don't push it," the nurse says, distracting him while she talks. "We have a lactation specialist who'll be here in the morning to help. In fact, it's possible your milk won't even come in for another day or two."

Sicily imagines two days of Noah screaming and all at once feels an enormous weight drop on her. "What are we supposed to do until *then*?"

The nurse starts to answer, but her words are lost on Sicily, who begins to sob. She can't understand what the nurse is telling her. She feels stupid for thinking any of this would be easy. It's as though an enormous, uncrossable chasm has opened between the person she used to be and the person she is with Noah, changed into a helpless, incompetent mess overnight.

"Sicily, it's okay," the nurse is saying. "You need some sleep, okay?"

She leaves and then returns with some pills, which Sicily manages to take with a cup of water. Everything is blurry and wet, and her nose is running uncontrollably. Noah is fussing again, and she's getting her tears on him. She feels horrible.

"Noah is in good hands." The nurse takes him, puts him somewhere nearby. Her voice sounds very far away. "Just get some rest."

~

But when Sicily wakes up in the bleak light of morning, the dead weight is still there. The tears come again, and she can't turn them off—she feels like she'll never stop crying. And Noah cries along with her.

Late morning, when the nurses can't get Sicily to eat or calm down, a doctor from the psych unit comes by to talk to her. He sits in a chair next to her bed with his legs crossed and his glasses perched on his nose. Behind her fog of gloom, Sicily has a passing thought that he looks like he should be a high school math teacher.

"It's normal to feel sadness or hopelessness after birth," he says. "You've just gone through an enormous change in your life, and you have a lot of new responsibilities. Plus, you're exhausted."

Sicily nods. She's stopped crying for the moment, but the puffiness and pressure behind her eyes lets her know that she could start again any minute. If only she could produce as much milk as she could tears.

"What's most helpful, at this time, is knowing you're not alone and looking to your support network," the doctor continues. "Now, I'm not prying—but I'm familiar with your work, Miss Bell, and I seem to recall you have a pretty large family who travels with you."

He glances around the room, as if expecting to see them right then and there. But, of course, the chairs against the wall and the hooks for coats and overnight bags are empty. There's no one here for Sicily except the security guard who's still stationed at the door. The concern in the doctor's face is not lost on her.

"Do you have anyone coming for you?" he asks, and the question creates a little break in Sicily's heart. "The baby's father, your own parents, a close friend—anyone who can come spend some time with you while you're recovering here?"

Sicily shakes her head. Kendra won't be back for a few more days, when Sicily is scheduled to depart to Arkansas. She's not about to tell the doctor that no, her family doesn't want to be here, and she, Sicily, is not supposed to be here, either. She doesn't want to tell him how much shame she's brought to them all. Because then he'd ask more and more questions, and she'd have to answer them, and she'd have to admit to both him and herself how awful everything has been and how terrified she is to be a mom.

Sicily takes a deep breath and wipes her eyes, folding her hands together to hide the fact that they're trembling.

"I'll see my folks in a few days anyway," she says, careful to add a lighter note to her voice. "And they're so excited to meet our newest bundle of joy. I'm feeling better, I promise. It helps just to talk things through with you, Doctor."

With a practiced effort born from years of performing onstage, Sicily smiles.

SEVEN

MIRANDA

2008

. . . you don't treat me like you should. You're so bad, but so, so good . . .

Miranda sings along as she draws a thick black line across her eyelid and follows with mascara, blinking when she's done and evaluating her reflection in the mirror. She's dressed in a tube top, robin's-egg blue, with a black leather jacket to give the pastels an edge. The top works with her low-slung jeans to show off her belly-button piercing. She's curled her hair and put on her favorite hoops.

It's her best outfit, and she wants to feel good today. Because today she has finally—and ironically—reached her twenty-first birthday.

Miranda takes the stairs two at a time and makes coffee and breakfast—peanut butter toast with grapefruit on the side. She's not doing the green smoothies anymore. They were too much work; so were the gratitude exercises, and so was the accountability partner, a woman who was rumored to have also relapsed, and whom Miranda has not heard from since.

But Miranda is feeling good. Things are stable. *The Bennington Bookshop* wrapped without incident, and she hasn't had to see George or Tyler since. She even has a meeting with her agency this afternoon about a new movie—a real one, with an A-list costar.

She hums to herself as she drinks her coffee and scrolls through her messages. There's one from her mom and one from her agent, both wishing her a happy birthday. Miranda replies with hearts and sets the phone down.

After a few minutes she picks it up again. What she's really hoping for is a message from Zane. When TLOYL returned from Venezuela, she set aside her pride and texted him several times before he replied and finally agreed to meet up. She felt that he owed it to her, at the very least. Miranda imagined it would be a grand reunion, something straight out of the old Hollywood movies; she wore a black dress with a plunging neckline and even had one of the MUAs on the Holiday Heartwarmers set do her makeup beforehand. The bar they met at in Westlake was classy, famous for star sightings. She felt her heart race uncontrollably when she saw his car pull up outside.

But Zane was underdressed in a T-shirt, jacket, and Chuck Taylors. Well, dressed for New York Fashion Week rather than the old glamour she'd been going for. And he didn't look happy.

"Hey," she'd said softly, moving in to give him a hug that he stiffly returned. "You look great." Their outfits may have been mismatched, but he was tanned, a little sunburned, and his hair was windswept as though he'd walked straight from the hacienda's fields and into the bar. He'd grown out his facial hair, the baby face he once had replaced with a more defined jawline and harder features. He was the most beautiful thing Miranda had ever seen.

"So what's this all about?" Zane asked as they sat down.

Miranda's smile froze on her face as she tried to read his expression, confused. "What's this all—you're back. We're back. I wanted to see you as soon as I could."

"That so?" He was looking at his hands, avoiding her eyes. A waiter came, and Miranda, trying to keep up appearances for him, ordered a root beer. She caught Zane watching her while she did and looked down at her lap. They'd spent very little time together during their relationship that wasn't fogged by the influence of one substance or another. The moment that the thought crossed Miranda's mind, she wondered whether that was what he had meant in the courtroom the day he got his sentence. Were they recognizable to each other without their vices?

He ordered a Cherry Coke.

"Zane," she said when the waiter had left and then returned with their drinks, and still Zane hadn't picked up the conversation again. "Come on. What's wrong?"

He ran his hands through his hair, looked out the window. "I heard you were fooling around with someone on the set of your movie. So—I was kind of surprised you wanted to get together, that's all."

Miranda's heart twisted painfully. She tried to think of something to say. Instead, she took a sip of her soda.

"So you don't deny it," Zane said, finally looking her in the eyes.

"Did we have some kind of agreement when you were in Venezuela? Because the way we left it," Miranda said slowly, "I wasn't sure if I'd ever see you again. Your family sure didn't want me to. And you were giving me all sorts of mixed signals. Whatever I did on set, it was after I hadn't heard a word from you for nearly six months."

Zane shook his head. "I don't know. I guess you're right. I just didn't think you'd run into the arms of the first guy out of rehab who looked at you sideways."

"Ohh-kay." Miranda rolled her eyes. "Well, that's just—"

"No, it's fine." Zane wrapped both hands around his glass; below the high-top, his knee was bouncing. "Sorry. I don't mean to be bitter. Maybe we just—met too young. We have our whole lives ahead of us, you know?"

"I know," Miranda said flatly.

"Maybe we just need to grow up."

Miranda shrugged and looked out the window. There was a couple across the street walking a dog. The man sneezed, and the woman took a Kleenex out of her pocket for him, taking the leash so he had both hands free. For some reason it made Miranda want to cry.

There was a time Zane might have done that for her. Back in their party days she would lean into him at the end of the night, letting the sounds of the music get muffled on someone's couch somewhere while Zane stroked her hair and made up stories to keep her awake. She wonders whether he even remembers that, the way he's acting now. She would have asked him if he wasn't being such a jerk.

So instead she said, "Whatever." And threw back her root beer.

After what she'd been through the past two years, she felt plenty grown up. And it was Zane's loss if he didn't recognize that.

They hadn't spoken much since then—Zane's dad made him work as a roadie on a summer old-rock-star-revival tour, and their lives continued to go in different directions from there.

Miranda wakes up her phone again, closes and opens the messaging app to refresh it. Because still, it's her birthday. Maybe he'll call, or at least text. Maybe he'll send her flowers or a note or something, any kind of message. He never said they couldn't be friends. Miranda tiptoes to the front door to make sure she hasn't missed a package.

Nope.

Whatever—today is not about Zane, and besides, she already has romance in her life. Lately it comes in the form of Taha, a minor prince from the Emirates, who has enough money for a whole fleet of Audis and three yachts in three different parts of the world. And he's throwing her a huge party tonight at Delphi, a Calabasas club he bought out just for her. It's going to be the best birthday party she's ever had, he's promised—cage dancers, open bar all night, hip-hop duo Deez and Straight A performing live, fireworks on the back patio.

Everything will be incredible, Miranda's sure. But she's *not* sure if any party could be the best she's ever had without Germaine and Sicily.

Miranda settles back down to finish her coffee. There's a ding on her phone, and she scrambles for it, but it's Sicily.

Happy birthday biyotch!!!! You better party your ASS off for me today!! Don't ride the bull <3 <3

Miranda laughs to herself just as a message from Germaine follows.

BIRTHDAY GURRLLL!! Live it up babes. If you see any bulls, don't ride them xx

They were both referring to Miranda's eighteenth birthday—the last one, she realizes, that they celebrated together. They'd been flush with cash and confidence. Miranda had just wrapped shooting on her second movie, and Sicily was about to go on tour for the first time. Germaine didn't seem thrilled about her parents' plans to send her to business school, but she brought the glamour and aloof confidence.

They started in Santa Monica and moved east, with a limo booked for the whole night, hitting a five-star restaurant for dinner and then on to the Sunset Strip, pretending to complain about all the paparazzi who followed them around—but, really, the attention made them giddy. They were stumbling over themselves by 9:30 p.m.

Miranda doesn't remember much about that night, but she does remember that at some point the driver started swerving to avoid a pap car coming up fast on their left. After a few maneuvers—and no directions from the three women in the back seat as to where he should go, because they were all laugh-crying about Tyler Xavier's new haircut—he must have made the executive decision to flee into the hills. Eventually he pulled over and knocked on the partition.

"Excuse me, misses," he said. "I'm sorry, but we have gotten off track. Where would you like to go next?"

Miranda had squinted out the window. It looked like they were on a neighborhood street. "Where are we?" she muttered.

"Yes, sir, where are we?" G demanded in a voice that sounded like her father's. Sicily giggled.

"Somewhere around Eagle Rock," the limo driver said. "But I can take you wherever you'd like to go."

"We could stay here, couldn't we?" Sicily said. "It looks nice here."

"I don't know." Germaine looked a little disgusted. "What's around here?"

"Sir, can you drive around and see if there's a bar?" Miranda asked.

He nodded, pulling out of the side street and onto a main road. They all looked out the window until Sicily pointed at one.

"What about that? The Pour House?"

Miranda glanced at Germaine. She was the oldest and most worldly; she'd traveled farther and had more money than Miranda and Sicily ever hoped to. They looked up to Germaine. She'd preceded them on *Kidz Klub*, and it was a secret kept between Sicily and Miranda that they'd both been *super* intimidated by her at first.

Germaine made a face. "Looks like a place with *super* sticky floors."

But this time Sicily pushed back. "It looks cozy," she said. "It's Miranda's birthday! It's up to her."

Miranda squinted out the window. It seemed like a dive. But she was drunk and happy, and if they took the limo all the way back to LA, she wasn't sure she'd be able to stay awake for another bar.

"Pour House," she said, starting to clap. "Pour House! Pour House!"

"Pour House! Pour House!" Sicily joined in, both of them getting up in G's face.

Germaine huffed, pushing them away. "Okay, okay! Driver, to the Pour House!"

It was pretty small inside and very much a local place. A few men in flannel shirts glanced their way when they walked in, but to the girls' surprise, they turned and ignored them.

"Three shots of Fireball for the birthday girl!" Sicily said, pushing Miranda forward to the bar. The bartender was a large man in a stained T-shirt who looked at them suspiciously. Either the people in this bar didn't know who the 3AM Girls were, or they didn't care.

"You ladies got some ID?" he asked.

Miranda scoffed, but Germaine said, "Of course, my good sir!" She reached into her sparkly clutch and pulled out her wallet. "Let me know if this works." She slid two hundred-dollar bills across the bar.

The bartender glanced at the other patrons, who weren't watching, and examined the Benjamins in the dim light. "Some IDs, huh?" He folded the bills together and slipped them in his shirt pocket. "Well, happy birthday."

They whooped and hollered, throwing back Fireball and cheap rail drinks. The bar was playing old country music, and Sicily put her hands on her hips and taught them how to two-step.

They sang Tammy Wynette's "Stand by Your Man," putting their arms around each other and swaying in a circle.

It was nearly closing when G pointed into a dark corner and said, "What is *that?*"

It was a mechanical bull.

"*YES!*" Sicily yelled. "You have to, Miranda!"

"No way," Miranda said, but she was laughing. Before she knew it, they'd pulled the bartender from behind his counter so he could operate the bull, and Miranda was straddling the worn old seat. She grasped the handle on the saddle and raised a hand in the air.

"Go, Miranda! Go, go, Miranda!" the girls screamed on the other side of the partition.

The bartender turned it on, pulled a lever, and made a face at the sickening mechanical screech that came from the machine.

"Doesn't see a lot of action," he said. "Most of the guys' backs are too bad for it."

And that was probably why, when the bartender went for the lowest setting, it malfunctioned and jumped to high.

The front end of the bull rushed toward Miranda's face at full speed, and the next thing she knew, she was on the ground.

"Okay, okay!" Sicily was saying brightly. "Let's get you outside. G, some towels?"

But Germaine, ever their defender, was upbraiding the bartender. "I could sue your ass so hard that your *grandchildren* will have debt."

The man put up his hands. "There's a sign right there, lady. Ride at your own risk. I know my rights."

"Towels?" Miranda asked thickly. Her face felt wet. She touched a finger to it and gasped when it came back covered in blood.

"G, come on!" Sicily snapped.

They took Miranda out and sat her on the curb next to the limo.

"It's just a bloody nose," G said, helping Miranda tip her head back and dabbing at her face with a wad of napkins.

"It better not be broken," Miranda groaned. "I can't go to the premieres with a jacked-up nose."

"I'm sure it's not." Sicily patted her shoulder.

"I'm going to get some water to wash that stuff off your face." Germaine balled up the used napkins. "You look like *Carrie*."

Miranda half nodded and kept her head back as G walked inside. The night was warm. From her vantage point, she could see the dark sky beyond the flickering neon of the bar. She couldn't see the stars— she rarely ever could in LA—but it seemed darker, quieter here than downtown, and she could imagine them out there somewhere.

"You have a good birthday?" Sicily asked.

Miranda laughed. "The best."

"We'll do it again next year."

Miranda could hear the smile in her voice. But where on the globe would Sicily be a year from now?

As if reading her thoughts, Sicily rested her head on Miranda's shoulder. "I hope it's always like this," she said quietly.

Miranda touched the side of her cheek to the top of Sicily's head. "What do you mean?" she asked, even though she already knew.

"I hope we don't grow up and get boring. Get too busy for each other."

Miranda shoved her a little. "You think I'd ever get too busy for you, Sis?"

"No."

"And I know you won't, either. And neither will G."

Sicily shoved her back. "I know. So it's a deal?"

"Deal."

That was Miranda's best birthday ever.

Tonight there will be hundreds of people at her party, but how many of them will be actual friends? Most of them will be hangers-on— Hollywood hangers-on, oil-money hangers-on. Every guy with a designer suit and leased European car will call himself a producer. Miranda's mother will be there because Miranda couldn't convince her not to be, and she'll probably end up sleeping with one of them, now that she's broken up with Doug and then, after him, Manuel, a plastic surgeon who remade her face. It was a very unsettling feeling, seeing the mother who bore and raised you come home with an entirely new face.

By the time Miranda realized Bobbie had stopped going to therapy, it was too late to convince her mother to course correct. It's a pattern: whenever Miranda's on the upswing, Bobbie stops parenting and starts celebrating. When Miranda crashes, that's when she puts on the *Mommie Dearest* persona, all tough love and discipline. But if having a party girl for a mother is the price Miranda has to pay for career success, so be it.

Bobbie keeps saying that she and Miranda can be the 3AM Girls now. Miranda keeps ignoring her.

It doesn't matter, Miranda tells herself as she drives to her afternoon appointment. The party will be fun. Taha will make her feel incredible at the after-after-party, when everything is over and it's just the two of them.

And she's working! Miranda adjusts her top and feels extremely professional as she walks into the agency office with her script in a binder in the crook of her elbow. She shakes hands with Sam, who took her back as a client after *The Bennington Bookshop* wrapped, and the others, excited about the potential project.

"I've read the script and I absolutely love it," Miranda says, sitting up as straight as she can and being as enthusiastic as possible. The film is a fictionalization of the international pop scene in the seventies, centering on an ABBA-like group and their rise to superstardom. It's going to be a career maker, sexy and glamorous with a rock-star edge. Miranda is vying for the part of Tove, one of the young women in the group.

"Well, I thought it'd be a great part for you," Sam says. "*Bookshop* brought you back to the land of the living, and I know you've got the chops to really shine in a role like Tove's."

"Right." One of the other agents, a tall man with slicked-back hair, scratches his nose. He's more executive level, the ringleader, Miranda can tell, and the two younger agents besides Sam are new faces. They exude the hunger and swaggery confidence of young men who have been promised a highly lucrative career. "So you're up against Ellie Dakota and Jade Dempsey. But we managed to get you an earlier audition time than them."

Ellie and Jade were even younger than Miranda, and both had already been on the last cover of *Vanity Fair*'s "Young Hollywood" cover.

"Maybe I need to get on that *Vanity* cover to complete my résumé," Miranda jokes, laughing a little.

"That ship has sailed," Sam says flatly.

Miranda looks at him, but he avoids her eyes. Instead, he looks down at the script and says, "Let's see what you've got."

Miranda stands and reads a monologue of Tove's, in which the character is contemplating the trajectory of her life in an Amsterdam Red Light District club. They give Miranda advice as she goes, helping her tweak her delivery and consider different emotions Tove might be feeling. Sam does a scene with her, and then they talk about audition strategy.

Miranda feels confident, and the lines come easily—she loves the idea of Tove. She could bring so much to the gritty, struggling-star character arc. She wants to *be* Tove, in a way—this movie could bring her the success that Eurovision brought to the complex, fictional rock star.

But she can't get Sam's comment out of her head. It nags at her more and more as they go on.

One of the younger agents' cells rings, interrupting them.

"Sorry," he says. "Gotta take this."

Miranda takes the opportunity to excuse herself and go to the restroom. At the sink she runs her hands under cold water and presses them to her face. The unflattering overhead lights make her look older than she is.

"I'm twenty-one," she says aloud. "If I weren't here, I'd still be in college."

And if Ellie and Jade weren't where they were, they'd still be in high school.

Miranda shakes her head. It isn't age that matters. It's talent. And she still has plenty of that to share.

Setting her jaw and squaring her shoulders, she heads back to Sam's office. But voices outside the door make her pause.

". . . deluded," one of them is saying. "The only ship that's sailing for her now are those Arab yachts where she's a whore for hire."

"Yeah, if Taha wasn't giving so much for this picture, I wouldn't even consider her for it," the other says. "She wouldn't even get hired as an extra."

"All right, come on." Sam sounds tired.

But the first man laughs. "Honestly, she should just jump to porn now and stop wasting everyone's time. Including her own."

"Okay," Sam says, not as sharply as Miranda would have liked. "Take it easy."

The floor is unsteady under Miranda's feet. She feels like she's about to throw up. The thing is, she's not deluded at all about the mistakes she's made, or the chances she's thrown away, or the talent she's wasted. But apparently she's been deluded about one important thing: how little people think of her.

She doesn't pay much attention to the rest of the meeting. Sam picks up a little gift bag from his desk as he walks her down to the parking lot.

"You okay?" he asks. "I thought that went all right."

Miranda just nods numbly.

"Okay," he says doubtfully. Then he lifts the bag. "Happy birthday, Montana. Hope you have a good one tonight."

She takes it and walks away without saying goodbye.

~

In the car Miranda finds a bottle of pink champagne and a cheesy little birthday card.

A familiar feeling of fury and oblivion overtakes her as she rips off the foil and pops the cork right there in the driver's seat, taking a long and painful swig. Then another.

Then she pulls out of the lot.

Why do so many people despise her? Plenty of other actors have had problems with drinking. Plenty have had bad relationships. Some have the most flagrant affairs and bitter divorces; some are estranged from their children or vilified by their parents. But these things don't seem to destroy their careers. Tyler X has been to rehab, and he was just cast in a superhero movie. He was on the cover of *People* magazine only last month, for god's sake, with an angelic smile on his inane face.

Miranda presses her foot to the gas. All she wants to do is get home and hide from the world in bed for a few hours. She'll drown herself in champagne until she feels numb enough to go to her own party.

The yellow light a few yards in front of her on Mulholland is stale, and it suddenly turns red as Miranda barrels through the intersection.

She swears, and then swears again when the whoop of a police siren sounds behind her.

"Shit," she says, pulling over and looking for a place to stash the champagne. It spills on her a little. "Shit, shit, shit."

The officer is at her driver's-side window surprisingly fast.

"Ma'am?" he says sternly, and there is no doubt in Miranda's mind that he sees the bottle in the purse shoved haphazardly behind the passenger seat.

"Yes?" To her horror, it's followed by a hiccup.

"Step out of the car please, ma'am."

She can't. The day can't end like this. "Officer, I'm sorry, but I'm really late for something. I'll pay a fine, a speeding ticket—"

"Out of the car."

The paparazzi will find out. She won't get the ABBA movie. Sam will drop her again.

Miranda picks up her wallet and slowly climbs out, mind racing. The car is registered to Taha—he has more than enough money to smooth things over. Sam didn't write her name on the card. All identifying information is in her wallet, in her hand. And maybe the cop doesn't recognize her—he doesn't seem to, at least.

"Step away from the car," the officer says, and Miranda takes a big step. "License?"

"Um," Miranda says, trying to stall.

At that moment, a cyclist on the shoulder swerves around the cop car, and a second car honks loud and long, making the police officer turn.

There is a bus pulling up to the corner. Miranda takes one step, then another, clutching her wallet and feeling like time is moving in slow motion. This is overwhelming, but if she can just slip away—

Then she speed-walks.

She has one hand up, hailing the bus driver, when the cop closes his grip around her wrist.

So that's her twenty-first birthday. DUI and a penalty for resisting arrest.

The mug shot is up online before Bobbie comes to bail her out.

"Miranda," Bobbie says in that pitying voice Miranda hates.

"Just—don't," she says.

Miranda's making headlines again, for all the wrong reasons. She won't be able to get insured to make the movie. It's over.

EIGHT

GERMAINE

2008

Germaine frowns down at her phone, sipping rose bandung through a straw. She sets the drink down on the marble table of the sidewalk café, then composes a text to Miranda.

> Just saw the news. I'm so sorry, hun. Call me whenever, don't
> worry about time difference.

Germaine is in Singapore—not because she's there to play any sort of professional role in the opening of her family's glossy new hotel, but to serve as eye candy. Although, after a knock-down, drag-out fight, they did allow her to help book the music. Because no matter how much her parents would have preferred string quartets, they're trying to appeal to a wealthy younger generation with this location, the children of Singapore's elite—the earlier you hook them, the longer the profit potential, Terence likes to say.

"I suppose you're more familiar with the rowdy pop bands than we are, given your . . . entertainment background," Céline said dryly.

Germaine had rolled her eyes to disguise her excitement, but she relished the work of compiling lists of candidates. Which group had enough of a presence in Southeast Asia to garner attention? Which was up-and-coming—or, conversely, a nostalgic get? Who would have the crowd on the floor all night? She dug her teeth into it, staying up late with Shibuya napping in the crook of her arm while she compared recent releases, media coverage, and *Billboard* charts.

But then she came across No Exit. And she decided to do Sicily a little favor.

"Marie," she had said, looking up from her laptop as the family's stylist laid out clothes from Germaine's closet for the upcoming trip. "How would you get revenge on someone who had wronged a close friend of yours?"

Marie froze in her task of draping a dress bag over a silk hanger. She's older than Germaine, or maybe younger—Germaine isn't really sure. She was the apprentice of the family's last stylist and recently took over the position, but they've barely spoken. That's the case with all the St. Germaine-Chang staff, though.

"Miss?" Marie had said. "Revenge, you say?"

"Oui, madame."

"On whom?" The stylist cocked an eyebrow. "A man?"

Germaine decided in that moment that she liked Marie. "Isn't it always?"

"How bad is it?"

"Abandoned-her-after-an-unplanned-pregnancy bad," Germaine said. "And basking in all the media attention while the same outlets call her a train wreck."

"Mmm. So the very worst, then." The stylist narrowed her eyes. "Well, in that case, I would stop at nothing to make sure he finally faced some consequences for his actions. To balance the scales for him, so to speak."

"Murder?"

This would have sent the other house staff running, but Marie shrugged as she expertly folded a pair of capris over her arm. "Vous êtes le chef, miss. It's your call to make," she said. "But I would stick to something legal so you don't get implicated. Something to embarrass him, perhaps—men can't stand being embarrassed."

"*Framing* him for murder," Germaine tried, and in spite of her blasé exterior, Marie cracked a smile.

Germaine doesn't know Hugo Smythe personally, but she knows his type. Somehow it's always the gross heartthrob men that Sicily goes for, the kind to sweep you off your feet in the name of "romance" and then hang you out to dry when you get knocked up. It was only a matter of time before that happened. Germaine never dated seriously in her Hollywood days—much to the chagrin of the tabloids and to Sicily and Miranda, who constantly tried to set her up—and she has zero interest in commitment now. Celebrity guys have always seemed kind of scummy to her. And she knows too well how many men in the world will stab you in the back once you've been at your most vulnerable with them.

Hugo Smythe is no different. The press gushes about how he wants to be involved in his child's life—how fantastic, the bare minimum, let's get him a trophy, Germaine thinks. She knows better, anyway, from many a tearful call from Sicily. Hugo wants nothing to do with their child. He tried to talk her into getting an abortion, in fact, when Sicily first broke the news to him.

So Germaine booked No Exit. And tonight, after they've begun their Singapore debut, Germaine will pluck something of value from the hotel—one of the Finnish statuettes from the ballroom, maybe, or a bottle of fifty-five-year Yamazaki single malt from behind the bar—and plant it in the greenroom. Preferably in Hugo's bag, if she can figure out which is his. Nothing expensive enough to get them thrown in the Changi Prison Complex, but enough to insult her parents and ensure that No Exit is banned from ever playing at a St. Germaine-Chang hotel again—or any of the many subsidiaries over which they have influence. She'll be sure to send out a neat little press statement about it, too.

The embarrassment and indignation he'll feel will be the tiniest taste of the shame he's brought to Sicily.

Until then, Germaine has zilch to do. She's on her third day of boredom.

She had told Miranda that she was busy with company business on their last call, but the reality is much more mundane. Like most tourists, she's spending the time either shopping in the air-conditioned bliss of the Orchard Road malls or lying by the hotel pool with iced Milo, bubble teas, and bandung in the swampy heat. Her work with the bands was handed off to some lackey once the contracts were signed. So far she's appeared in one family photograph at the ribbon cutting and a celebratory brunch this morning.

Asking to be excused from these public appearances is a mistake, but Germaine had to try at least once.

"You know what you are?" Greg had spoken up. "Selfish. If you're not in the photos, people will ask why. You never support the cause."

"It's like you don't even want to be part of this family," Giles added.

Germaine wanted to tell him what she really thought of *this family*, but her No Exit plan had already been put into place, and it wasn't worth the breath. Plus, she doesn't want to risk financial banishment again—not here in Singapore. She wouldn't put it past her mother to strand her in a Four Asian Tiger country with nothing but a pair of sweatpants and a handful of dollars, not after the last stunt. Germaine knows it sounds like an exaggeration, but her possessions are all she has.

So she's keeping her mouth shut.

Germaine must smile for the photos if she wants to spend. And she really, really wants to spend. She's already hit Louis Vuitton twice today—the chairs adjacent to her table are stacked with bags, and her limo driver is waiting with more in the car. She wants to buy every single thing in Singapore and surround herself with beauty, so when she's back home and staring down another ugly, empty week of nothing before she can go to her next dance class, she'll be able to distract herself with genuine silks and tortoiseshell sunglasses and soft top-grain leather.

They'll never love her back like she loves them. But she can't help herself.

Germaine sighs, taking one more sip through her straw as it hits ice in the bottom of the cup. She's goddamn lonely is what she is. People cast interested glances as they walk past the sidewalk café, but it's only because she's a spectacle with all her bags. Maybe they recognize her, but if they do, they care only about her family name and celebrity reputation. They don't really know Germaine. The only two people in the world who do—who should be sitting in the chairs across from her rather than these totes and boxes—are many time zones away, probably fast asleep. Maybe she *does* need to have a fling.

Germaine checks the time on her phone and pushes the thought aside. It's now time to do what she's come to consider a job.

She gathers up her things and returns by limo to the sparkling new St. Germaine-Chang hotel, strutting across the marbled lobby floors past the three-tiered contemporary-art fountain and taking the glass elevator to the suite on the top floor. The chauffeur and bellhops follow with her purchases of the day, wheeling them in by the luggage cartful and stacking them alongside yesterday's many items.

Germaine knows it's a lot, but the piles make her feel secure. She also can't be expected to wear any old thing from home for all these splashy publicity events.

"You've had a busy day, miss," Marie remarks when she arrives in the suite, looking around at the consumerist carnage.

"I can't have you calling me *miss* if we're in cahoots together," Germaine says. "My name is fine."

"Cahoots?" Marie raises her eyebrows as she lays out her tools. "I know nothing of the sort, Miss Germaine. You have no evidence on me."

Germaine frowns, but in the mirror she catches Marie's wink.

They put on Sicily's newest album, *Carnivale*, and get to work considering Versace, Dior, and Prada as they examine each look in the mirror. Could Marie be a friend, Germaine wonders, as she watches the woman's hands fly? It's tricky. At this stage of life, every relationship feels transactional.

Thankfully Céline is busy with her own preparations and doesn't interfere with the process this time. So Germaine settles on something she actually likes—a Givenchy, the palest robin's-egg blue. It hugs her figure to create a striking silhouette, finished with glossy satin twill that wraps around her throat and waist before falling at the sides to create an asymmetrical hem.

The stylist wraps Germaine's hair in a soft, low bun, curling the pieces that fall from it, and bringing her a pair of Graff pendant earrings that drip with diamonds.

"Thank you, Marie," Germaine tries, the note of gratitude feeling unnatural and yet necessary.

"Voilà. Parfait," Marie says as she adjusts the strap of Germaine's dress. "Good luck tonight, Miss Germaine. I hope all goes according to plan."

In a moment of madness, Germaine wants to ask Marie to come with her, or even just stay and talk for a while. But the stylist is already gathering up her things.

"What will you do tonight, Marie?" Germaine asks. What does she or any of the house staff do, Germaine suddenly wonders, when they're not waiting on her family hand and foot?

"If you would believe it," Marie says, a mischievous look in her eye, "I have a date."

"Good for you!" Germaine laughs as Marie scurries out of the room. But then the door closes, and Germaine is alone again. Even Marie, with her absurd working hours and erratic travel, has someone. A life independent of the St. Germaine-Changs.

Germaine fiddles with her fingernail, then catches her reflection in the mirror and checks to make sure the look is complete. She smiles approvingly, allowing her eyes to take in the spectacle for a moment, and then quickly fixes her gaze elsewhere. The first glance at a new haute fashion outfit is always a rush. But if she looks too long, she will get so, so bored. Excitement fades quickly.

Germaine dons a winning smile when she arrives at the opening gala downstairs, posing with her father, mother, and brothers for pictures that would fool anyone into thinking they were the happiest and most functional of families. The five of them, mercifully, are seated at the head tables on the ballroom stage, facing outward. She won't have to make conversation with anybody. She's still onstage, still has to perform for the cameras that flash incessantly, but Germaine can fall back on an old trick she's beginning to rely on more and more.

There's not much to it—she just makes her mind go completely blank. She lets her body run on autopilot, smiling and raising her eyebrows, taking the daintiest bites of food. Outwardly, she's having the time of her life and celebrating the unstoppable success of her family. Inwardly, she withdraws, imagining herself shrinking down so small that she can curl up somewhere hidden and wait this out. If she isn't present in the moment, she's learned, it will go by quickly.

But after dinner, when the guests mingle at the adjacent rooftop bar while the ballroom is turned over for dancing, a familiar face catches her eye and breaks her trance.

Hugo Smythe.

She glances around as he approaches, evidently coming in her direction. Does he know about her relationship to Sicily? Could he have guessed her plan? Of course not, she chides herself, but she's surprised to see him out here—and, yes, definitely headed for her. He looks very different from the grainy tabloid photos. Terence and Céline stipulated that the band should be a bit more dressed up than their typical ripped jeans and leather, but Hugo is still managing to make pressed dress pants and a white button-down look positively obscene. He's got the top few buttons open, the sleeves rolled up, tousled hair, and a devilish grin. No wonder Sicily fell so hard for him.

"Evening," he says, setting his whiskey down next to her flute at the edge of the balcony. He wipes his brow. "I thought the heat would get better once the sun went down. Shows what I know."

In spite of herself, Germaine cracks a smile. "Very—what is that accent?—British of you," she says.

He laughs. "You nailed me. I couldn't be more out of my element."

"Are you with the band?" Germaine can't help playing coy. Any man overconfident enough to invade her space at a party deserves to be taken down a peg.

But he takes it in stride. "Hugo Smythe, No Exit." He puts his hand out to shake, which Germaine finds refreshing. His palm is cool from holding his icy glass, welcome in the oppressive humidity.

"Germaine St. Germaine-Chang," she says.

"Oh, you need no introduction." Hugo smiles. "I thought I should come over and thank you and your family personally for inviting us to play tonight. It's quite a gig."

Germaine shrugs. The gratitude would make a lesser person feel guilty about how Hugo's night is going to go, but she is steadfast. "Shouldn't you be setting up?"

He sips his whiskey. "Did setup and sound check this afternoon, so there's nothing left to do but wait for them to change over. The rest of the guys are hiding in the greenroom—you might be surprised to learn that high-society functions aren't really their thing. I'm sure you love it, though."

He doesn't know anything about her.

"They're all right," Germaine says vaguely, sipping her own drink. Champagne, as usual.

"It's truly something," he says, and she looks at him to find that he's gazing at the glittering city that sprawls before them, stretching out into the vast hazy darkness of the sea. "I haven't gotten sick of traveling with the band—not just yet. I keep discovering new things that take my breath away."

This time he's looking at her, and Germaine raises her eyebrows. She's surprised by the pleasant warm prickle at the back of her neck. Hugo isn't her type, but she doesn't mind being flirted with. It doesn't happen very often.

"I guess it depends on who you're with," she says, thinking how much more fun it sounds to travel the world with a group of friends than with her family, in particular.

"The guys are great," he agrees. "Still. It can get lonely sometimes."

That one hits Germaine in a slightly more uncomfortable way. Like her own vulnerabilities are being recognized. It sounds like another half-baked line, but Hugo's looking away again, and Germaine wonders whether he's thinking of someone else.

She doesn't like what she's feeling, and it makes her want to punish him, just a little. Just an appetizer before tonight's main event. "So," she says slowly. "I do know Sicily Bell."

He looks at her, face falling. Germaine gets a thrill from it.

"Oh," he says, the easy confidence dropping from his voice. "Then you must not like me very much."

Germaine isn't quite sure what she's doing; this conversation wasn't part of the plan. She had no intention of *meeting* Hugo, ever, and it isn't helpful that he's more charming, more self-aware than she expected. Germaine had built him up in her mind as a villain based on her conversations with Sicily and Miranda—a boorish, joint-smoking rock star who was as dumb as the next pretty face.

But now she's confronted with the fact that he's a real person. And he's interested in her, thankful to her.

Germaine waves her hand like it's nothing. "We worked together on a TV show." She drinks again, stalling. "When we were kids."

She feels an odd, delicate contradiction of wanting to push Hugo away but wanting his attention at the same time. It's something she rarely experiences—being flustered. Just a little bit.

"Oh my god." He laughs. "*You* were on *Kidz Klub*? How did I not know that?"

Germaine smiles sheepishly and rolls her eyes. "My parents would be thrilled that you don't know. I'm pretty sure they'd like to erase that chapter from the family legacy."

Among others, she thinks. *Among most of the things I've ever done.*

"Does that mean you're a singer, too?" Hugo asks, halfway between teasing her and sounding sincere.

"God, no." Germaine shakes her head. "Acting and dancing for me. I mean, they made us all sing—but I was never close to Sicily's league."

"You've stayed in the industry, though?" Hugo asks. "I'm sorry I'm not more familiar with your work. Seems all you Blast Off! folks have enjoyed more or less thriving careers since then."

"Oh." Germaine lightly touches the back of her neck. She decides a bit of fibbing won't hurt. "Um, here and there. I still dance a little. But it's mostly handling the music for events like these—which I'd like to do a lot more of."

"Very nice." Hugo nods. "You know, we're looking for a new booking agent, if you're ever interested."

Germaine feels everything in her lurch forward. The sounds of the party seem muted around her as all her focus zeroes in on Hugo's words.

"Seriously?" she says.

"I mean—" He laughs, shakes his head. "God, I'm sorry. I don't know what I'm thinking. You've probably worked with *way* better acts. You're friends with Sicily, for Chrissake. I'm sure you've got opportunities lined up around the block."

"Oh, no, no," Germaine says. "I didn't mean it like that. I just like your guys' sound, and—yeah, I'd consider it. If you're still looking after all this is over."

"Really? Great!" Hugo says. "Your name would really open doors. Totally, no pressure, but yeah. I'll give our manager your number, and you two can talk in the next few weeks. I think we have your contact info from the contracts, yeah?"

"Yeah." Germaine smiles.

They're drinking together and laughing. When they finish their whiskey and champagne, they pluck seconds from the trays of the waiters who rove about the party. Germaine catches more than one of the other women casting envious glances her way. She likes it. She likes it a lot. The idea of a relationship floats back to the surface of her mind—not Hugo, of course. That would be weird. And she wouldn't hurt Sicily like that. Sicily never gets over guys, and because of the baby, Hugo is part of her life forever.

Germaine can't imagine a long-term relationship, even if it's with a baby daddy. She *does* want a fling. Greg and Giles can pull any girl they want—no consequences, no scrutiny. They brag about it so much that it's beyond gross. Why couldn't Germaine do the same? She should have been wilder in LA when she had the chance.

But still, Hugo's attention makes her feel a little giddy. And that job offer . . .

She could still do the revenge, right? No one would have to know it was her. And then she could make up for it by being the best booking agent ever. That would balance things out—right?

Germaine wonders what Marie would do.

"Oh, he's just, his nose is like a little button," Hugo is saying, almost with an ache in his voice. He's asked her if she knows about Noah, if she wants to see pictures. "I never knew why they called it a button nose before, but you just want to press it—*boop*. Like you're calling a lift." He laughs hard, and Germaine can't help joining in. "I've never seen anything so perfect."

He pulls his wallet from his pocket and unfolds a few pictures that have clearly been handled many times.

"He's a sweetie." Germaine smiles, but she notices that the majority of them are clippings from tabloids. Only one is a printed picture of Hugo and Noah in an easy chair, both of them smiling widely. Germaine knew that Sicily doesn't have much to do with Hugo, and she thought the feeling was mutual—but it's clear that Hugo doesn't get to see his child nearly as much as he'd like to. In fact, he sounds positively obsessed with the boy.

"You're really into him, huh?" she says quietly.

Hugo looks into the distance and nods. "I'm sure Sicily told you, but—I wasn't at first. I said some awful things to her. My whole world was turning upside down, you know? I didn't know how I could be a dad. Wasn't ready. But the first time they let me see him, when he was still so wrinkly and small . . . Oh, Germaine. I did want to be a dad. Ready or not."

She flinches at her name in his mouth.

"I've thought about suing for custody." His voice is suddenly brusque. "I don't know. I don't think I'd have much of a case."

"Really?" Germaine says. The timing between her thoughts and speech has slowed a little, and she inwardly admonishes herself; she needs to stay sharp for the revenge. "That seems—extreme, doesn't it? Have you tried talking to Sicily about any of this?"

He shakes his head. "That family has those two under lock and key. My visits with my own son are like being buzzed into a prison. That Uncle Henry guy's always standing somewhere in the background like a warden—arms crossed, sunglasses on. It's not healthy for a little boy. Not healthy for Sicily, either, I don't think. There's something weird about that lot." He frowns. "I've tried to talk to her when I'm there, but she doesn't have much to say to me. Doesn't return my messages or calls when I'm gone, either. I go straight to voicemail, like my number's blocked."

"I'm sorry," Germaine says quietly. She's long known that there's something off about Sicily's family, but it feels even more stark hearing it come from a stranger's mouth. And maybe her experiences with her own family had dulled her senses to it.

"I feel like I just count the days between one visit and the next," Hugo says, refolding the pictures and rubbing his nose. "It's awful. I see Noah, he's a little tyke. I go on tour, I come back, he's walking and talking. I'm waiting for the day that I visit and he's suddenly an adult with a job and a cup of coffee. And I'll realize that I missed his entire childhood . . . and he won't know who I am."

Hugo laughs hollowly. He looks down into his empty whiskey glass with such despair that Germaine feels a twinge of annoyance. Sicily either wasn't honest about how Hugo really feels, or her family has shielded her from his true nature. Hugo has no reason to lie to Germaine about his love for his son. And doesn't Germaine know what it's like to feel lonely, far away from the people you really care about? Sicily has her family with her, even if they're frustrating sometimes; she has Noah. She has everything.

"When we were young, she did used to joke about having to give any eventual baby up for adoption so her family wouldn't make it into some kind of sideshow," Germaine says with a chuckle.

But Hugo doesn't look amused. "Really? She said that?"

"Yeah, I mean—I don't think she was *serious*. But."

"For her to even mention it, though, there must be some risk of them exploiting our child."

"I guess. I don't know."

"Because if she knows it's a bad environment for him to be in—and if it's already been bad enough for her these past few years—" Hugo shakes his head, looking intently into the distance.

Germaine is feeling dizzy all of a sudden, a little unsettled in the stomach. Something in their conversation has shifted. Hugo's not as bad as she thought, but Sicily would be hurt if she knew how Germaine was talking to him. Sweet Sicily, always the nicest girl in *Kidz Klub*, always the hardest worker.

"You should be gentle with her, though," Germaine says. Sweat is breaking out in even greater earnest along her brow, not from the heat of the night now but from guilt. "She's always tried so hard to be good. I'm sure she's doing all she can to be the best mother. I mean—she even tried to be a good influence on me and one of our other friends when we were young, you know? I think it ended up being the other way around, though." She laughs nervously. She's babbling now, trying to say anything that will make things better. Germaine can fix this.

"Oh, really?" Hugo grins.

"Yeah. We were the ones who were always dragging her out to clubs, parties, talking her into being a 3AM Girl—do you remember that name they gave us? I don't know, it was silly. We were good-looking teenagers with too much money, and I guess that's what happens to good-looking teenagers in Hollywood."

"Yeah," Hugo says. "That's wild. *3AM*—what was that all about, anyway?" She doesn't notice how quiet he's gotten. She doesn't realize how closely he's listening.

"I don't know." Germaine laughs, and so does he. "We didn't always . . . Oh god, it's so embarrassing now. We were hot messes, not the kind of girls you'd take home to your mother, and we didn't always wear underwear. And the paparazzi caught it when we'd get out of limos."

Hugo grins. But his eyes are hard. "Her parents let her do all that as a minor, huh?"

"She wasn't a minor the *whole* time." Germaine shakes her head again and again, trying to get a grip on the situation. "But Sicily was always so *good*. It was our fault, convincing her she needed a sexier image if she wanted to sell records to anyone older than ten. We told her she needed a hot boyfriend, the clothes, the publicity."

"Couldn't have hurt the Bell moneymaker scheme, could it? She really went through the guys, I hear."

"No." Germaine's eyes are wide. "No, they went through her. I mean, she was always going after someone way out of her league—not because she wasn't gorgeous, but because LA was teeming with all these skinny, leggy girls who would do anything—and I mean *anything*—to be a star."

"Still," Hugo says. "She got quite a reputation."

"It was the guys' fault," Germaine says pointedly. "They'd stick around for a few weeks, or maybe a month or two, and then find someone wilder and more exciting. Someone without a family like the Beverly Hillbillies managing her entire life."

"3AM Girls, wild relationships, parties . . . you sure paint a vivid picture," Hugo says, and there's something soft and dangerous in his voice. "What an environment to grow up in. And the same people who 'raised'"—his tone drapes air quotes over the word—"the mother of my son are now, in a sense, the guardians of my son. Interesting."

"We were young. It's what you do when you're young in Hollywood," Germaine says, feeling defensive. And incredibly uneasy.

But his eyes are bright, so bright. He's gotten exactly what he needs from her.

"Hollywood. It's a nice place, huh? I've been thinking about moving to Los Angeles myself, in fact." He winks, then checks his watch. "Look at that—about time to get warmed up."

"Hugo, wait." If Germaine could just think, if she could just get her story straight, defend the way Sicily was raised—but she doesn't want to do that, either. "I don't want you to misunderstand me."

Hugo shrugs, overly casual. "What's there to misunderstand? It was *lovely* meeting you, Miss St. Germaine-Chang. I'll be in touch about that booking gig, okay?"

Then he's gone.

Germaine stands still, rooted to the spot, even after the guests return to the ballroom and music begins to sound over the rooftop balcony. A million paths unfold before her—she should warn Sicily, she should sabotage Hugo, she should bribe all the lawyers in LA—but all seem like dead ends. What has she done?

Revenge forgotten, Germaine walks slowly back to her suite. She shouldn't have told Hugo about Sicily's misgivings regarding her family, that there was uncertainty about their fitness as parents even back then. Because he was right, wasn't he? All the jokes Sicily had told, all the little quips they said to each other in their party days—they hadn't been jokes at all. They'd been denial.

The 3AM Girls really were girls—kids, essentially, who were allowed to run wild and do dangerous things because their parents were too unaware, like Germaine's; too absent, like Miranda's; or—worst of all—because the racy press was lucrative, as the Bell family well knew.

Germaine hadn't seen it that way at the time. They all felt so grown up; and besides, she was there to watch over Sicily and Miranda.

Germaine goes to the bathroom, stands in front of the mirror over the sink, and begins to rub her makeup off. Her eyeliner smudges a dark streak across her eyelid.

But she hadn't always been perfect at the protector thing, either.

Germaine took her status as the oldest 3AM Girl seriously. It was a role that had chosen her, not the other way around. A vocation, if you will. She was the most worldly in *Kidz Klub*, the most sophisticated, having come from a wealthy and business-oriented background that the other kids hadn't.

She hadn't expected to make friends on the show when she first began at age fourteen. She was there to begin her career—that wasn't what her parents told her, but it was Germaine's plan. And she didn't make friends, not until Miranda and Sicily were added to the cast and gravitated toward her. Germaine never knew why they chose her. And though it took her time to warm up to them, she soon couldn't imagine things any other way.

The three of them came of age together, Germaine and the two little ducklings that followed her around. She guided them through the rules of the soundstage, having been on the show for one season more than they'd been. She was there for their first sips of alcohol, holding their hair back, their introduction to parties and nights out.

It was quite a debut. Her eighteenth birthday was the first night all three of them went to the clubs together, with Miranda's mom finally deciding fifteen was old enough to go out on the town, and Sicily telling her parents she was sleeping over at Miranda's. Germaine had an au pair as her stand-in guardian for the duration of the Los Angeles stay, but she was largely free to do whatever she wanted.

She helped them dress up in their most revealing outfits, painting on eyeliner for them and helping them straighten their hair. She'd been out a few times with other cast members, but this would be way more fun. This would be her first time going out with real friends.

"We're not going to get blackout drunk, right?" Sicily had said, worried.

"Is it even going out if you don't?" Miranda scoffed.

"You pace yourself, girls," Germaine chided. "We have all night. Sicily, pull that neckline down."

Sicily had been fussing with her shirt all evening, pulling the scoop neck up way higher than it was supposed to go. Germaine readjusted it so the lacy top of her bra just barely showed.

"You're so lucky to have cleavage already," Miranda sighed, looking at her enviously.

"*Stop.*" Sicily giggled, pulling the shirt up again and turning bright red.

"Come on, we all have something to flaunt," Germaine said. "Miranda, get some blush on that cherub face of yours."

Miranda wrinkled her nose. "I'd rather have a skinny face like you."

"Hush. Body trends come and go, but natural beauty is forever," Germaine quipped as she placed a fake lash over her own waterline. "You're gorgeous, both of you. Now hurry up, the limo's almost here!"

They each took a shot of Fireball and passed around a dose of Oxy, courtesy of Miranda's generously dispensed leftovers.

Giddy and loud, the girls hurried down the elevator of Germaine's family's penthouse suite and into the limo, piling into the back seat.

They sang Avril Lavigne's "Complicated" at the top of their lungs, careening through the Los Angeles streets as the substances made their bodies feel awake and alive.

When they arrived at the club, Germaine brushed past the bouncer and indicated that the others should do the same. The dance floor was alive with silhouettes and laser lights, with remixes of Ja Rule and

Missy Elliott songs interspersed with David Guetta pounding through the crowd.

Germaine was proud to see Miranda's and Sicily's eyes light up at the thrill of the party. She ordered drinks at the bar for all three of them, shouting her order, and then they stepped into the fray, vodka cranberries in hand.

Germaine loved the clubs, and she knew the girls would, too. You could lose yourself here, forget about anything outside that black set of doors, and simply be moved by the music and the people.

She caught the eye of one guy a few feet away, smiling at her, and nodded back when he winked. He headed over to them and danced closer to Germaine, moving his hips with hers and eventually shifting behind her. Germaine leaned into him, exhilarated by the anonymity, high on the drinks and the pills and the sexuality she was able to explore so far from her family.

Miranda was giggling; Sicily's jaw had dropped. Germaine just smiled and winked at them.

Soon two other guys approached, one for each of them, and they were all dancing even closer together.

"You want to go somewhere quieter?" Germaine's guy murmured in her ear. "They got back rooms here."

Germaine's heart jump-started. She'd never been invited to a back room before, and she never would have gone herself, but now that the others were with her . . .

She raised her eyebrows at Miranda and Sicily. "You want to go somewhere quieter to talk?"

Miranda grinned and nodded. The little group navigated through the crowd, slipping through a door into a room with black leather seats and red velvet walls. The lights were down low.

Germaine sat on the couch with her guy on one side of the room, and Miranda and Sicily sat on the other with theirs. Germaine's man put his arm around her, leaning in close.

"How old are you girls, anyway?" he said with a chuckle.

Sicily's guy laughed. "Don't ask questions you don't want to know the answers to, man."

The guy drew Germaine closer, and she went in for a kiss, smelling the musky scent of his aftershave and sweat. She pulled back for a breath, expecting to catch Sicily's and Miranda's eye and communicate *How wild is this?* with glee. But her heart sank.

The two of them were perched stiffly on the couch. Miranda looked halfway into her guy, but her body language was clear—she was nervous. And Sicily's eyes were as wide as saucers, terrified. Her guy was kissing her neck even as she was trying to lean away.

"Wait, wait," Germaine said, straightening up. "Hold on. Are you two cool with this? Or do you want to go back out?"

Miranda half shrugged, but Sicily nodded her head very quickly.

"Yeah? Should we go dance some more?"

"I think they want to stay," Sicily's guy said, pulling Sicily into him with both arms so that she was leaning on his chest. Sicily froze.

"No, I think we're good here," Germaine said, standing up. She'd messed up. She should have been paying better attention to how her friends were feeling, but now she would fix it. They were her responsibility.

"Baby, come on, be cool," Germaine's guy said, even with his eyes half-closed from whatever he'd taken.

"You can dance with me more out there, yeah?" Germaine said. "Come on."

Miranda's guy looked equally out of it and reluctant to move, but Sicily's gave a mean smile. "Okay, you all go. We'll stay here."

"No," Germaine said. "Let her go." Sicily looked like she was about to cry, and it made white-hot anger flare in Germaine's chest.

"Maybe you'd like to take her place? I could go for a thai massage," the guy said, standing and sizing himself against Germaine's height while still gripping Sicily's wrist. He came up short.

"I'm Vietnamese, you fucking idiot," Germaine spat, and swung her leg to kick him hard in the crotch with her stiletto heel.

He crumpled with a high-pitched noise, falling back onto the couch, and Germaine had led Miranda and Sicily back onto the freedom of the dance floor.

Germaine stares into the middle distance, somewhere beyond the sparkling earring that Marie fixed on her ear earlier this evening. That's who Germaine was. Who she always thought she was, who she wanted to be—their protector, their advocate. She made mistakes, sure, but she didn't let anything bad happen to her girls.

Until the moment she did.

NINE

SICILY

2008

Hugo's lawsuit hits Sicily like an incoming missile.

She rereads the papers on the floor of her bedroom, panic growing with every line until it feels like it will break her apart.

She's an unfit mother, he claims. Little Noah is being dragged from country to country, from hotel to hotel, with no stability in his life, just so Sicily can keep acting the fame whore. A good family would provide a permanent home for their baby, but Sicily has been on the road for 257 days out of the past year.

Worse still, he's using her own words against her. Someone told him about a joke she used to make—an anonymous source; Sicily has combed through the documents, but there's no indication of who—about giving any future baby up for adoption.

That's all it was. A joke—right? The fact that Sicily was afraid of her parents stealing Noah away in the heat of labor doesn't matter. Maybe not the healthiest fear to have, sure, but she wasn't thinking straight.

All families have issues. This is what Sicily has always told herself. But Hugo seems to think the Bells are beyond repair—and he's using her joke to form an argument that she knew her family was unhealthy.

That she's deliberately keeping Noah in that environment. Hugo thinks they're all grifters, and this along with the thorough foundation he's laying of her wild days as a 3AM Girl is the foundation of his case.

"None of it is airtight," the family lawyer had said. "But he's certainly bringing a lot of ammunition. And press leverage."

Sicily's whole body is trembling, but she manages to read what he proposes. Hugo wants custody of Noah for *at least* half the year, when the boy will live with him and his parents. They've just moved from England to LA to make it as straightforward as possible. Even if Hugo has tour dates, his parents will be home all the time to look after Noah—unlike Sicily's family, who tour the world with her, concerned only with selling more merchandise.

Sicily takes a deep breath and leans back, her head thudding against the wall behind her. There's a crack in the paint on the ceiling and some kind of stain; she wonders how long it's been there, whether it's water damage.

Of course, the move to LA will also be very convenient for Hugo's budding solo-artist recording career, but that doesn't get mentioned anywhere. No, everyone just sees how he's crossing oceans and continents for the sake of his baby boy. All because he doesn't trust Sicily or her family.

Kendra's daily roundups have always been bad, but lately Sicily has found them unbearable. She's used to criticism. But the publicity around the court case has made the scathing articles skyrocket.

She's a sweet girl, said one "friend" of Hugo's, words that had been circulating around several outlets. *But her focus is on stardom, not motherhood, and her family enables that. She's their meal ticket. They never wanted her to have the baby.*

That may be true, but neither did Hugo. Neither did he! Sicily doesn't understand where this is coming from. She wanted to reach out to Hugo to see whether they could settle things out of court, but Day admonished her.

"Let the lawyers handle it," he said. "This is no time for emotions to get involved."

Then, when Hugo's little press tour didn't let up, she wanted to publish the messages he'd sent her, imploring her to rethink the pregnancy and reiterating the distance he wanted to keep. But she was met with another no. A good mother wouldn't publicly lash out at her baby's father. A good mother isn't bitter; she's demure, and she takes bad news on the chin.

"No sob stories yet," Uncle Henry had said. "We're keeping the high ground as long as we can. Save that ammo for when things get nasty."

And when it can be sold at a higher price, Sicily had thought. But she wasn't sure how much more she could handle.

Her family's prayers of thanks at the dinner table—for tour bookings, for Sicily's quick bounce back after Noah's birth, for their growing fortune—are beginning to get on Sicily's nerves. They sound hollower with every deposited check.

All families have issues.

Things should be calm for the moment, at least. She's home now—or what home became after the Blast Off! Network: the huge Bel Air house that she shares with Day, Carole, Uncle Henry, Kendra, and various other relatives on the payroll. Hugo should be thrilled she's introducing some stability into poor neglected Noah's life.

"He's the one who's poor," Sicily murmurs to Noah in the playpen next to her, pressing a finger to the mesh and touching his little hand. "Your daddy can't handle the consequences of his own decisions, huh, Noe?"

Sicily wipes her nose on the sleeve of her sweatshirt, watching Noah babble in response. His crib is right next to her bed so she can wake at the slightest noise of discomfort, the earliest sign that he's hungry. They had on-and-off luck with the latching, but she's supplemented with pumping and formula, and he's doing okay. They're doing okay.

She's already started introducing baby food. Soon he'll be able to move on to solids, and it will break her heart.

None of that matters, though, because LA is a snake pit of people who make money off the misfortunes of celebrities. It's gotten harder and harder to go anywhere. Every time she leaves the house with Noah, someone is lying in wait to take compromising photographs. Kendra just has to google *sicily bell bad mother* and there are dozens of shots: Noah sipping from her glass of soda, Noah baking in the sun without a hat, Noah wailing his lungs out in the car while Sicily talks on the phone or buys herself an iced coffee. She's criticized for holding Noah the "wrong" way, for wearing UGGs while she's driving. There's even a site that keeps track of how many times she goes out *without* her baby and mocks her for going to the gym more than she goes to playgrounds or parks.

She wants to scream at them, tell them that he's too little for playgrounds, that she would never leave him home alone, that he loves feeling the sun on his face, he just cries when he's tired and cranky. Like all babies do. Like she constantly wants to—but then she would be hysterical. They'd say she was a basket case.

"Don't act all crazy, now," Uncle Henry has said, one too many times. He's been watching her even closer, ever since a horrible day last week when Sicily dinged someone's parked car in the Nordstrom lot. She'd rushed from her car with Noah, locking herself in the women's bathroom while she called her father. Day had arranged for repairs, and Uncle Henry had tracked down one photographer who was lurking in a Starbucks across the street, paying him off.

"You need to be more careful," Day said that night, rubbing his eyes after a call to insurance claims.

"I'm sorry," Sicily said, but she couldn't help feeling indignant. People got in fender benders all the time. She wished everyday errors didn't feel so life-and-death. "It was just a mistake."

"We can't afford mistakes, especially not now," Uncle Henry had cut in. "You have to take better care of yourself and your child. Noah could have gotten hurt."

Sicily can't win.

The weird thing: her parents don't seem all that worried about Hugo's claim on Noah.

"It might actually help us out," Carole had the audacity to say. "Like a built-in babysitter."

"I know it's not an easy situation, honey," Day had said. They had a family meeting about it just yesterday, with all of them gathered around the big dining room table. "But . . . you didn't make things easy in the first place. And, well, he *is* the boy's father."

"And he's willing to sink a lot more money into this than we are, apparently . . . ," Kendra muttered under her breath. Next to her, Emmylou snorted.

"Has he *acted* like a father?" Sicily said, seething. "Has he given a shit until now?"

"Language," Uncle Henry said sternly.

"Noah doesn't even know these people!" Sicily protested. "You'd be totally fine if he just spent half his life in an unfamiliar house? With people who are basically strangers to him?"

"All right, no need to raise your voice," her mother said.

"He's my *child*!" Sicily said, getting only louder. "If I'm not going to fight for him, who will? Apparently not you people!"

"Now that's enough!" Uncle Henry barked. "Go take care of your son. The adults are going to talk about this."

Sicily was too angry to stay, to say that she, too, was an adult.

Now Sicily bends over the playpen, kissing Noah on the top of his head. He's oblivious to her, endlessly busy with whatever imaginary world he's wrapped up in. He has a little wooden puzzle and is trying with all his might to figure out how to make the pieces fit.

"What are we going to do, huh, little bugaboo?" she says softly. "I'm not going anywhere for half a year, no way. We're sticking together."

It's almost his lunchtime. She's been keeping to herself as much as possible, grateful for a door that she can close to be alone with her son. But the formula is in the refrigerator downstairs.

The house is quiet, and Sicily wishes she could get there and back without running into anyone.

But no such luck—there are voices in the kitchen, speaking low.

". . . not anything extreme, of course," Sicily's mother is saying, nearly whispering. Sicily stops at the bottom of the stairs.

"It's been hard on all of us." She can tell Day is covering his mouth, hands likely laced together at his chin in thought.

"Well, I'll tell you one thing," says Uncle Henry. "She can't deal with the pressure. She's going to crack. Who wouldn't?"

Sicily's mother is starting to say something else, but Sicily goes up a few stairs and then stomps down them, loudly. She bustles into the kitchen in a huff, and they all turn to look at her. So inconspicuous.

"How are you feeling, sweetie?" Carole asks. The oversympathetic concern in her voice grates on Sicily's nerves.

"I'm fine," she says flatly, retrieving the formula from the fridge. "Just lunchtime."

"We think you should take some time off," Uncle Henry says. "Take a vacation or something. Kendra was talking about this spa—"

"And leave my baby?" Sicily's voice is too high with mock hilarity. She can see the headlines now. "And go pamper myself while I'm embroiled in a tooth-and-nail fight for custody of my son? What a great idea! You really know how to call 'em, Uncle Henry. Sounds perfect." She lets out a peal of laughter that does not reach her eyes, letting it get shrill and stale as she marches out of the room.

"Sicily!" Kendra trills as they pass in the upstairs hallway. "There you are. E! just had an interview with Hugo, and—"

"No, Kendra." Sicily pushes past her without hesitating. "Not today."

"You can't shut it out," Kendra calls. "We need to stay on top of his press, too."

Sicily slams her bedroom door.

She can deal with pressure. All Sicily ever does is deal with pressure. It's been a survival tactic since she started singing her heart out on *Kidz*

Klub, performing for the whole world and becoming her family's only source of income.

But nobody was worried about the pressure of an eleven-year-old girl back then, not when the checks started rolling in.

Sicily lifts Noah in her arms and cuddles him to her chest, filling up with pride when he grabs the bottle and drinks from it greedily.

They just need to get away. They just need a little time to themselves.

"Change of plans, bugaboo," she coos. "You want to go on an adventure today?"

~

"I have to run some errands." Sicily slings the baby carrier over her elbow and picks up her keys from the hook by the fridge, casting what she hopes is a casual glance at her mother. Day and Uncle Henry have disappeared somewhere, and Sicily is glad to find Carole alone.

She frowns. "Is that a good idea, sweetheart? Let's just—"

"It's just diapers, Mom. And pads. You want to come with?"

Carole frowns and gives a little shake of her head. "We can send Kendra for that. It's not a good idea to be out right now—the whole thing last week, and with the case going on . . ."

"How about I take your car? They won't recognize that one." Sicily sighs, trying to make herself look small and vulnerable. "I just need some fresh air, Mom."

Carole purses her lips and looks uncertain, but she waves her hand. "Go then. Quick before the boys notice you're gone."

Sicily switches the keys and is out the door before Carole can change her mind.

She buckles Noah in his baby seat in the back seat of the hatchback, kissing his sweet nose. He is the only important one—Sicily needs to get away from everyone but him. Behind the wheel, she starts the engine and pulls out of the back driveway before deciding where to go. She has no definite plan in mind.

Is she an adult, like she wanted to blurt to Uncle Henry? She's never had to make plans by herself, not once in her life. She's never had to open a bank account or pay a bill or choose a phone service or call a cab. She's never had to buy groceries. She's never done the laundry.

Everyone has taken care of those things for her—has kept her too busy to ever learn how.

But she's a mom. Aren't moms supposed to be able to do that stuff? Sicily glances in the rearview at the baby seat, facing away from her. She's there for Noah's every cry, playing with him and singing to him and fumbling her way through changing his diaper. But when she throws his clothes in the hamper with hers and forgets about them, someone else takes care of it. When he grows up, she won't be able to teach him how to fill out a college application or file his taxes.

Maybe she *is* useless, like everyone has been trying to tell her. Maybe she's an unfit mother.

Lost in thought, Sicily drifts a little too close to the next lane on the highway and is startled by a honk. She quickly corrects, pushing her sunglasses closer to her face and hunching down as a pickup truck passes her on the left, the driver peering into the car. She sneaks a glance; he's wearing a baseball cap, and his eyes are narrowed.

She presses her foot to the gas to get ahead of him, but he speeds up with her. She slows down, and he does, too. He's staying right next to her, trying to look in the car—he knows who she is.

Finally, Sicily drops her speed to thirty and puts her blinker on, slowly moving behind him. She exits as soon as she can, and he's gone.

"We didn't like him, did we, Noah?" she says in the rearview mirror. "No, sir."

Sicily finds herself heading east on the 10 and realizes, after seeing signs for Malibu, that she's instinctively driving toward Miranda's beach house. For just a moment, she relaxes. How incredible would it be to see Miranda right now? She hasn't met Noah yet, even though they're both in the same city again. Just seeing her face would make Sicily feel grounded. She imagines opening a bottle of wine, having Noah play on the floor between them while they talk like they used to. Just talk, for hours on end, swapping stories and complaining about work and the men in their lives and how fast the world is moving, how hard it is to keep up.

But no—there could be no wine, no drinking at all. Sicily isn't sure whether Miranda is even home right now, between the DUI, the arrest, and what's rumored to be jail time due to poor behavior while on probation. It sounds like things really went downhill when her most recent guy dumped her. Miranda's temper is not serving her well lately, and Sicily has been giving her space; not to mention that Sicily's plate is now full with this court case.

Really, Sicily shouldn't even be driving this way. It's an obvious route to Malibu, and she shouldn't give the paparazzi any opportunity to draw a link between her and Miranda and bring up the 3AM shit again. Sicily checks her mirrors; there's a white Chevy that's been behind her for a few miles. Is it following her? There's no saying how quickly that man in the pickup might've called a press connection to let them know he'd seen her. A tip like that could get you some nice pocket change.

Who's to say she isn't being watched now, trailed by the cars around her, even in front? The paps could be ruthless. One of them risked getting T-boned by pulling out in front of her limo, forcing it to stop. Sicily suddenly feels claustrophobic on the open highway, wide but filled with cars and eyes that are craning to see her.

She swerves for the next exit without putting on her blinker. The Chevy follows, signaling right.

"Shit," Sicily says under her breath. "Hang on back there, okay, bugaboo?"

There's a yellow light at the end of the off-ramp, and she runs it, turning onto Lincoln Boulevard and then off down several side streets, twisting in an unpredictable route. At the end of every alley, she expects the white car to screech in front of her, trapping them. Her hands are like vise grips on the wheel. She needs to get out of the city, away from her family, away from these awful people.

At last she reaches Venice Boulevard and gets back on the 10, this time heading west and then exiting north. She drives as fast as legally possible, weaving around the cars so none of them get too good a look at her or Noah.

Where can she go? What can she do? Everybody in America knows her face. It was so much easier to disappear, Sicily thinks, in the days before social media. In Old Hollywood. If she'd lived back then, maybe she could have changed her hair, moved to Iowa, and worked at a diner somewhere. Paid a local retiree to babysit Noah during the day and spent her evenings watching him play in the fields. The vision feels so achingly beautiful to Sicily that all at once she feels like she could cry.

That won't cut it nowadays. The media will find her, no matter where she goes—if her family doesn't get to her first.

As if picking up on her panic, Noah fusses and begins to cry. Maybe it's the way she's driving, or the hot sun coming through the window, or maybe he needs a change. Whatever it is, Sicily can't do anything about it just now. She turns on the radio, switching stations when she can take her eyes off the road for a second and trying to find one he likes. His whimpering pitches up into a scream.

"Hey, Noah, it's your mama!" she says over the din when "So Bad, So Good" comes on. "Listen to Mama . . ."

She sings the chorus when it comes around, hating the way her voice sounds. Tears come to her eyes, and Sicily brushes them away angrily.

When they reach the Los Angeles city limits, she keeps driving.

~

By the time Noah finally quiets, it's getting dark. They're in the desert—Sicily isn't sure where. She's never driven this far by herself, and she doesn't have a GPS or a map, having shut her cell phone off and tossed it in the back when calls from Mom, Dad, Uncle Henry, and Kendra started rolling in. She wasn't paying close enough attention to the road signs, either, while watching for cars that might be trailing them.

But maybe she's close to Palm Springs. Maybe she could get to Vegas. Maybe she'll just keep going until they find a new town of their very own, and she and Noah can just curl up to sleep in the back seat like two animals in a burrow, safe and sound.

Hours pass. Or maybe minutes. And then the engine starts to stall.

"Oh shit," Sicily whispers to herself, looking at the fuel gauge. The dial has sunk below empty. She wasn't watching it. This is all her fault. "No, no."

She pumps the gas pedal as the car sputters and slows and finally grinds to a stop.

Then everything is silent.

Sicily remains frozen, staring at the horizon through the windshield as a heavy blanket of panic wraps around her. A long, lone road stretches out before the car with miles of desert scrub brush on either side. She's facing east. The dusky light of the evening is slowly sinking into the foothills behind her.

Sicily unbuckles and gropes in the back seat for her cell phone; it's there, fallen near the door. She still doesn't want to talk to her family—and she's starting to worry that Hugo has some good points about them—but maybe there's someone else who can help her.

The phone still has a battery charge. But zero service.

"Come on," Sicily says, holding it higher. She dials 911, once, twice, but the call won't connect. At last she slumps back in her seat.

"We got our wish, huh, bugaboo?" she whispers. "No one out here to take our picture."

Or to save their lives.

Sicily shakes herself. She has to move. She has to keep going or she'll lose it. Doesn't the desert get deathly cold at night? But they can't stay here in the car; Sicily isn't sure she wants to meet anyone who finds them on this road all alone.

It's been miles since they passed any signs of civilization. By the odds of it, she figures, there should be something just ahead. The road slopes upward about a mile off—maybe there's a gas station she can't see, a little desert town just over the crest. People didn't recognize the 3AM Girls in that bar on Miranda's eighteenth birthday, so maybe they won't recognize one former, miserable 3AM Girl here. She hopes.

Because she has to keep going forward. If she goes back, deep down, she knows that Noah is already lost.

He's sleeping when she unbuckles him from the car seat, and she feels horrible for waking him up, horrible that he hasn't eaten in hours.

"Let's go for a little walk, huh, Noe?" She kisses his furrowed brow and hefts the baby bag over her shoulder. There's just one bottle of formula in there—she hadn't planned on being gone this long. She didn't have a plan at all. Sicily presses the bottle to his lips as they walk, leaving the car dark and locked.

She sings him a lullaby, ignoring how heavy everything is in her arms.

The moon is coming up over the rise. She checks her phone again every few yards, but they're in too much of a valley.

When Noah's had half the formula, she stuffs it back in the bag and burps him while he fusses.

Sicily continues to hum, heart pounding as they reach the top of the slope, and she cranes her neck to see the road ahead.

Her stomach twists when the crest reveals nothing but more desert in front of them, black road cutting through the gray brushland like a snake.

"Just around the next rise, then, right, bugaboo? Just by those rocks?"

She keeps going. Her arms ache.

As the darkness deepens from navy blue to black, she catches sight of two pinpricks of light far behind her—a car.

Relief and terror mingle in her chest. It could be anyone. They could do anything to her and Noah.

But when the headlights stop at the dark, far-off shape of her parked car, blue and red police lights flicker on. Sicily has the urge to run as it approaches, but she can't; there's nowhere to go. And this particular mistake is really starting to feel like life or death.

The officer who pulls up on the shoulder is wearing a patch on his uniform that reads NEVADA PD. Sicily didn't even know they had left California.

"The hell do you think you're doing, young lady?" he asks when he steps out of the car.

"We ran out of gas," Sicily says in a small voice, clutching Noah closer. There's still a chance he doesn't know her, that he's just a small-town cop from nearby.

"Sicily Bell, right?" he says, a little incredulous. "Your family is beside themselves, called every police station in the American Southwest. Goddamn celebrities. Do you have any idea what could have happened to you out here? With a baby?"

Sicily says nothing. She just lets out a long, desperate sigh that feels like her last breath.

~

By morning, they are back in LA. Sicily and Noah are picked up from the police station in a limo sent by the Bells' lawyer. As she sits numbly in the back seat with Noah against her chest, Sicily realizes they are not en route to home.

"Where are we going?" she calls, knocking on the partition. The driver glances in the rearview but does not answer.

Instead, he eventually pulls up to what appears to be a medical facility in Thousand Oaks. Her mother, father, and Uncle Henry are waiting by the front door.

"What is this?" Sicily says when Carole opens the passenger door.

"We just think you need to take some time to relax," her mother says.

"No." Sicily tries to shrink back into the car even as Carole takes her by the arm. Despite the homey lobby and nurses' uniforms that are simply embroidered with SUNNYVALE, she knows what this is. It's a private mental health facility—the kind you don't check into voluntarily.

"It wasn't cool, what you did last night," Uncle Henry says, taking her other arm. "It wasn't good for Noah."

Sicily twists around, surprised at the strength of the two, trying to see what's happening to her son in the back seat of the limo. Kendra is there, taking him out of the baby carrier and burping him over her shoulder.

"Kendra!" Sicily shouts. "Bring him over here!"

But Kendra only shoots a guilty-looking glance at Sicily and turns away, carrying Noah back toward the parking lot. Sicily feels something that has been growing tighter and tighter in her chest suddenly snap.

"Do you realize what could have happened, Sicily?" Her father is coming up to her now, a small paper cup in his hand. "If you and Noah had starved to death out there—if anyone with ill intentions had come across you—and worse, if they realized who you were . . ." He shakes his head, hand trembling a little. "It's over now. And it's not going to happen again."

"It won't!" Sicily cries. "It won't, Dad, I promise. Please—can we just go home?"

"Come on now, hun," he says, lifting the cup. "These will help you calm down."

Sicily screams and elbows the cup from his hand, sending pills clattering to the ground. She doesn't need drugs. She needs to be alone with Noah. She lunges and kicks until two burly aides hurry over. It takes five people total to hold her back from running to her son.

Of that, at least, she will always feel a little proud.

～

The year ends with Sicily spending more time with the family lawyer and his associates than she's ever spent with a boyfriend. Hugo easily wins the custody suit, moving Noah to his house in Pasadena.

And Sicily's parents win a suit of their own, between the institutionalization, the court cases, and the tangle of legalities: a conservatorship, with Day and the family attorney being granted the right to oversee Sicily's life. Along with Hugo's case, which laid out the evidence of Sicily's past life so eloquently—the drinking, the spending, the drugs, the parties that lasted into the early morning—how could any reasonable judge not see the need for some oversight? Sicily is an obvious mess.

This means that Day and the attorney are in charge not only of her finances, but of everything: the new apartment in a high-rise tower so she can't slip away, the revoked license, the limited time with Noah. Sicily can leave the building only under supervision, usually straight to the rehearsal rooms where she's learning routines for the new tour.

Because there's always a tour. The family still needs her to make money, however low she feels, however much she misses her baby.

The show must go on.

PART II

TEN

SICILY

Sicily hums to herself as she strolls through Utsubo Park, drinking Earl Grey milk tea. July is probably her favorite month, she thinks to herself, even if the cherry blossoms in Japan have gone by now. Deep summer is super romantic, too.

But maybe that's just because she's in love again.

This time it's with Squeak, one of the backup dancers on her comeback tour. Is it too late to come back? The question has nagged at her, but no, the answer is that it's definitely not too late. Gwen Stefani made it *huge* as a solo artist in her thirties, so why can't Sicily— especially when she was a solo artist to start with?

Along with promoting her new album, the tour comes with a big prize at stake. If all this goes well, and Sicily proves that she can still sing, dance, and draw major crowds, then a Vegas residency is practically guaranteed.

And she really, really wants a Vegas residency.

Toned, taut, and tanned—she's been back at it, doing all she can to lose weight and get into peak shape again over the past year. But it's not for her; the tour is called "Second Chances" for a reason. She clicks the lock on her phone, as she's already done a million times today, to see the picture of Noah that serves as her wallpaper. He's posing in his scuffed baseball uniform, a toad he found somewhere displayed carefully in his palm and an expression of pure glee on his face. His dirty-blond curls are a glorious mess, and he's missing his left incisor tooth. Sicily has never seen a more perfect picture. She hopes that someone will improve on Google Glass someday so she can project the photo in the corner of her vision constantly.

Noah still lives with Hugo and Hugo's insufferably sweet Zoë Kravitz look-alike of a wife in LA, on a big all-American plot of land with a front porch and ranch-style backyard that would make anyone forget that Hugo is an expat.

But Sicily gets Noah one weekend a month, when she's not traveling; every second holiday; and three weeks every summer, every second of which is spent spoiling him as rotten as possible and practically gluing him to her side.

It's still never enough. And she's begun to feel the tension, the way he pulls back or looks embarrassed when she runs her fingers through his hair or kisses him on both cheeks. A sharp Hugo-esque chin is starting to show through the baby fat.

Sicily hates every second she spends apart from her son. But a Vegas residency—that would start in the new year and give her what she craves most: stability. Financial stability, professional stability. Sicily could stay put for a while, and Chad—her new manager—says he can negotiate one Saturday a month off so she can spend as much time with Noah as possible.

Chad is the manager she never knew she needed. Sicily has not spoken to her father or Uncle Henry in five years, the exact amount of time that has passed since she successfully challenged the conservatorship and got back control of her life.

It had been a long and difficult battle. The seeds were planted when someone who had formerly been on Day and Uncle Henry's legal team leaked a voicemail to a pop music podcast—a voicemail of the two of them discussing how to take away Sicily's car after they caught her driving it after curfew. She had been twenty-six at the time. The whistleblower also alleged that the conservatorship was supposed to be in place for only two years as an emergency measure, but that Henry and Day had extended it as a means of control and had abused Sicily under its pretense.

It had taken Sicily a long time to realize that this was true. She'd bent to her family's will for so long—she'd been raised to do it. She was placed on a pedestal by all of them, almost a sort of messianic figure that elevated them out of their rural background and brought them more money and fame than they ever could have dreamed.

But they didn't see her as a human. Sicily doesn't like to think of those long, dull days that were just eat, rehearse, train, sleep, repeat. The two men even limited the amount of time Kendra spent with Sicily, though Sicily didn't learn this until later. The daily roundups stopped; they didn't want her to hear too much from social media, especially when the "SilentSicily" hashtag started trending and groups popped up all around the world, banding together and demanding her release from legal restraint.

Sicily still doesn't know who that whistleblower was. But she's forever grateful to them.

Day and Uncle Henry were dismissive of the "conspiracy theorists," then irritated, then paranoid. The days got darker before they got better; the suspicion that had begun to plague Sicily when she drove to Nevada spiraled when the outrage from the public—while affirming—made it clear that her mistrust of her family had never been in her head.

A lot of horrible things came to light—everyone was out to get her. She discovered that Joe, her cousin who was in charge of accounts, had been skimming money. Candy, another, was taking secret photos and selling them to the tabloids. Yet another had a side business where they sold pairs of her socks and her old jewelry and other junk on eBay for hefty sums.

But the worst of all was Kendra, whom Sicily caught texting Elliot—one of the other members of No Exit.

"It was you," Sicily had said softly, startling Kendra as she read the screen over her shoulder. Sicily had become very good at sneaking around, watching, observing. They had underestimated her.

"Jesus Christ, Sicily. What?" Kendra clambered to her feet and shoved her phone in her jeans. "What was me?"

"You told Hugo all that shit about me. You set him up with everything he needed for the custody case."

"Sicily, shut up." Kendra was upset. "You don't know anything. I've never spoken to Hugo."

"How am I supposed to believe that? How am I supposed to believe anything you people say? You're texting Elliot Stowell!"

Kendra's face was bright red. "So I got some with Elliot while you were getting some with Hugo. So what? You think I voluntarily signed up to be dragged around the world as your personal assistant? I *never* get to have normal relationships, Sicily!"

"You never? *You* never?" The rage felt like a living animal inside Sicily, hot and writhing. She doesn't quite remember what happened next, but some of the ugliest words ever exchanged among the Bell family were contained within that single argument. It might have gotten physical if Carole hadn't come in to break things up.

Sicily stopped speaking to Kendra after that.

After six months of social media fervor and denied requests for press statements from Sicily that only fueled the flames, a lawyer from Corcoran and Associates messaged Sicily privately on Instagram to offer her services. Her name was Deborah, and she was a no-nonsense tank of a woman who agreed to take Sicily's case out of goodwill.

She spoke to Sicily plainly and very matter-of-factly, like a doctor trying to understand a health concern. Sicily was grateful.

Under Deborah's advice, Sicily did not let on that she was speaking with counsel until she'd managed to gather as much evidence as possible about her father and uncle's legal control and the ways they had abused the conservator system.

Sicily had hoped it would be one and done with a single court case, but no—there were hearings and sessions, follow-ups and recesses and delayed court dates. Deborah said that Henry and Day were trying to starve her out.

But Sicily had Germaine and Miranda on her side, the first public figures to use the "SilentSicily" hashtag, and who pooled their money to offer her a safety net for anything she needed.

Plus, the press was vitriolic against Day and Henry. Someone doxed them, and Uncle Henry even got a rock through his Audi window.

At the end of the battle in court, it was Day who made the choice to finally, voluntarily, terminate the conservatorship. Sicily walked freely out of the courtroom with Deborah that day without casting a second glance back at her father or uncle.

She posted a picture of herself on the steps with the simple caption: #SilentNoMore.

Her mother is still in her life, for now. Kendra is not. Sicily still keeps in touch with some of the other cousins who had about as much agency in getting yoked to the family machine as Sicily did—like Emmylou, who could still do Sicily's hair and makeup better than anyone. But the rest of the Bells are kept at arm's length.

Chad, on the other hand, treats her like an adult. A real, actual adult—and it took some sinking in for Sicily to realize that she was no longer a kid. He's asked for her opinion on things, dropped plans when she expressed reluctance toward them. It came as a shock. But the stable guidance gave Sicily the confidence to follow Gwen Stefani's footsteps, all the way to Japan, where she is playing an Osaka gig at the Ookini Arena on Maishima Sports Island tonight.

All seven thousand seats will be full, Chad promises. And she believes him because he tells her the truth.

Sicily's phone dings, and she glows when she checks the screen, due not only to the picture of Noah but also to the text from Squeak: You manage to escape again?

She grins around her tea straw. Whose business is it? she texts.

Mine, because I think I see you by the fountain.

Sicily looks around, excited by the thrill that he's somewhere nearby. Soon she spots his tall, muscular frame approaching down the park path, his grin equally wide to see her.

He's all brown skin and tattoos, the physical opposite of Hugo, and much more caring. She found his name mismatched for someone of his broad and athletic build—Sicily looks petite standing next to him. When she asked about it, he told her about his favorite dish called "bubble and squeak," the one that he ate every day growing up in Brisbane. He loved it so much that his mom gave him the nickname, and it stuck.

Utterly charming, Sicily thinks. *Irresistible.*

He kisses her on the forehead and Sicily melts.

"What are you doing out here?" Squeak asks.

"I could ask you the same thing," she chides. "I thought rehearsal was still going on."

"We're breaking for lunch. And *you,* my SiSi, should eat something more than boba before we need to load into the tour bus."

His nickname for her. Sicily loves it. Their couple name is apparently circulating as "Squeaksy," which is embarrassing—but at the same time she can't get enough of the sappy articles. If she and Kendra were still speaking, Sicily thought she might have even looked forward to the daily roundups.

"I had something earlier," Sicily says, laughing and pushing him away lightly. She doesn't want to let on how nervous she is; she doesn't think she could keep anything down until after the show. There has never been so much riding on it.

"If you say so." He still looks concerned and loops an arm around her waist. "You're going to be killer tonight, you know that, right? You always are."

She leans into him, his body solid and secure against hers. "Thanks, you. Walk me back to the hotel before they drag you away again?"

They walk through the park slowly, hand in hand, watching kids play in the fountain and fly kites on the green. This is a life she once never imagined could be hers.

Sicily and Squeak run into Chad just inside the hotel and instinctively drop hands, though everyone must know what's going on between them. Chad pretends not to notice.

"You haven't been keeping her, have you? How long are these lunch breaks supposed to last?" he says to Squeak, half joking, half not.

Squeak grins sheepishly. "I was just getting back." He waves goodbye to both of them, holding Sicily's gaze for a lingering second that makes her a little lightheaded.

"Could you be ready in forty-five minutes?" Chad asks her once Squeak is gone.

She loves that it's a question. She could say *No, sorry, I need more time*, and Chad would make it work. But it's for this reason that Sicily never wants to let him down.

"For sure." She nods. "Give me thirty."

"Fantastic. Right on the money." He's always saying corny stuff like that—it's the best. Chad heads toward the elevators, then turns back like he's suddenly remembered something.

"Hey, I'm happy for you two," he says. "You more than deserve the chance to blow off some steam. Just play it cool, yeah?"

Sicily feels her face redden a bit. "I will."

"A dancer romance is for tour, not for happily ever after."

She shifts her weight. "I know."

~

Seven thousand seats full and then some. From the stage, Sicily swears she sees people standing in the top rows, in the aisles, packed as tightly as they can in the arena just to see her perform. She's been practicing her routines for months to perfect them, but once the stage lights hit her, it all comes back like magic—the energy, the charisma, the feeling that she's incapable of making a single misstep. The crowd loves her every move, roaring their enthusiasm and singing the lyrics along with her by heart.

Sicily feels fluid, hitting all her marks and even catching Squeak's eye during one song to wink at him in excitement. The nod he gives back, as if to say *I told you so*, seals it. She and the dancers bring down the house to thundering applause.

Sicily runs offstage and is suddenly hit with a wall of exhaustion. She's breathing hard and sweating. Squeak was right—she should have eaten. But this feels like more than regular nerves to her, and, anyway, the hardest part of the night is already over.

"Let's do an encore," the stage manager says into their headset, signaling for Sicily and the dancers to go back out. She takes a deep breath and braces for the hot lights once more.

Sicily makes it through, but the arena swims before her eyes, and she doesn't hit her marks quite as sharply as she did when the adrenaline was helping her. The crowd doesn't care—she's already won them over.

But back in her dressing room, nausea brings her milk tea back up in the sink. Yet it's a familiar feeling, and something is nagging at the back of her mind, a gut instinct that doesn't go away the next day and the next.

A pregnancy test from the drugstore finally confirms it.

Sicily did it again: she's pregnant.

ELEVEN

MIRANDA

2018

Wat is with you and failed contraception?" Miranda exclaims into her phone. "I had to find out from *Hollywood Today?*"

"I know, I'm sorry." Sicily is laughing on the other end, crying a little, too. "They leaked it. I think someone on the Ookini crew overheard."

"But the Vegas residency," Miranda goes on. "I thought you had all these plans . . ."

"It was definitely a surprise." Miranda can hear Sicily blowing her nose. "And Vegas is on hold for now. But it just . . . happened! I don't know. Things aren't always foolproof."

"I'm aware that none of us went to high school. But you do know how babies are made, right?" Miranda says flatly.

Sicily laughs. "Yes, yes, shut up. You could be happy for me, you know."

"Are you happy about it?"

There's a pause on the other end and a big sigh. "Yeah. Yes. I really am. The timing is bad. I'm bummed that Vegas is off the table, but . . .

this *guy*, Miranda. Perfecto. And to be able to love on a little baby again? I've missed that so bad."

Miranda bites her lip. If she had a dollar for every time she's heard Sicily gush about a guy, she'd have been able to buy her own yacht instead of riding around on the one she's on now, which belongs to another boyfriend. But Sicily deserves happiness whenever she can grab it.

"Then I'm happy for you, Sis," she says. "I'm over the moon for you, you know that. But the godmother thing still stands!"

Sicily laughs.

When Miranda gets off the phone, Bobbie, lounging on a deck chair nearby, clucks her tongue.

"Was that about the new Bell baby?" she asks. Miranda's mother is much more in tune with the Hollywood gossip than Miranda, for reasons Miranda doesn't understand.

"Yeah," Miranda says. "Baby number two."

Bobbie shakes her head. "That girl has no sense. I mean, jeez, I made that mistake, but I only made it once."

Miranda pauses with her cosmopolitan halfway to her mouth and shoots a look at her mother. "Thanks, Mom."

But Bobbie is adjusting the sleeves on her billowy white caftan and peering out at the sea through her sunglasses, apparently unaware that she's said anything wrong. She sets down the magazine she's been reading and gives an exaggerated yawn.

"All this lazing around is exhausting. Think I'll dress for dinner."

Miranda knows that's code for having a bubble bath and drinking champagne. She rolls her eyes as her mother drifts off into the cabin, hardly sparing a backward glance at her daughter.

Bobbie has nothing to complain about. Aren't they sailing around the Mediterranean on a yacht, no particular destination in mind, no foreseeable end to the vacation? Without the "mistake" of Miranda, Bobbie would still be living in the Midwest and sweeping hair off the floor of some suburban salon. Or worse—stuck in an abusive relationship with a semipro baseball player, which is exactly the scenario that made Miranda agree to bring Bobbie along on this trip. As difficult as their relationship has been, Miranda couldn't in good conscience leave her mother to her own devices in LA.

It isn't Taha's yacht. Taha was five guys ago—and to his credit, he didn't bail immediately after the DUI. But when they kept her from joining the ABBA remake and Sam dropped her for good, Miranda lost control. Taha walked somewhere between the second DUI, the Oxy relapse, the belligerence, and the jail time. Miranda can't blame him.

Two years of prison. It was just like rehab—worse than rehab—but at least in prison, people didn't subscribe to the positive-thinking kumbaya crap. Miranda found her way through it. She could make the other women laugh with her impersonations of famous people and get Bobbie to smuggle in contraband that she could trade for cigarettes and Altoids. Sure, there was a big brawl in the shower and she got stabbed. But the scar is small, a white line right above her left hip, and the attack won her respect from the other inmates and a sympathy vote from the parole board. She's thinking about getting it covered with a tattoo someday—of what, she doesn't know. On the other hand, it makes her feel pretty tough.

When she got out, a lot of people stopped returning her calls. Auditions dried up completely. The only bright spot was when Zane broke his long radio silence and called to see how she was doing. Surprised to see his name on her phone, Miranda breezed cheerfully through the conversation. She could have fooled anyone into thinking she was getting back into Hollywood's good graces instead of becoming one of its outcasts.

"It could be worse," she remembers saying. "I've got a cool scar now, at least. And a few commercials lined up."

It was a lie; there were no commercials. There was nothing. Why didn't she tell him the truth, cry, and let it all out and admit that he was the only one who could make her feel better?

"Hey, good for you," he said. "I'm glad to hear it."

"How's everything in your world?" Which meant, *Are you seeing anyone? Are you eating enough? Are you okay?*

He let out a long breath. "Things have been better, things have been worse. My parents split because my mom's running off with someone back in Venezuela. Well—I shouldn't say 'running off.' They're getting married and all, it's legit."

"I'm sorry," Miranda said. "I mean . . . good for her? I don't know what to say. How's your dad handling that?"

"He's been better." Zane barked a short laugh. "Bankrupt, now. His last business manager was . . . no bueno. Bad at his job. But maybe it's for the best—all those years of jumping around onstage has been catching up with my dad. Joint pain like you wouldn't believe."

He said it sort of like a joke, so Miranda chuckled, but she felt sorry for Zane.

"Yeah, I know what that's like," she said. He knew about her foot injury.

"Well, you better stay healthy." Zane laughed. "Otherwise, I'm going to have to take care of my dad *and* you."

Miranda said nothing to that, but it was because she was smiling quietly to herself.

"Means all my famous inheritance has pretty much dried up, though." Zane sighed through the phone. "I'm getting the realest taste of regular life since Venezuela, and . . . it bites."

"Yeah? How bad?"

"Like, I'm-heading-into-a-shift-at-a-family-friend's-restaurant-in-twenty-minutes bad."

Miranda laughed. "That sounds bad."

"Eh. It's okay. We get a lot of Laguna Beach bums. But, hey, I have free fries for life."

"Can't beat that."

They both trailed off. Though he was trying to make light of it, Miranda could tell he was embarrassed. She had thought, more than once, about what she should have said in that pause—that they should get coffee sometime, that she'd come to his restaurant to say hi, that it was okay their lives weren't turning out the way they'd always hoped they would.

But instead, she said, "Well."

And he said, "Yeah."

And they bade an awkward goodbye, the conversation fizzling out as quickly as it had started. Miranda had meant to call him again sometime, or make a trip down to Orange County just to see how he was doing. But she thought that showing up unannounced might embarrass him further. And truth be told, maybe Miranda was embarrassed, too. They'd both grown up like he'd said they should—kind of—but their lives were a mess.

And now there's Amir, who owns the yacht on which she's now lounging. He's okay. Miranda can't really summon up much more enthusiasm than that. She's begun to see a cookie cutterness to all these megawealthy men and the way they conduct business from their phones, buying the attention of women and media, partying, sailing to a new place, repeat. But traveling the Med on his yacht is not a bad way to escape the heat of summer—not to mention the heat of the bad press surrounding her most recent movie, a horror flick that was supposed to be the summer sleeper hit that relaunched Miranda's career. Again.

But *Ghost Slayer* opened in June to scathing reviews and poor box-office numbers. It didn't do anything fresh, they said; it had some of the novelty of old eighties slashers but kept Miranda, the lead, in a tired damsel-in-distress trope. A winning marketing team would have pitched it as campy, but this studio's publicity was mediocre at best.

Sam would have never suggested Miranda audition for a role like that. But, like Taha, he and Miranda haven't spoken since the DUI. Miranda thinks it's final this time.

But who cares? Like Miranda would ever want to walk into his agency again, after they called her—what was it?—*some whore for hire who spent her summers on an Arab yacht.* They could keep on saying it, along with every gossip site. Plenty of models and actresses did the same thing. She knew half the girls in the marina at Saint-Tropez. What's wrong with having a rich boyfriend who buys you gifts and takes you places and lavishes you with money? That sounds close enough to love for Miranda.

She presses a finger to her bare thigh and the skin pales, then pinks. She's had enough sun for the day. For her lifetime, maybe—but she'll be grateful for the tan when audition season comes around again.

She sighs and checks her phone. There's a group text from Germaine to her and Sicily: Remember when we went to the Griffith on the 4th of July and that guy was so startled when the fireworks started that he fell over? I think of it every 4th and it KILLS me. Btw you should both come to Bali if you get the chance. Rooms on me!

Miranda smiles and texts back. So far away from America, she'd forgotten that it was the holiday. And he almost knocked that kid over!!! I thought he was going to roll down the hill for sure XD

Maybe she could convince Amir to spend August in Bali. Miranda taps into her messages from him; sometimes he sends her a shirtless picture from elsewhere on the yacht to signal that he's in the mood. But Miranda hasn't seen him in an hour or so.

She walks the length of the boat, squinting to make out the coast of Malta on the horizon. They're headed to Catania next, she thinks; she's actually not completely sure. All Miranda's days seem to blur together out here. She's losing her sense of time.

The door of the cabin suite she shares with Amir is slightly ajar. When Miranda ducks into the room from the bright-white deck of the yacht, she blinks the sun out of her eyes. It's dark in the hull.

"Amir?" she says.

Her vision adjusts gradually. But she can still see well enough to witness the two figures in the bed and hear the startled rustle of sheets.

"Miranda! There you are," Amir says, smiling widely.

He's coming into focus now—naked, relaxed, arm around someone with tousled bottle-blond hair.

Her mother.

"Come join us, babe." Amir winks. "There's room for one more."

There's a silence that stretches painfully and then snaps when Bobbie giggles nervously and waves. "Well—why not, honey?"

That she at least has the decency to look sheepish is lost on Miranda. There is hot, white light flaring at the edges of her vision, boiling water coursing through her veins. Reaching down, Miranda takes off one of her Manolo Blahnik sandals and hurls it with all her strength at Amir's face. He dodges it and puts up his arms, annoyed.

"You're *sick!*" Miranda screams. "You are both *sick* and I *hate* you!"

"Hey!" Amir barks. "Uncalled for!"

"Oh, it is SO called for," Miranda snarls, taking off the other sandal. "And YOU!" she shrieks at Bobbie, launching her shoe. "What kind of godforsaken, hoe-ass *bitch*—"

Bobbie covers her head, but the sandal still hits her. "Okay. Miranda, okay—"

"They do it in porn all the time," Amir mutters.

"Fucked up, sick—both of you. Perverted *motherfucker*—literally— thinking he can get me a few Hermès bikinis and that'll buy his way into a threesome—"

She has no control. She feels like she could vomit acid on both of them. Miranda wishes for another shoe, a heavy pot she can throw, anything.

"You're supposed to be my *mom!*" she bellows, nearly sobbing.

"Don't go being a crazy bitch again," Amir says.

"You ruined my childhood." Miranda can't stop—her anger feels like a sharp, hard point right now, and she wields it at Bobbie. "You ruined *me!* Where the hell were you? When I got hurt? When I needed an adult in my life? When they doped up your thirteen-year-old daughter with *drugs?*"

Bobbie shakes her head. "Miranda. I didn't—"

"I want to leave." Miranda suddenly stops and stands up very straight. "Amir, I want off of this stupid, *fucking* boat. Immediately."

"Well, I'd say that you can jump overboard and swim to shore," Amir says, sneering at her. "But I'm not going to be the one to rescue you. So tough shit."

Miranda just stands still for a minute, breathing heavily. Bobbie is looking pointedly down at the bedspread, sheets pulled tightly across her chest. Amir is glaring at Miranda.

Then Miranda turns, barefoot, and walks below deck. Amir has stuff, she knows it. She's been good, she's been sticking to alcohol, but wouldn't anyone agree she's earned this? Yes, she thinks, digging through the drawers of the wet bar with shaking hands. She's been through enough. She needs this now.

There's harder stuff, and she tells herself she's being disciplined by choosing the benzos. Just a little Xanax. Just something, anything, to block out what is happening right now.

A tepid high begins to envelop Miranda as she makes her way back up to the forward deck. She places her hands on the railings, starboard side, and stares down into the blue water. It's too choppy to see her reflection. She puts one foot on the lower rail, then the other, leaning out until she can feel her center of gravity shift.

She could jump, like Amir said. She could dive down as far as possible and let the sea take over. Swim until her body just gave out, finally putting an end to all this.

But instead, Miranda lets herself fall backward, slumping down onto the deck. She doesn't have the nerve.

Her phone buzzes a text.

And Miranda kept us rallying until 4 am, writes Sicily, answering the group text. With Zane's help! ;) God what's happened to us haha. Old and gray now

Miranda sits on the polished wooden beams, numb and cross-legged. She watches the sun go down and wonders how she can escape this life.

TWELVE

GERMAINE

2018

Germaine places a carefully manicured nail between her teeth as she examines the layout of the lobby. She bites slightly before stopping herself, folding her arms across her chest instead and frowning. If her mother sees her with a bitten nail, Germaine might as well die.

"Why are the orchids orange?" she says to the harried-looking woman standing next to her in a sharply pressed black suit, holding a clipboard. "I thought I *specifically* said blue."

"You did say blue," the woman says, her voice taut like she's trying not to raise it. "But then we learned that someone else bought out our vendor's stock of blue, so you said orange would be okay. If you recall, Miss St. Germaine-Chang."

Germaine puts her nail back in her mouth. "We're not going for *okay*, Melati. We are going for haute. Pristine. Immaculate. Try again for blue. Let's go to the fountain."

Germaine walks briskly to the center of the high-arched atrium lobby, which is filled with foliage, marble statuary, and natural light. She's followed by Melati, the manager of this new St. Germaine-Chang boutique hotel, and half a dozen stewards. The fountain, ordered from

Milan, is a particular point of pride, with intricately carved stonework that boasts five tiers of bowls that spill water in uniform curtains down to the bubbling pool below. It's enormous. There are schools of iridescent gourami fish in the lowermost level, their scales flashing in the light.

"How many fish did we put in here?" Germaine asks.

"One hundred and fifty," says Melati.

"Let's do three hundred. No—two seventy-five."

Melati scribbles a note and hurries after Germaine, who is strutting for the courtyard.

Germaine sighs as she notes the off-center art books on one of the marble café tables, and decides that the gamelan music playing from a speaker somewhere is a touch too loud. The music is important—it's Germaine's favorite part. She's begun contracting with local musicians in each region of her family's empire to create bespoke soundtracks for the hotels. It's gotten great press, and it brings an added dimension to the boutique hotel's design.

Germaine turns and touches a finger to her ear. "It should be an atmosphere, not a school band concert."

"I'm so sorry, Miss St. Germaine-Chang," Melati says. "Banyu!" she hisses behind her, miming turning the volume down.

Germaine doesn't have time for apologies. The linen curtains on the cabanas aren't tied evenly; the bottles of shampoo in the bathrooms should be Moroccanoil, not the generic brand. In one king suite, she smells the musty scent of dust.

"All rooms were cleaned this morning before your arrival, Miss St. Germaine-Chang," Melati assures her.

"I swear I smell it." Germaine wrinkles her nose. "Like the back stairwell of an old building."

Melati very subtly sucks her teeth and orders the staff down on the floor to inspect under the four-poster bed, the velvet-upholstered chairs. Someone procures a hand duster from somewhere, running it carefully over each surface.

"This is the thing," Germaine says aloud, to no one in particular. "It can't just look good on Instagram. It has to *be* good—perfect, in fact—in real life."

Social media has turned into quite the customer-feedback machine. While Germaine's family hasn't experienced much more than the standard slate of positive and negative reviews, some of their competitors have seen serious PR damage from patrons slamming them via the "expectations vs. reality" trend. One hotel was brought particularly low when the gorgeous "aquarium" they publicized so widely was little more than a fish tank in person.

Germaine will make sure that doesn't happen to her family's empire. It is her job to guarantee that everything is flawless and exactly as advertised—or better. Under her purview, not a single customer will moan on social media. Particularly not this new boutique spot in Bali.

She has carved out this niche for herself in the family business for three main reasons: one, she's good at it, having been trained her entire life to be a picky, bossy princess who knows what she wants. Two, it gets her away from her parents and brothers while keeping onside with them. Family dinner at the penthouse? Sorry, she has to be in Venice to inspect the new hotel. An afternoon charity tea with Céline? Nope. Germaine is meeting with the design team for the renovation in London. She can completely avoid them while demonstrating how hard she's working for their benefit—it's perfect. And the funding for her lifestyle continues to flow.

And three, it's stopped them from trying to marry her off to some hotel heir in Taiwan, or has at least put that master plan on hold for now. Both Giles and Gregoire are married and have babies, the ultimate heirs to the empire. When they're together, Germaine feigns interest in her little nephews. They're cute, sure. In a sticky, loud kind of way. But their main function, in Germaine's eyes, is that the grandchildren distract Terence and Céline and make them forget to nag and criticize their only daughter. Their *unmarried* daughter.

Germaine still does not want to get married. Maintaining her status as her own single woman is fulfillment enough. When Germaine was young, she thought that success meant being an entertainer, appearing on TV, getting the paparazzi to follow her around and the magazines to write features on everything she wore, bought, ate, and drank.

But when her parents yanked her back to New York a short three years after her Blast Off! contract and offers for any work outside the family business dried up, Germaine was just back to her old life: poor little rich girl.

She catches a glimpse of her reflection in one of the wall-length gilded mirrors in the hall. She's in her thirties now, still looking great, of course. Unlike Miranda, whose life is one long spring break where she keeps baking herself to a crisp in the sun, Germaine takes care of her skin. She exercises and drinks green tea, gets red-light therapy and gua sha treatments and acupuncture. The 3AM Girls feel like another lifetime now. Germaine is a moderate drinker these days and is the first to leave a party instead of being the last to arrive.

And she is focused on this job that has given her much of the independence and purpose she wants—not all of it, but close enough. As a bonus, it distracted her from Sicily's spiraling life, which was Germaine's fault. Completely. Germaine even had some of her hair fall out when she heard about Sicily's institutionalization. She wanted to run to her, admit that she'd started Hugo on this terrible trajectory, but what would that have solved?

So she kept her head down and her mouth shut and contemplated fabric swatches in Milan while her friend suffered, like the garbage person she was.

This hotel was supposed to open in April, at the start of the dry season, but there was a red-tape issue with permits, and everything got delayed. This opening has been long anticipated and very widely marketed, and Germaine wants to make sure that the guests are stunned.

Especially two guests in particular: her parents.

They are set to arrive the next day, after Germaine has done one more painstaking loop with Melati, fixed what can be fixed on this timeline, and resigned herself to the rest. Everything must be as perfect as physically possible.

Germaine's breakfast is rushed. She picks at her red rice porridge while running through to-do lists in her head. Returning to her suite, she changes into a fresh blouse, something cream and drapey and cowl necked, paired with tailored soft-brushed tweed pants. She accessorizes with pearls, small ones, not overly stated. Suede kitten heels. She wants to be elegant but pared back, professional. The blowout she got the day before is at its perfect, effortless peak, and her nails are remanicured, unbitten.

Germaine tries to adjust her face so that it displays an expression of unbothered, reserved confidence as she watches the cars pull up, although her heart is thrashing in her chest. She's nervous about this property but very proud of the work she's done on it, and hopes that—for once—Terence and Céline might give her some praise. However grudging.

But as she watches them alight from the first chauffeur-driven car, she looks behind them and sees that they've brought a surprise in the next car. And the next car after that.

Germaine walks down the grand staircase and puts on her best PR-appearance smile, since it works better for hiding her irritation.

"There she is!" Terence smiles, putting on a good show for a couple of nearby journalists, who have arrived early for the opening.

"Darling." Céline nods.

"So glad you made it safely!" Germaine greets her parents, along with their snooty daughters-in-law, two noisy grandchildren, and a total of four bossy nannies that have come with no warning whatsoever.

"And what a lovely surprise," Germaine exclaims, kissing her mother on both cheeks. "Elizabeth, Aalia, hello!"

"I knew you wouldn't mind," Céline says. "New York has just been so dreary and cold, they had to get away."

"Absolutely. I'm very excited for you all to see the place." Germaine beams and ushers them all inside; bellhops are already transporting their many, many pieces of luggage from the cars.

"The grand lobby," Germaine notes, gesturing at the opulent room filled with topiary, secluded sitting nooks, and an adjacent coffee bar. The smell of espresso blends with spiced sandalwood, and the gamelan, though still a touch too loud in Germaine's opinion, melds pleasantly with the bubbling of the fountain.

"Cozy," Terence says. Céline says nothing.

As the family heads to see the pool, Germaine signals to Melati.

"Make up my suite for Elizabeth," she hisses to the manager. "As fast as you can."

"But, miss, where should I put your things?"

"It doesn't matter—pack them into my office. Put a cot in there. We won't have enough suites otherwise; the rest are booked."

"Right away." Melati does a little nod of her head and gives Germaine a look that might be sympathy, but she isn't sure before the woman runs off.

Germaine hurries to rejoin the party. Her mother is inspecting one of the cabana curtains, feeling it between her fingers, just like Germaine knew she would.

"Belgian flax?" she asks when Germaine approaches.

"French," Germaine says, nodding.

Céline raises her eyebrows just slightly, but not in a bad way. Even this very minimal reaction sends warmth through Germaine's body.

"Well," Terence says, signaling he's seen all he needs to. Aalia has her arms crossed, unimpressed; Elizabeth is rebuttoning her son's polo that he keeps unbuttoning.

"Oh!" Céline says, like she just remembered something, and the sly look on her face is unsettling. "We do have one more surprise guest."

"Oh?" Germaine laughs. "They never cease, do they?"

"He's just a ways behind us because he had to stop downtown on some business. But we convinced Eddie Chou to join us—you remember Eddie, I'm sure."

Germaine feels the warmth dissipate into a chill. It seems to her that the whole courtyard has been paused, creating a vacuum void of sound.

"Eddie?" she says when she finds her voice. It sounds to her a long way off. "He's—he's here?"

"He will be," Terence says. No one seems to notice the change in her demeanor. "We told him about all the work you were doing, and he was interested in seeing a new property. We were glad he accepted the invitation."

Germaine nods and makes a vague gesture, trying to get them upstairs, up to the rooms. She does remember Eddie, the boy wonder of real estate who's made a killing in Dubai, Macau, and Los Angeles.

Their families had always been friendly with each other, but it wasn't until Germaine was home for the holidays in the three years between the end of *Kidz Klub* and the beginning of her permanent New York stay that she and Eddie finally struck up a conversation.

Germaine had some flings out in LA, just harmless rebellion, but she had been surprised to find herself completely besotted with Eddie. He felt just as hedonic and dangerous as the West Coast guys, but he understood her. Germaine and Eddie? They were cut from the same cloth, born of wealth and high society—and equally high expectations.

For this reason, they kept everything a sworn secret from their parents.

Slipping away from the New Year's party at different times, so as not to be noticed; using the phones of their house staffs to communicate; even planning a secret Valentine's trip to Houston. They kept their long-distance relationship on the down-low when Germaine returned to LA. Miranda and Sicily got only hints—it was that high of a clearance level. Germaine and Eddie didn't want to take any chances.

Eddie's not a boy anymore and not quite a mogul, though he has the arrogance of one. Germaine does not find it hard to guess her parents' ulterior motives for bringing him here.

"I'm going to check on dinner while you get settled, all right?" Germaine calls brightly after them. "Take your time!"

Germaine can't see him. She doesn't want to. She breaks away from the group and hurries back through the lobby, going for a side staircase that leads to her office. Maybe she can invent some emergency at one of the other properties or fake food poisoning. Maybe—

Too late.

"St. Germaine-Chang!" His voice booms across the lobby.

She turns. PR smile.

What she remembers most about Eddie is their final weekend together, stolen in Aspen while Miranda was on the audition circuit and Sicily was busy with family. It was the weekend she realized that he filmed them in bed—and not for the first time.

"What is that?" she'd said, startling him when she came out of the bathroom, finding him fiddling with something.

"Nothing. Pager," he said. But she'd already seen it. A camcorder, small as a handheld radio—placed in the pocket of his bag on the hotel chair, by the looks of it.

"Were you—were—?" She couldn't get her mouth to form the question.

He looked sheepish for just a moment, and then recovered. "Oh, come on. Everyone does it. You should take it as a compliment, you know."

The guys in LA would have said the same thing. Germaine had hesitated, unsure. "What do you do with it?"

He smirked. "Watch it. Reminisce."

"Sorry, Eddie, I just—I don't think I want to be filmed."

Her infatuation with him had made her soft. She would have socked a different man in the face. But they had been vulnerable together; they'd talked late into the night, complained about their parents, shared stories about their grandmothers and their culture. She thought it was different.

She was wrong.

"Okay, it's okay, baby." He approached her, embraced her. "You'll get used to it. All the guys say I'm the luckiest—"

That, at least, was when she stiffened and pushed him away. "The guys? You—Eddie. You've never shown these to anyone, right?"

Instead of sheepish, he looked annoyed. "Don't get huffy with me. It's just what guys do."

"Oh, no. No. Eddie, please, *tell* me you didn't—that you'll never again—"

He dropped his arms and all pretense of trying to placate her. "Calm down. Jesus. It's not like I distributed the tapes beyond my inner circle."

His fucking inner circle. Him and all his idiot finance friends who acted like they were forming the New World Order. Germaine had indulged all his talk, his obsessive excitement about real estate and investing—she'd even thought it was endearing. Until that moment, when she knew that all those creeps had seen her naked.

The love went out of her like a switch was flipped. She sat down on the bed.

"You'll regret it," she said, her voice low and cracked. "I'll make you regret it."

He raised his eyebrows. "Um, okay. And I'll make you regret *that*. If you ever bad-mouth me, or say *anything* to my family. Because, you know. I think I have the upper hand here."

And he left her there in the hotel.

"Eddie!" Germaine forces her feet forward across the lobby, one after another, to meet him at the door. He's got his hair slicked back and a suit that doesn't fit him quite as well as it's supposed to; he's still figuring out new money. She can smell his cologne from across the room.

"How are you doing, sweetheart?" he says, going in for a hug that she tries and fails to turn into a handshake.

Maybe he's changed. Teenage years were ancient history; maybe he's grown and forgotten the finer details of their relationship.

"Fine, Eddie," Germaine says, stepping back as briskly as she can. "Just fine."

"You know," he says in a low voice, leaning in with a wink. "I still have our home video, if you're ever interested in making the sequel."

Germaine feels the world crumble around her.

THIRTEEN

SICILY

2018

The doorbell rings once, twice.

"Emmylou?" Sicily yells, staying as still as she can while her cousin's makeup assistants dust her with powder and apply heat to her hair. Sicily feels a kick in her belly and places her hands there as if trying to reassure both herself and the child inside that everything will go smoothly today. She's going to be an early-thirties mama—she's still young. She can muster up all the energy she needs.

Probably.

The doorbell sounds again and Emmylou hollers that she's coming. Sicily isn't sure why anyone is ringing it—there have been crews coming in and out of her house all day for the magazine shoot covering Sicily's lavish baby shower. Emmylou is the official host, coordinating media and family and gifts. She would have provided the venue if Sicily had let her, but although Emmylou and her music producer husband's house may be the size of the Grand Ole Opry, it's decorated like she still lives in a double-wide trailer.

Emmylou is . . . okay at coordinating things. Sure, she had a typo on the invitations, and she waited too long to book Sicily's first catering choice. But her heart is in it. And Sicily is grateful for her help now that she's not speaking to Kendra, whose number has been blocked for a good three years.

She found a chink in Sicily's armor when the pregnancy was officially announced—DM-ed Hey. Congrats on Sicily's Twitter—but Sicily didn't respond. It still hurts too much.

Downstairs, Emmylou has turned up the music a notch too loud for a baby shower. Sicily has held raging parties in this house for album wraps, New Year's Eve, the Fourth of July, and just for fun, but this feels more stressful and crowded than all of those combined. Carole is somewhere nearby, fretting over everything; there are plenty of Bell cousins as well as Squeak's mother and sisters, with everyone dressed in faux furs and cashmeres for the Winter Wonderland theme.

There's clearly some unspoken competition going on.

"Look how *cute* you are!" Carole had exclaimed to Squeak's younger sister, Jessie, when they arrived. By the look on Jessie's face, Sicily immediately knew it had rubbed her the wrong way. Jessie was nineteen and probably going for hot, not cute.

But Squeak's mother, Eileen, had breezed past it. "And you look so *elegant!*" she exclaimed to Carole. "This dress—is it a Jessica Howard?"

"Jessica Howard!" Carole laughed aloud, her smile getting tighter. "Oh, you're a riot. No, dear, this is Alexander Wang."

"Absolutely gorgeous." Eileen waved her hand. "I tried on a few Alexander Wang, actually, but in the end I went with Carolina Herrera. Felt a little more sophisticated to me."

"Well, nothing's too good for our Sicily. My goodness, Squeak must really bring home the bacon, hmm?" Carole quipped. "I didn't realize the backup dancers made enough for a Carolina Herrera . . ."

And so it went on. There were similar tussles at the gift table, with Squeak's older sister Raquel clearing space for her enormous box, and Sicily's cousin Stephany making a show of placing an even larger gift bag next to it. Everyone stepped in front of each other to display their best sides to the cameras, obviously posing but trying to make it look as casual and *oh-I-didn't-see-you-there* as possible.

Sicily wishes she had never agreed to it.

The makeup team finally releases her with one final touch-up, and she heads downstairs, careful not to trip on her long red velvet gown—à la Mariah Carey—that shows off her significant belly bump and is paired with a furry white shawl. She groans inwardly to see that the doorbell ringer was Jaime, Hugo's flawless wife, who's arrived with Noah.

"Hey, bugaboo!" Sicily cries, forgetting her caution and hurrying the rest of the way down the stairs. Noah smiles but looks a little beside himself in the sea of chattering women and magazine staff. He's unbelievably handsome and adorable in a white polo with a smart forest-green suit jacket.

After the horrible smoke of the court case and the institutionalization and conservatorship had cleared, Hugo had called Sicily and invited her over for a long talk.

She'd been stunned by the contact. They hadn't spoken to each other directly since before the court case—first they communicated through lawyers, and then Jaime or Emmylou acted as intermediaries—and it took some gentle prodding on his part to convince her to stay for a cup of coffee one of the weekends she dropped off Noah.

She sat on a barstool in the vast expanse of his kitchen as he bustled around, surprisingly domestic, working a coffeepot and adding sugar, cream, and a touch of almond syrup. He still remembered her order.

It was a strange feeling to be served by the man she'd viewed as her mortal enemy for more than ten years. Sicily felt her adrenaline starting and her muscles tensing as if bracing for a fight.

When he'd poured his own cup, he sat across from her at the long marble island and cleared his throat.

"I want to start by acknowledging how much you love Noah. Probably more than I could ever understand."

She gave a short nod. With that, at least, she could agree.

"This one is going to be harder to believe." He wore a small, wry smile. "But I also love Noah. From the very first moment I held him, I knew I was a goner."

Sicily had once hoped it would be true—and, of course, she wanted to believe that she was sending Noah to a loving home whenever her time was up—but it was somehow hard to hear from Hugo.

"Covet has seemed like a more appropriate word in the last few years," she said quietly. "Covet, not love."

Hugo sighed. "That's fair. How could you not feel that way? I—took him from you, I suppose. By force, it must feel."

Sicily had nodded.

"I didn't want that." Hugo started speaking more quickly. "This is what I want to make clear: I wanted both of us to be in his life, and if I wanted to *take* him from anybody, it was your family—not you. You're his mother." He paused, looked at her earnestly. "And over the years, I've realized how disgracefully I've treated the mother of my child. The most important person in Noah's life."

Sicily said nothing, but took a sip from her mug.

"I've made mistakes, I dragged your name through the mud, I hurt you. And Noah, for putting him through all that," he went on. "I did it for Noah, to get him out of that toxic environment your dad and uncle had built. I think you see it now for what it is."

Sicily stared into her coffee for a long moment. Then she said, "I do. And if nothing else, I'm glad you got Noah out of there."

Hugo pressed his lips into a line. "I'm glad you both got out. I wish I'd handled it better. It didn't have to come to all that."

"It was always going to be ugly. It was so ugly."

"It was." Hugo sipped his coffee and was quiet, as if remembering. "But I want us to be together on this. I want to make things right."

Sicily didn't make any promises to him after that conversation. And it took a long time for her to trust his words—years. But gradually, she realized how happy Noah was with Hugo. He looked up to his dad.

Hugo wasn't the absent parent Sicily was sure he'd be, but an actual father who knew how to parent with discipline and love.

So they'd found a new path forward.

"Hey, Mom," Noah says, accepting her hug stiffly. The teenager is coming—she can hear it in his voice.

"Sicily!" Jaime trills, going in for a hug when Noah is released. "You are positively *glowing*."

"Thanks for coming, Jaime." Sicily smiles.

Jaime tosses her blown-out hair over her perfectly bronzed shoulder, exposed by the off-the-shoulder skintight dress that displays her slim and toned figure. "Oh, I wouldn't miss it. I am just so thrilled for you. And I'm going to try to keep it together, because you're just—so beautiful—"

She places both hands on Sicily's belly, gazing at it tenderly, and Sicily resists the urge to either roll her eyes or step back.

"And it really is a miracle, you know? Every woman should be able to experience the miracle of birth, if they want it. You and Squeak, you are blessed, you know."

Sicily wills Jaime not to bring it up. She is not about to bring this up right here, right now, at a baby shower, right?

Wrong. "I wish Hugo and I could be so lucky. It is hard on us," Jaime goes on.

"You're struggling to conceive?" Raquel has drifted into the conversation. "Oh god, I'm so sorry to hear that."

"Yes. But—" Jaime puts up both her hands. "This is Sicily's day. We don't have to get into that."

Sicily nods her head graciously. "The open bar is over there, and you can put gifts on the table—"

"That's so tough, though." Raquel is holding a glass of wine and doesn't seem to have heard Jaime or Sicily. "I can't tell you how many times my husband and I tried before our first kid."

"I wish it was a matter of time or effort." Jaime shakes her head. "But the doctors say it's just not in the cards for me."

"You've tried IVF?" One of Sicily's cousins has sidled up to the conversation.

Jaime gives a deep, full-body sigh. "IVF, IUI, you name it—we've tried everything. I've been poked and prodded until I've felt like a pincushion. I just—"

She touches her fingers elegantly to the bridge of her nose, and Sicily, again, wills what's about to happen next not to happen.

But Jaime begins to cry. "It's just really hard—and to see all the baby stuff—and all your friends having babies—"

Someone's aunt is there at Jaime's shoulder, comforting her.

"What's meant to happen will happen. It's going to be okay, sweetheart."

The other women murmur noises of sympathy. Sicily purses her lips and beckons to Noah. "Does Jaime have a gift, hun? You want to put it over on the table? Come on, I'll show you where it is."

The doorbell rings again, and Sicily turns toward it, irritated. But then, like something out of a dream, in walks Miranda.

Sicily isn't sure how she makes it so quickly through the crowded room, but suddenly she's at Miranda's side, in her embrace—one real friend in this house of people who are just here for publicity.

"Oh god. I'm so glad you came," Sicily says, squeezing Miranda tight. But when she pulls back, she sees that Miranda looks stricken.

"I am . . . *way* underdressed," Miranda says. "Why didn't you tell me?"

She's wearing jeans and a Christmas sweater with a snowman on it. The invitation did say "Creative Black Tie" in a slightly smaller font than "Winter Wonderland," but Sicily doesn't want to make her feel bad.

"No, you're fine!" Sicily says. "You're totally fine. No one's going to notice."

Miranda tucks her hair behind her ears and looks nervously at the photographers roaming the event, one of whom is getting close to where they stand.

"C'mere, come on," Sicily says, taking her hand. "Can you help me with the food in the kitchen?"

There are no photographers there; very few people at all, actually, since the catering staff is out serving food. Miranda seems to relax instantly.

"I feel so stupid," she says, running her hands through her hair. "I mean, you're pop royalty. Of course it would be a huge event."

Sicily smiles wryly, getting a glass of water from the fridge. "*Was* pop royalty."

Miranda shakes her head. "Still are. I'm sure you only pay attention to the bad press, because that's all we ever focus on, right? But I see the headlines, the social buzz. People were *really* excited about the Second Chances tour. All your fans from the old days, grown up with you. It was sweet."

Sicily smiles. "The tour did its job, I guess. Then I sort of nose-dived again." She pats her belly.

"But you'll get back up there."

Sicily glances at her and nods. Miranda has a serious, almost challenging expression on her face. Sicily wants to say *And so will you*— the phrase is hanging in the air between them, practically audible. But that would mean acknowledging that Miranda is *not* currently "up there." And Sicily knows that Miranda will retort immediately, saying what they're both thinking—that maybe she won't. Not everyone gets second chances.

Sicily is already worried about Miranda. She was surprised to feel how much weight she'd lost when they hugged, her frame now more angular and wiry, her bone structure more prominent, changing the apple-cheeked face that Sicily knew and loved. Miranda has been lying low for the past few months, refusing to go out or see anyone. Sicily knows she had to give up the Malibu house. From what little Miranda has told her and Germaine, Sicily gathers that she's living in a rental in Tarzana now. She has not spoken Bobbie's name in months.

So instead, Sicily says, "Can I get you something to drink? We literally have everything—rosé, stout, milk, kombucha, apple juice . . ."

Miranda finally cracks a smile. "You know, apple juice actually sounds super good right now."

Sicily opens the large stainless-steel fridge and displays the shelves like she's on *Wheel of Fortune*. "If you would believe it, we even have the super-cute little Martinelli's jars."

"I would expect nothing less from the rising queen of pop royalty."

Sicily smiles indulgently and hands her the bottle, but she wishes Miranda would stop saying that. "Anything to eat? Please, I'm going to be drowning in leftovers."

Miranda shakes her head as she pops open the cap. But she says, "I do actually have some news."

"Yeah?"

She nods. "My agent talked me into doing a reality show."

Sicily raises her eyebrows. "That sounds . . . interesting. What's it called?"

"*Crashed and Burned*. They put a bunch of former child stars together in this fancy house and see what kind of drama comes out of it. It's brand new. Should be fun." Miranda takes a swig of juice and laughs.

"Yeah, wow," Sicily says, laughing along with her. "I've always wanted to know what reality TV is really like behind the cameras, seriously. Maybe it'll actually be very chill?"

"I think so. Have some catfights, make up some fake gossip . . . Should be easy money."

"Totally." Sicily nods, hesitates. She has to ask. She would be a bad friend if she didn't. "Were you . . . Are you still doing the sessions with that therapist?"

Miranda shrugs. "Yeah, but I don't know. I'm not really into it. Makes me feel like—somebody's neurotic mother."

Sicily knows she was going to say Bobbie. "Yeah, but it's good, right? To have someone to talk things through with? I mean, you can always talk to me and G," she says. "But I'm about as qualified to give life advice as you are to be a godmother."

She winks at the last part, and Miranda snorts. "Yeah, I know. I know."

"I was just wondering if you'd be able to continue those sessions while you're shooting the show, I guess."

Miranda takes another drink and re-caps the juice. "Nah, probably not. She thinks it's bad for me to pick up new projects, and it's like— okay? So what am I supposed to do? If I'm going to have a therapist, it needs to be someone supportive."

Sicily nods. She's not surprised that Miranda's therapist thinks it's unhealthy for her to stay in show business—it probably is. But where is Miranda's safety net if she drops out of the industry? What kind of skill set could she apply to a regular job? This is the only life she knows, and that goes for Sicily, too. Maybe Germaine.

Sicily would give her a job, any job, if she knew Miranda wouldn't be too proud to take it. Germaine would do the same. Doesn't Miranda know that? Doesn't she remember the promises they made to each other?

She glances at Miranda's fingernails, plain and short. Sicily's are covered in bright-red acrylics; it's been a long time since she's done them herself. But they used to have a ritual, the three of them, at the end of every *Kidz Klub* season: when filming wrapped, they all gathered in the wood-paneled basement of the house Bobbie rented in Burbank, as close to the studio as she could afford, and paint their nails. The producers of the show forbade nail paint of any kind—all the kids were supposed to look as clean and uniform as possible.

So the very same night they had their last studio audience, Sicily, Germaine, and Miranda would pull out the bins and bins of the Sally Hansen bottles they'd bought with their show money and paint every nail a different color. Their hands flashed the rainbow until August. Plus, it helped Germaine to stop chewing on hers.

It's the summer before the final season that Sicily is thinking of now, when they'd all learned that the show would be wrapping.

It was a weird time for Sicily. At fifteen years old, she knew it was time to grow up, but she wasn't sure how. *Kidz Klub* was for—well, kids—and she was still mostly treated as one in her pigtails and Blast Off! Network T-shirt, even though her chest was filling out quicker than everyone else's. And people had noticed.

But she didn't want to grow up. She'd sort of convinced herself that the show would just turn into her career; she didn't know what she was supposed to do when it ended. And she was afraid of losing touch with Miranda and Germaine, whom she really looked up to—even though Miranda was younger. They seemed so wise. They knew so much about the world, and perhaps more importantly, about sex, of which Sicily had had only one very troubling experience. Another mistake on her part—hadn't her parents warned her to be chaste before marriage? But there had been a boy, and Sicily was infatuated, and she ruined it. Ruined everything.

She wasn't ready to talk about that. It made her want to hide her chest even more.

But she could paint her nails. That still made her feel good.

"What are we going to *do*?" Sicily had said, for the hundredth time, as she struggled to operate the little nailbrush with her left hand.

"Something better than this song-and-dance crap," Miranda said, painting her thumb lime green. "My mom has connections. She said she's going to get me an agent."

"I told you, Sis, you'll be drowning in offers." Germaine swiped a coat of turquoise confidently along the nail of her index finger. "I've already had a talent scout reach out from Unlimited."

"Unlimited? Are you serious?" Sicily's jaw dropped. It was the most exclusive dance studio in town. Dancers from that studio traveled all over the world with the hottest artists. "Will your parents let you?"

G snorted, switching to magenta. "Who cares what they think? I'm a working woman now. They'll have to drag me back to New York. Oh shit," she said, as the nail polish tipped onto the old shag rug.

"It's fine," Miranda said, brushing the thick carpet fibers this way and that to hide the stain. "My mom won't care."

Miranda's mom was cool—she didn't care about anything. In fact, Sicily wasn't even sure where she was that afternoon, or whether they were in the house alone. Bobbie had left them a pile of chips and Go-Gurts and Fruit by the Foot and Dr Pepper on the kitchen table with a note that said CONGRATULATIONS!! with hearts under the exclamation points, but they hadn't seen evidence of her beyond that. Miranda said she was out for drinks, maybe with the very agent she'd been talking about.

At least it sounded like Germaine's and Miranda's home bases would still be in LA. But Sicily didn't know what the end of the show meant for her; her mom and dad had been deep in discussion about the announcement the night before. She'd heard her father make a call to Uncle Henry, asking his advice.

"I hope I get to stay here, too," Sicily murmured. She was never able to get the polish on straight; even as she spoke, her left hand trembled and veered across her cuticles. She couldn't do it as well as G and Miranda.

"Come here," Miranda had said, taking hold of Sicily's right hand and adding a careful coat of sunflower yellow to her ring finger. "You're going to make it bigger than all of us, obviously. Have you heard yourself sing?"

"You won't be here, because you'll be all over the world giving concerts every night, you beautiful idiot," Germaine added, taking her other hand. "Stop worrying!"

"And even if for some bizarro reason you don't get hired—" Miranda continued.

"Not possible!" G cut in.

"I'll get you a job on all my movies."

"And I'll make you head of operations at my dance studio," Germaine said.

Sicily laughed. The nails they painted are perfect: shiny and smooth.

"Okay, deal," she said. "And I'll do the same for you."

Now Sicily wishes she could. She wants to take Miranda's hand and squeeze it, ask if she wants Sicily to paint her nails for her, returning the favor eighteen years later. The party outside doesn't matter. She needs to know Miranda's okay.

But Miranda shoves her hands in the pockets of her jeans.

"It'll be good, though," she goes on. "They actually have counselors and stuff on the show; we're supposed to work through our 'past' with them, or whatever. Those people will understand the industry better than some lady in an Encino office park."

"Nice. That sounds like an amazing opportunity, Miranda." Sicily comes over and gives her a hug. "You're going to have to tell me all about it. I bet they take your phone away during filming, you think? But afterward—even if you've signed an NDA."

"A piece of paper won't stop me." Miranda smiles.

"When do you start?"

Miranda talks about the production timeline, what she's allowed to bring, the other stars they've gotten so far, and Sicily nods along supportively. But it all sounds awful. *Crashed and Burned*? If the name itself is any indicator of how the producers will treat their cast, it's going to be downright exploitative.

But Miranda needs the money and the work, and Sicily understands—that's the reason there's a stupid photo shoot at this baby shower. Without the financial stability of the Vegas residency, Sicily needs money, too.

"They got Dora Sanchez?" Sicily exclaims as Miranda recaps the rumors she's heard about the cast. "I *totally* forgot about her. I thought she was—"

Suddenly Sicily notices that the sounds of the party outside the kitchen door have gone eerily quiet. Above the much more muted chatter rises an exchange of loud voices.

"What's going on out there?" Miranda says.

Sicily hurries back out into the living room just in time to hear her mother say in a sarcastic voice, "Oh, Squeak would just *love* that, wouldn't he?"

Eileen is opposite her, shoulders squared and face angry. "Just what are you implying?"

"Mom." Sicily hurries her way over; most of the guests have turned to watch this confrontation. "What is going on?"

Carole folds her arms. "All I said was that I don't understand why Squeak's family seem to want the two of you to rush into marriage."

"It's the right thing to do." Eileen's nostrils flare. "It's what's right for the baby. The child should have some security in life, two parents who love each other and who make a public commitment to each other."

"Eileen, I can assure you that Squeak and I are very much in love," Sicily says, holding up her hands.

"Marriage is all well and good," Carole says. "Especially for wallets, when Squeak is elevated from the minor role of backup dancer–baby daddy to the husband of an international pop star!"

Angry exclamations burst out from Squeak's family. Eileen gasps and clutches her chest.

"Mom, *stop it*," Sicily hisses. "Apologize."

But Eileen has a few words of her own. "How *dare* you. When I'm the one who has so many reservations about my son's involvement with your daughter and your batshit family. Tacky court battles, your public fighting—not to mention her"—she glares at Sicily, saying the next phrase almost under her breath like they're dirty words—"mental health problems. How am I going to get through each day knowing that I could get a call that she's absconded into the desert with my grandchild?"

"You watch your mouth!" Carole cries, but there are murmurs of assent. Next to Eileen, Jaime crosses her arms and nods slightly, looking concerned.

Emmylou jumps into the fray. "You're just jealous because you want everything she has!"

"Oh? And what's that?" Raquel snaps. "A dying career and a desperation to stay relevant?"

It is spiraling out of Sicily's control. As she looks helplessly around the room, she sees two people make their exit: Miranda, out the front door, and Noah, into the backyard. The two people she needs here more than anyone.

Sicily ducks down and hurries after Noah as the fight turns into an uproar.

After a moment of hunting, she spots him sitting in the mouth of the tube slide on the enormous swing set she bought just for him. This has been his spot at her house to sit whenever he's upset, which is . . . a lot, unfortunately. His knees are tucked up, arms around them, legs getting too long to fit comfortably in the slide anymore. Sicily hitches up her dress and squats down next to him. He doesn't look at her.

"Hey," she says. "I'm sorry you had to hear those mean things. Your grandmas are just . . . dealing with some big emotions."

"Squeak's mom isn't my grandma," he says flatly.

"Well, that's true. But Squeak is going to be part of the family, and I hope—"

Noah turns and glares at her. "Didn't you have enough family? Wasn't Dad enough?"

Sicily feels the familiar pit open up in her stomach; it grows every time she knows Noah is mad at her. The whole world could hate Sicily and she wouldn't give a damn as long as she and Noah were okay. But knowing he's unhappy—because of her—is the feeling she hates most.

"Your dad and I have a lot of love for each other," she tries. "But he's *in* love with Jaime, who also loves you very much. And I'm in love with Squeak—I need someone, too, you know."

"Is that why you sleep with a ton of guys and get pregnant all the time?"

Sicily feels like he's punched her in the chest. "*Noah!* I do not do that. Where is this coming from?"

"It's embarrassing, Mom!" he says, fully angry now. "It's all anyone ever says about you!"

"That's so—I don't even—" She shakes her head and rubs her hands over her eyes, surely smudging any professionally applied makeup there. Noah turns away from her, leaning against the wall of the slide. "I don't want to talk about it."

"Please, Noah. It's not like that. This is only the second baby I've had, and I'll love you both equally—no one could ever replace—"

"I said I *don't* want to *talk* about it!" Noah yells, his voice reverberating off the slide.

Sicily's heart sinks to her toes.

"Okay," she says. "I'd . . . better go check on things inside anyway." She stalks numbly back across the yard, unsuccessfully fighting away tears.

Nothing has improved inside. Sicily hunts down the magazine editor, disliking the way she's talking intently to the photographer and pointing out people around the room—primarily, those who are most embroiled in the fight.

"Hey," Sicily says to her. "I think the party's over. Can your people wrap up here and head out?"

"For sure, in a few minutes," the editor says cagily. "We're just getting some final shots."

She side-eyes Sicily, steps away, and starts texting furiously on her phone. Sicily rubs her temples, knowing that this whole debacle will be up on TMZ before the cupcakes are even eaten. She's making her way back up the stairs to try to appeal to the stylist to gather the team and leave when the door opens again and a late guest enters the party.

"What the hell is going on here?" Sicily's father shouts over the din.

Sicily freezes; the angry party guests fall quiet. Carole, relaxing the finger she was jabbing at Squeak's aunt, looks from Sicily to Day to Sicily.

"Surprise!" Carole says, voice faltering.

"Mom," Sicily says, the word sounding unnaturally loud. She hasn't spoken to her father in almost six years. "What is this?"

"Sicily, honey—I wanted—I just wanted you to have a chance to reconcile with your daddy," Carole stammers. "I thought he could come and see you on your big day."

Scrambling for context, Day glances from his wife to his daughter and folds his hands penitently in front of him. He looks very pitiful.

"It's good to see you, sweetheart," he says quietly.

It's too much—Sicily can't deal with this. All eyes are on her, including the photographers' and the editors'. They're eating it up. But she doesn't want to see her father. She just wants this baby shower from hell to be over.

So Sicily lets her eyes go wide, and she clutches her stomach. "Oh—oh god—"

She grasps the stair rail and sinks to her knees. The crowd murmurs in concern.

"Sicily!" Carole cries. "Honey, what is it? It's not your water, is it?"

"I don't know—it's terrible cramping. All this stress—" She begins to cry, looking around wildly. "Can someone help me? My baby—"

"Call 911!" Eileen shouts to no one in particular.

~

When the ambulance doors close and Carole is distracted with interrogating the EMT, Sicily allows herself a long exhale and a very small smile.

Her great talent may be singing, but she can still act when she wants to.

FOURTEEN

MIRANDA

2018

Miranda adjusts her dress, a lilac-colored Lycra number with ruching on the sides. She can still taste the teeth-whitening strips she popped in before everyone came down to the fireplace room to shoot the first few moments of *Crashed and Burned*. Miranda looks around the room, staying as positive as she can, but it's clear the producers haven't put a lot of thought into set design. Miranda, the other cast members, and much of the crew are essentially quarantined together in a mansion in Topanga that was once used for filming *The Bachelor*, before *The Bachelor* moved on to bigger and better locations. It looks like the decor hasn't been touched since before Miranda was running around as one of the 3AM Girls.

But she's smiling sweetly at the cameras, and she's going to make the most of it.

The cast is making their on-screen entrance one by one, and Miranda is fourth out of ten. The others who have already lined up in front of the fireplace include two women with whom Miranda will be sharing a room, all bunked together like the sisters in *The Brady Bunch*—if Marcia, Jan, and Cindy had been addicts who went to jail together instead of junior high. Dora Sanchez, a fortysomething whose career transitioned from bubble-pop girl group to cage fighting, leans against the mantel in black leather and a jacket with tassels on the arms as she eyes the others through darkly lined lashes. She's a chain-smoker—Miranda can smell the cigarettes from her spot by an ostentatious potted plant, and she's sure she'll smell it on herself soon enough.

There's also three-times-divorced Lucy La, once famous for being typecast as wiseass daughter with glasses on various hit rom-coms, but who's now better known for getting married on a beach in Rio wearing nothing but a lei.

Brandon, a man with very tall, glossy hair and teeth far whiter than Miranda's strips could hope to achieve, is their host. He wears a tan suit and an impermeable smile as he introduces each of the former child stars.

"Let's hear it for Miranda Montana, lovely as ever," he exclaims to an otherwise silent room. "And give it up for yet another Blast Off! channel alum—Tyler X!"

Miranda's heart sinks as she sees Tyler walk into the room, hollow eyed and slightly potbellied since she last saw him. He raises his eyebrows at her in mutual surprise, but otherwise gives her no acknowledgment as he lines up next to her spot. Miranda knew about her roommate assignments ahead of time and had heard rumors about a few of the other cast members, but the production has been largely secret so that stars' reactions to each other can be captured in real time. Miranda stares straight ahead, unwilling to give the producers any insight into her former relationship with Tyler.

But she watches him out of the corner of her eye as the others file in. He looks just as worse for wear as the rest of them, his star power having taken a nosedive after one too many roid-rage incidents on set and the subsequent bad press.

"Welcome, everyone, to *Crashed and Burned!*" Brandon says once everyone has arrived. He looks each of them in the eye, seemingly very sincere. "Now, you're all here for a reason. Each and every one of you came into the public eye thanks to your extraordinary talent, your drive, your charisma. But for one reason or another"—he puts his hand to his chest, sympathetic—"you crashed and burned. I'm here to tell you: it's *okay*. Because we at *Crashed and Burned* believe in second chances. We know you still have that fire in you, that spark. And we're going to put it to the test!"

Once filming has wrapped and all the editing is complete, this episode will play on TVs across the country with heartfelt music and poignant close-ups of the contestants. But right now, without any of that magic, it just feels like standing in a room of has-beens listening to a man who's definitely younger than everyone acknowledge how much you suck now. Miranda can practically feel the disdain wafting off Tyler.

"During your time here, you'll get the chance to prove yourselves through exciting team challenges, peer bonding, and personal growth," Brandon continues. "You'll also be asked to participate in group sessions and confessionals to reflect on the career paths of your fellow contestants, and similar challenges you might have faced along the way. We have trained therapists, right here on set—just for you. And they're here to *help*. So honesty, authenticity, and sincerity will be rewarded. But that won't be the only reward."

Brandon pauses for effect; one of the camera operators adjusts a lens.

"Because the contestant who sticks it out the longest will win one *million* dollars!"

Everyone cheers at the top of their lungs; they don't need to be cued up. But while Miranda knows that a million (after taxes) probably won't make or break anyone here, the publicity and chance at a renewed public image makes it an even shinier prize. Plus, it's not like any of them have something better to do.

"So rest up, rock stars!" Brandon says, pointing both fingers at the group. "Because you have a big day ahead of you tomorrow." He swivels on his heel to face a different camera and reads from a cue card:

"Think you know who has what it takes not to crash and burn? Follow along each week and vote for the contestant *you* think can rise to the challenge. Get it right, and you might just win a chance to meet your favorite celeb in person during our season finale."

He holds the pose for a moment, displaying a winning, infectious smile.

"Clear," calls the floor director.

Brandon's smile drops from his face immediately, and he wipes his nose on the sleeve of his suit. He takes his phone out of his pocket and walks briskly out of the room without a second look at anybody.

Miranda crosses her arms and follows the others up the stairs to the bedrooms.

"Thought there'd be better craft services!" Dora mutters to Miranda as she passes. "Dry chicken breast and broccoli for dinner and then it's off to bed? What is this, an orphanage?"

"Breakfast better be good," Miranda agrees.

"Better be sausage, if they want me to be running around like a kook." Dora pats her jacket, undoubtedly looking for cigarettes.

"Hey," Miranda hears someone say behind her as she reaches her door. Tyler is standing a few feet down the hall, a menacing look on his face.

"What?" Miranda says in a low voice, mirroring his expression.

"You tell anyone about us and you're dead."

"Like I would do that," Miranda hisses back. "What is your problem?"

His mouth curls downward. "I don't want anyone to know I sunk that low."

She scoffs. "Yeah, well. Same with you."

Tyler shakes his head and turns for his end of the hall. "Yeah, it doesn't work like that."

"Oh, fuck off."

But as Miranda closes the door tight behind her, she knows it's true—no one would have sympathy for her. They'd only care about Tyler.

~

"Look at all your bright smiling faces!"

Miranda could throttle Brandon. It's eighty-six degrees, and they're all standing in the direct sunlight of the mansion's sprawling backyard, staring down a makeshift obstacle course. Dora has swapped her leather for a black tank top, and Lucy's white sports bra leaves little to the imagination. She leans over to Miranda.

"I'll break your arm if you break mine," she says under her breath. "That'll get us out of this, right?"

"I don't think there was anything in the contract about that," Miranda mutters back.

"This morning you'll be evaluated on team spirit, self-esteem, and winning mentality," Brandon goes on. He's wearing long-sleeve linen and no sunglasses but is somehow not sweating or squinting at all. Brandon is flanked by a team of four therapists, who all wear white coats, and the cast and crew form a semicircle on the grass.

Brandon continues his spiel. "You'll be split into two teams, and you need to complete this obstacle course via relay, getting to the prize—that golden star—at the end of the course. Whichever team—red or blue—reaches it first is the winner. Ready?"

They divide up and don jerseys for their respective colors, and the producers tell them where to line up on the course. To her dismay, Miranda is sandwiched between Tyler and Dora—neither seems too jazzed about it, either. Tyler has to ride a tricycle over to Miranda to hand her the baton; then Miranda has to wade through a kiddie pool of chocolate syrup to Dora, who will climb over a rock wall. The looks on Tyler's and Dora's faces match how Miranda feels.

"Get ready," Brandon calls. "Get set—go!"

Miranda puts one foot in the pool as she watches Tyler furiously pedal toward her, baton in hand. His face is beet red, and he's steering erratically, his legs way too long and his body too big to properly work the bike.

"Come on, come on," Miranda says. Lucy is passing up Tyler in the next lane.

"Shut up!" Tyler shouts. But he puts on speed and swerves into the side of the pool, splashing them both with chocolate.

"*Shit!*" he barks.

"Just give it to me," Miranda says, yanking the baton out of his hand. She slides across the pool, stumbling to her knees once, twice, and then shoving the syrup-covered baton to Dora.

"Here we go," Dora says uncertainly, sticking the baton under her arm. She runs for the wall and finds a foothold, then a handhold. But she's struggling. Desi Jacobs, in the next lane, has already scaled halfway up.

"Here!" Miranda runs over and steadies Dora's legs. "Let's go—put your foot on that one, up to the left!"

But Dora swings her leg out, her heel catching Miranda squarely in the chin. White light flashes in front of Miranda's eyes, and she stumbles backward, biting her tongue in the process.

"Thanks, cariño!" Dora says as she disappears over the wall.

"Ungh," Miranda grunts from the ground, holding her hands over her face and trying to stem the blood.

~

"Miranda," the blond therapist says, her coat enviably free of blood and chocolate stains. They're sitting together for the postgame analysis, in which each contestant is filmed speaking with the therapist and Brandon about how they ranked.

"You helped your teammate Dora and even risked your safety doing so," the therapist continues.

"Which we don't endorse," Brandon adds seriously yet jovially. "But what a hustle!"

"Yes." The therapist nods. "So those are some big points for teamwork and team spirit. But—we couldn't help notice how you hid your face from the cameras after you got hurt."

"Yeah," Miranda says thickly. The split on her chin has stopped bleeding, but her tongue is still swollen. She hopes that nothing will bruise. "I got the crap kicked out of me."

"We really want you to be more open, more willing to receiving help," the therapist says in the gentlest voice possible. "We know it's hard to be filmed with a disfiguring injury when so much value has been placed on your appearance. But hiding your face only enables further low self-esteem."

"Oh." Miranda nods slowly, trying to pick up on the thread the woman is laying before her. "Yeah. You know, you're right. So much of my life has just been my looks, my face." If she thinks hard enough about Dora's foot slamming into her jaw, she can almost will the tears back. "But—but I don't want to hide anymore."

Brandon nods approvingly. "And here on *Crashed and Burned*, you don't have to."

~

"What a load of . . ." Lucy trails off, sitting cross-legged on the floor of their room and french-braiding her hair later that night.

Miranda clears her throat and cocks her head to the corner of the ceiling, where a camera mounted to the wall records their every move. Dora eyes it and stretches her arms, giving an exaggerated yawn.

"God, that obstacle course took me *out*," she says. "You girls mind if I turn in early?"

Miranda shrugs; it's only nine thirty. But Dora winks at her. She grabs a sweatshirt from her bed, turns off the lights, and then hangs the sweatshirt over the camera.

"You think that'll work?" Lucy says doubtfully as the lights go back on.

"It'll get them off our backs for a goddamn second." Dora shrugs and pulls out a Svedka bottle from her suitcase, wrapped in a T-shirt. "Besides, a lady's gotta have a little privacy."

"Oh shit. Give me some of that," Lucy says. "They water down their drinks to hell here. I thought we were supposed to be able to get drunk on camera."

It has turned out, in fact, to be quite the opposite. Apparently the production team doesn't want to be liable for lawsuits or sloppy drunks, and there's a very strict two-drink-per-night maximum to get the cast feeling loose but not out of control. Many aspects of the show feel very much like rehab and hard time to Miranda—and although she cleaned up her act publicly and hasn't used since her breakup with Amir—not more than once or twice, anyway—it isn't as though you can accurately gauge whether your alcohol use is "affecting major obligations or causing problems with physical, social, or work relationships" when your only obligation is to sail around on a yacht with a cheater.

So the vodka is as welcome as ever. Miranda feels instant comfort as she tips back the mouth of the bottle, breathing in the fumes. It has been there for her when nothing else made her feel good.

"I needed that." Dora leans back and sighs, sitting on the floor with the other two. "I'm too old for this shit."

"What would you do with a million dollars?" Lucy asks, taking the bottle again. "If you make it to the end?"

"Probably pay off my credit card debt, then try to invest the rest." Dora purses her lips. "You?"

"Put it in a college fund so my daughter can go somewhere really good someday," Lucy says.

"I didn't know you had a daughter." Miranda takes the bottle from her.

Lucy purses her lips. "We try to keep it quiet. I want her to live as normal a life as possible, and my reputation—" Lucy waves her hand, as if the thought will finish itself. "My reputation doesn't really allow for it. But that was one thing I was dead set on. I told her po po—who's basically raising her, my mom—I said absolutely not. This girl will never, ever set foot on a soundstage. She will not perform. She'll go to school, she'll sign up for—I don't know, lacrosse—dig in the dirt, do whatever kids are supposed to do."

Miranda nods. She doesn't think kids are in the cards for her. But considering it now, if she had a son or daughter, she would never subject them to the child-star path she'd gone down. She would do everything she could to protect them from it.

"Anyway," Lucy says. "What about you, Miranda?"

Miranda takes a long sip of the vodka and is quiet for a moment. She needs money, but she doesn't have a lot of people she'd be willing to spend it on. Definitely not Bobbie.

"I'd buy a house, I think," she says. "Just a nice one, in a neighborhood where I wouldn't get priced out. Then I'd go on a vacation with my best friends, because it feels like it's been a lifetime since we've done that. And if I had any left over . . . I've got a friend who's trying to start a business. I guess I'd try to help him out."

"A *hot* friend?" Dora winks.

Miranda smiles. "Not like that. Not anymore."

"Yeah. Okay." Lucy rolls her eyes. "I've heard that one before."

Miranda kicks her in the leg and reaches again for the bottle. She doesn't want to talk about what happened just before she came to Topanga, when she was in a Santa Monica Whole Foods hunting for green smoothie ingredients in an effort to give herself a healthy boost before the reality show. She was debating between mangoes and papayas when a voice sounded behind her.

"Miranda?"

Miranda turned, all at once nervous and relieved—she didn't like the unpredictability of fan interactions, but it had been a few weeks since anyone cared what she was doing out in public.

And yet it was not a fan, not really, but Zane, standing next to a display of peach and pear LaCroix.

"Zane?" she said. "What in the world are you doing here?"

He laughed a little and lifted his basket. "Buying peanut butter cups. What are you doing?"

She shook her head. "Trying to decide between mangoes and papayas."

"Mangoes." He winked. "Definitely."

Miranda laughed and put two in her basket. "This is such a surprise! What are the odds? Do you . . . Have you eaten lunch yet? I have some time to kill. I was going to get something from the deli."

Zane checked his watch. It wasn't a fancy model; the leather band was worn, and it looked like it had been handed down, but it fit him. In a plain black T-shirt and jeans, hair a little shorter than usual, he still looked so good. "I could eat. I do have a weak spot for their orzo salad."

"Okay! Amazing," Miranda said, overly bright. She felt a bit like she was in a dream as they walked through the aisles together, just two adults shopping for groceries. It was as though she had sidestepped into a parallel reality where they had grown up healthy and normal, working regular jobs and stopping here to pick a few things up for dinner. Zane seemed at ease and talked about his drive from Laguna Beach as they picked up à la carte meals and went through the self-checkout.

When they were seated in the eating area and Miranda had opened her spicy thai noodles, she pressed again. "But wait, why are you up in Los Angeles? Are you still working at your family friend's restaurant?"

"Yeah, and it's actually going pretty well," Zane said. "This friend—he's basically like an uncle to me, and he's been teaching me the ins and outs of the business. How to set up the finances, manage the employees, all that stuff." He mixed his salad. "So—god, it still feels kind of silly saying it. But I was in touch with an old LA friend of mine, and he has a business degree . . . and, I don't know. We're thinking of trying to open something up together."

"That's not silly at all," Miranda said. "That's a great idea. Like a restaurant? Or something else?"

He shrugged. "Wherever we can find a good niche. He's got the book knowledge; I still have a few connections around here. So I came up to brainstorm."

"That's amazing. I wish there was some way I could help."

"Very honestly, it's going to be boring for a long time. I'm sure you have much better things to do—you were always such a go-getter."

The way he smiled at her, wryly, made him look just like his old self again. The boy she'd known as a teenager. Miranda had the overwhelming urge to reach across the little table and grab his hand, but she kept hers firmly around her plastic fork.

"I don't know," she said. "Analyzing the small-business landscape of Boyle Heights sounds better than doing a reality show to me."

Zane laughed out loud, but Miranda was only half joking.

"Wow!" he said. "Reality TV? What's the show?"

"Um." Miranda chased a sesame seed around the edge of her container. "I don't know if they've decided on a name yet—they don't give us all the details, you know. But yeah, it should be interesting. They pay us okay, so."

"That's incredible," Zane said, his voice sincere. "I'm really happy for you. I hope it goes well."

She smiled. "Thanks, Zane. This is one of my last days of freedom, actually. Then I'll be locked up in a Topanga mansion for the filming."

Miranda couldn't help feeling a little pleased at how his expression faltered.

"Oh," he said. "Then I'm glad I caught you when I did. They probably don't let you have a lot of contact with the outside world during all that, huh?"

"Airtight contracts." She clucked her tongue. "You'd think we were in the CIA."

"Guess we'll go back to our old routine of touching base every couple years or so."

"We do have a pattern going, don't we?"

He chuckled. "We do."

Miranda lifted one shoulder. She had to say something. If she didn't, she knew she'd kick herself for the full duration of *Crashed and Burned*. "Unless—I mean, after I'm out, we could always grab coffee . . . or dinner . . ."

Zane pressed his lips together and nodded. "It's always good to catch up. I should say—well. I guess I should mention—"

Miranda sensed his meaning with a jolt and put her hand up to stop him. "You're seeing someone?"

He smiled apologetically. "My business friend isn't the only reason I'm in LA."

She had to get ahead of it before she made a fool of herself. "Zane! That's wonderful. Truly, I mean it. I'm so excited for you." And she found that she did mean it—mostly.

"Thanks. She's a regular person. No industry background at all! Which is new for me. But it's been good so far."

"Probably a good thing," Miranda said, laughing. "Probably not as wild as the rest of us."

"Well, she only likes Whole Foods–brand peanut butter cups." He raised his eyebrows. "So only time will tell."

"For sure."

His smile grew tight, and then he looked down at his empty bowl. "Look, I'm sorry. I gave you shit for this exact kind of thing when I got back from Venezuela, didn't I? Seeing someone else even though we were broken up? I realize now how you must have felt. I didn't have any right to say that to you."

Miranda felt her face growing warm. Even though the polite conversation they'd been making had felt a little awkward, it wasn't as alarming as this sudden earnestness.

"It's fine, Zane," she said. "We haven't been together for a long time. You have the right to do whatever you want with your own life."

He fiddled with the edge of his compostable container. "I know. But I am sorry. And it's just that part of me always wondered if, somewhere down the road—if you and I got our shit together—"

Zane couldn't seem to say it out loud, but he looked Miranda directly in the eyes, and she felt her heart stutter.

"Me too," she said. "I wondered that, too."

"Yeah." He broke her gaze. "Yep."

Miranda gestured to the peanut butter cups. "So then why did you do this? Instead of calling me?"

Zane hesitated. In the space between his breath and his answer, his phone rang—a clattering, cheesy melody.

"Sorry," he said. "That's the restaurant. It can wait."

"No, no, it's okay. Take it." Miranda felt itchy and embarrassed as she gathered up her utensils and napkin; she didn't know why she'd asked that last question. The answer was clear: because they still didn't have their shit together. Or at least, she didn't.

"Miranda, come on," Zane started.

"No, really. I have to get packed anyway. And I don't want to put my foot in my mouth any further than it already is." She gave him a small smile. "It was really good to run into you, Zane."

"You too," he murmured, one hand on his phone, looking conflicted.

Miranda hurried off without saying much of a goodbye. As she pulled out of the lot, she caught a glimpse of him through the store window, still at their table, hanging up from his phone call. She couldn't help watching as she waited to make a right turn, seeing him tap around his screen and then smile at it in a way he used to smile at her. It didn't take much guesswork to know whose messages he was reading.

It was time to let him move on, she knew. Zane deserved someone who didn't come with so much baggage.

Lucy and Dora are still debating what they would do with a million dollars.

If she wins the show, Miranda thinks to herself, she'll see if Zane and his friend would like help with the business loans. But even surviving to the end of *Crashed and Burned* is feeling like a long shot after the first several hours.

"Well, here's to good company and vodka," Dora says, taking the bottle back from Miranda and shaking it. "If I can keep the three of you around, I might just make it out of this hellhole."

~

But the next morning, as everyone files in to sit in a circle of chairs for group therapy, a buzz of excitement among the crew tips Miranda off that something's up.

Once the cameras start rolling, Brandon steps in the middle and folds his hands.

"I think we need to be reminded that we're here to heal, and to help each other on the road to reflection and recovery," he begins.

Next to Miranda, Lucy lets out just the slightest exhale of air so the cameras won't catch her full-on snorting.

"But three of you are enabling—instead of encouraging—each other," Brandon says. He pauses for such a long and dramatic moment that Miranda wonders whether he's forgotten what comes next. But then he continues: "Last night, the crew learned that someone had smuggled in a bottle of illicit alcohol and shared it among their roommates."

Miranda groans inwardly. How did they know?

Brandon looks very disappointed. "The culprits tried to cover up their room camera, but we still picked up audio of the incident."

The rest of the cast looks around. Miranda's cheeks are burning—she knows any of them would have done the same if they'd had enough forethought.

"Miranda, Lucy, Dora—is there anything you'd like to say to the group?"

Lucy stands up. "I'm out. Stop filming. I'm done."

"Miss La." Brandon raises his eyebrows. "Now you know you signed a full waiver—"

"What do I have to do to keep you from airing that audio?" Her face looks as though it's been cut from stone.

"That's not really how we—"

"Brandon, whatever your name is, cut the shit. I'm walking. I'll take the penalty; I'll buy the audio back from you, in fact. But I'm done."

For once, Brandon seems at a loss for words. The penalty for bailing before week three is $100,000, four times what the participants are being paid for the show. He looks at the line producer, who sighs and runs his hands over his face. "Can we get that in writing, Miss La?"

"Whatever you need."

The producer waves his hand. "Allison, take her to legal?"

Lucy tosses up a middle finger as she struts off the set. "Bye, bitches."

There's an awkward pause—they haven't stopped filming—but Brandon seems to remember himself and readjusts his posture. He picks up where he left off, as though Lucy was never there. Miranda is sure they'll patch it with a voice-over later.

She feels something almost like physical pain in her gut. This is what Lucy was willing to do to protect her daughter. It even had a price tag on it—a hefty one—and she was ready to pay it like nothing. Imagining what Bobbie would do in the same situation makes Miranda want to laugh and scream at the same time.

"Miranda, Dora," Brandon says. "Is there anything you'd like to say to the group?" Brandon looks directly at Miranda.

"Not really," she says flatly.

"Miranda, we know you've had difficulties with substance abuse in the past. And we want to help you work through them. But it's not cool to drag others down with you." Brandon has the most genuinely concerned look on his face.

"What?" Miranda sputters. "But it wasn't my—"

She doesn't want to snitch. But she's furious right now, and she shoots a look at Dora, who's sheepishly examining a spot on her leather leggings.

"It doesn't matter whose fault it was—we're not here to point fingers," says Brandon. "But you're going to be the first to learn that if you break house rules, you'll need to make up for it with some house service."

Which is how Miranda finds herself missing out on the afternoon's activities—a group volleyball game, which she would have actually been good at—and pulling rubber gloves up to her elbows before cleaning the house bathrooms.

They've been there for only one day, but somehow the rooms are already filthy. Miranda starts with the women's, picking up sodden pieces of toilet paper from the floor and scrubbing makeup stains off the sinks. The men's is even worse. Apparently their busy careers as child stars meant no one had time to teach them how to aim.

In the third stall from the last, Miranda gasps when she opens the door. On the metal side of the stall, in huge, jagged letters, someone has written WASHED UP BITCH in Sharpie.

Miranda knows who. But there's no way to prove it was Tyler, since the stalls are the only places in the house without cameras.

She grits her teeth as she slops dirty water over it, scrubbing even harder to get the marker off. Miranda would pay a lot right now to retrieve her phone from wherever it's been locked, call her agent, and demand he get her off this show. But she doesn't know where the crew took everyone's personal items. And she doesn't have $100,000 to spare to escape the set early.

Miranda wishes she was back on a yacht so she could really jump off this time—ideally, right into the mouth of a shark.

FIFTEEN

GERMAINE

2018

Germaine sets her toothbrush down and looks out the bathroom window of the hotel, wondering whether there's any way she can get out of this. It's crisscrossed with lattice ironwork in a Tudor style, and although it holds a gorgeous view of the Jardins des Champs-Élysées, the design makes her feel even more trapped.

Germaine is here in Paris, the City of Love, for anything but.

She sighs as she picks up the cream-colored Cartier box on the sink—a gift from Eddie. Inside is a gold choker necklace with tiny pieces hammered to look like a garland of laurel leaves, inset with thirty-two obsidian gems and 129 brilliant-cut diamonds. The St. Germaine-Changs will meet with the Chous tonight at the Paris St. Germaine-Chang hotel for a Valentine's Day ball, and Germaine will be expected to wear it.

Officially, she and Eddie are on the road to a proposal and a lavish wedding. Unofficially, they can't stand the sight of each other. After Germaine made it clear that she was not interested in rekindling their secret romance, Eddie dropped all pretense of friendliness. At least they could be honest about their feelings toward each other. Their parents have set them up several times, finding reasons to send

Eddie and Germaine to the same galas, hotel conferences, and public appearances, even going so far as to force them into business together—the Chous wanted Germaine to complete a similar decor inspection at one of Eddie's properties, with Eddie, of course, close at hand—but all encounters have ended frostily. He tells her she's a cold stuck-up bitch; she calls him a little man with a micro-dick.

But they're both in the same position: they need to play along in public or risk antagonizing their families. Both the Chous and the St. Germaine-Changs see marriage as a political alliance, not a romantic pursuit; after all, this is their own experience. As far as they're concerned, Eddie and Germaine are the same age, and both are attractive, well presented, and well spoken. They come from similar cultures, both personally and in business. Marriage is a no-brainer. A merger, if you will.

Germaine does not feel the same. In the sacrosanct, passing daydreams where she's occasionally imagined marriage for herself, it was always with someone kind and easygoing and somehow antithetical to all her parents' calculating ideals.

Never, ever with Eddie Chou.

There's a knock at the door, and Germaine opens it to find Marie.

"Marie! Veuillez entrer," she says. "You know you don't need to knock."

Marie shrugs and smiles, eyes wide. "Yes—but I never know if your mother is in here."

Germaine laughs. Marie has become the only stylist that she will trust, and if it was up to her, she'd give Marie the highest of raises. They've developed a tenuous bond over the years, with Germaine becoming more and more aware of the power dynamics between her and all the other St. Germaine-Chang staff; neither she nor Marie strays from the formal verb conjugations when they speak to each other in French. But their almost-friendship is a relief, nonetheless.

With her face washed, Germaine sits before the mirror as the stylist goes to work.

She's impressed by Marie's skill. Germaine very rarely does her makeup herself; she's not great at it. She rarely does anything for herself. Her parents are proud of this fact—to them, it's a symbol that they've made it. They can pay others to do the mundane, everyday tasks for them, even down to picking out their own clothes. That's how royalty used to—and still does—live, and it's what the St. Germaine-Changs are trying to emulate.

Germaine knows that she would not get far without them. The "lessons" she's been taught have been clear evidence of that, and all her bank accounts are still linked in some way to her parents. Germaine makes a mental note to see whether that's something she can change without being noticed.

But it's about more than just money. However spoiled they both were as children, she and Eddie were raised to be obedient to their parents and to put their families' wishes above their own. Eddie could make enough money from his real estate business to strike off on his own path, but the estrangement from his family would be devastating. If Germaine were to cut ties with her family right here and now, the best she could hope for with her education and experience level is a hotel-management job, earning the kind of money real people get paid—that is, not very much. Her entire lifestyle would have to change. There would be no more jet-setting, no designer clothes, no house staff, no stylist. She probably wouldn't be able to afford a doorman building. She might have to work somewhere unthinkable, like Phoenix or Fort Lauderdale.

It occurs to Germaine, on some level, that this all sounds dramatic. She has things in perspective. Miranda, for example, is in a much worse spot—renting and essentially selling herself out for a paycheck. But Germaine also knows that Miranda is much tougher than she is. Always has been. Germaine's coolness, her aloofness, her poise, has always come from the fact that she can fall back on money. That's why the wealthy get to act the way they do—it's a symptom of no consequences.

But she knows she could face consequences—big ones. And walking away from her family's safety net would mean that she'd need to become an entirely different kind of person. She's not sure she has what that takes.

So maybe she's going to have to suck it up and marry Eddie Chou, after all, no matter how repugnant that may sound.

"We are going for Grecian, yes, Germaine?" Marie asks as she brushes and poufs.

"Oui, madame," Germaine says with a sigh.

"Ne vous inquiète pas. That style will be gorgeous on you."

"Thanks, Marie."

"And . . . everyone's favorite real estate agent? What's his dress?"

"Toga," Germaine says, making a gagging sound.

"One needs a very good body to pull that off," Marie says lightly, and Germaine snorts. In the politest of quips, Marie has made it clear how she feels about Eddie. "If I were his stylist, I'd—"

The door opens without a knock, and Céline comes in, dressed head to toe in a red-and-black ball gown with a high-collared Queen Anne neckline. A fascinator crowns her high-swept updo, complete with ace and jack of hearts cards. The Valentine's Ball is a costume ball, and Céline is going as the Queen of Hearts.

"Germaine! You're not dressed yet?" she asks as she enters. Then, to Marie, "Dépêche-toi maintenant, Marie, allez, allez!"

Céline's costume is fitting, Germaine thinks, because she's already got the character down pat—ordering everyone around and being a holy terror. Wasn't the Queen of Hearts super mean to Alice, too? Suitable.

Marie makes a few finishing touches and wordlessly brings out the rest of Germaine's ensemble, averting her eyes from her employer. Céline and Michelle, Eddie's mom, have handpicked the outfits for their children. Eddie is Eros, the god of love—and he already sent Germaine a selfie in his skimpy toga, carrying a prop bow and arrow. He knew how much it would annoy her, and she is not eager to see it in person.

Germaine will be Aphrodite. Marie shakes out a silken, diaphanous dress that's ivory colored and practically see-through. Even though her frame is slim, Germaine feels the urge to pull in her stomach as she examines her reflection in the mirror. It does not leave much to the imagination.

"Don't worry, Gigi, you can't see the cellulite," her mother says, leaning on a chair so as not to rumple her gown by sitting.

Germaine feels her neck and cheeks flush. She doesn't *have* cellulite. She's about to say so when Marie brings Eddie's necklace from the bathroom, completing the ensemble. Germaine's hair is in a curled Grecian-style updo with thin gold chains woven through, and there are dangling earrings to complement the necklace. She's glad they don't have to travel outside, because she has a feeling she'd freeze in this outfit.

"Magnificent," Marie whispers to Germaine before Céline ushers her out the door.

~

Germaine and Céline meet Terence, Eddie, and his parents in the grand foyer of the St. Germaine-Chang hotel, thronged with well-to-do guests in elaborate costumes. Michelle beams at Eddie in his skimpy outfit, with little attention spared for Germaine.

"Isn't he handsome?" she gushes. "Right out of the Parthenon!"

But Germaine's costume is not lost on Eddie. He makes a low whistle when their parents aren't listening.

"Okay," he says, looking considerably lower than where he should be if he wants to meet her gaze. "Not bad at all."

"Get bent," Germaine hisses, crossing her arms tightly across her chest.

Germaine's PR smile gets her through dinner, and then, just as she's beginning to wonder how soon she can excuse herself without seeming rude, the band Bad Society comes onstage. It's a young girl group, and a little edgy for this buttoned-up crowd, but Germaine's familiar with a few of their songs. She's not totally out of the loop in Hollywood, and she's impressed with the stuff some of these kids are doing—bringing grunge back, calling out sexual predators, getting politically active. Stuff Germaine would never have had the guts to do back when she was a 3AM Girl.

If Bad Society had been around when Germaine started booking bands, she would have scheduled them for every event. They're fresh, raw—nothing like No Exit had been all those years ago.

She wraps her arms around herself, chilled in her costume. She messed things up for herself, didn't she? Not only for Sicily, whose court cases Germaine watched with burning shame from the other side of the world. But for both of them. If she hadn't been so focused on revenge back in Singapore, she might have picked a band that she *really* liked to play her parents' opening. And who knows where that would have taken her? Sicily would certainly have fared much better. And Germaine might not have lost that feeling of a creative spark that came to her so rarely now, that had been quashed by spite and guilt.

But she is here, now, and Bad Society is making a weight inside her lift. They're killing it up there. Even with what Germaine perceives as a potential value clash between these up-and-comers and their wealthy audience, the music is good. Bad Society seems to read the room, and their stage presence is infectious. Soon the dance floor is packed. To Germaine's surprise, even Terence and Céline venture out.

Germaine isn't about to dance with Eddie—and anyway, he seems to be working his way over to a leggy blonde dancing by herself near the edge of the crowd—but she wanders closer to the stage, wanting to be part of the energy that radiates from it.

Then, as the band's current song ends—somewhat abruptly—the lead singer draws up short and peers into the crowd, hand shielding her eyes from the lights.

She's looking right at Germaine.

"We'd like to say a special little thank-you," the singer says. "Germaine St. Germaine-Chang, do I see you over there?"

Somehow a spotlight finds Germaine. She looks around, bewildered, and then waves, because she doesn't know what else to do. Everyone is staring.

"Yes?" she says in a voice that sounds unbelievably quiet in the sudden silence. "Hi?"

"When we got the call that Germaine wanted to book us for her family's event, I was floored." The singer grins. "I have a confession to make: I am a *Kidz Klub superfan.* I grew up watching the cast, learning their moves; I wanted to be one of those people someday. It was, like, my whole childhood. So you can imagine, holy shit—sorry, polite company—this is like the best night ever. Germaine, thank you for bringing us here."

Germaine feels herself blushing hard as the room applauds. It's incredibly awkward, but she hasn't been recognized like this in years—for something *she* did, not for being her parents' daughter. She just laughs, unsure of what to say, unsure whether she can even be heard from the stage.

"Okay, this is going to sound wild and you can totally say no," the lead singer is saying. She looks around to her bandmates for approval, and they nod. "But—would you want to come up and sing something with us?"

"Um . . ." Germaine presses a hand to her chest. "No. I couldn't—"

"Are you sure? It would be really cool. I know I'm springing this on you . . ."

Germaine glances around for a moment, as if looking for permission, but she doesn't see her parents or Eddie. And why should she need permission, anyway? This is basically her party. She owns stock in this hotel. She can do whatever she wants.

"Okay!" She raises her hands in defeat. "Okay, why not!"

The singer whoops and beckons Germaine onstage. Germaine hurries up, giddy with excitement.

"My favorite was always 'Treat You Right,'" the singer says, handing Germaine a microphone. "Do you remember that one?"

As if Germaine could forget. "Oh yeah."

"Well, let's go, then!"

The band plays the opening riff and sets off a flood of memories in Germaine—dancing next to Miranda and Sicily, running around in goofy costumes, spending hours at rehearsals waiting to practice one five-minute number. But she was good at it. And she comes in right on key, remembering every word.

We're going to party all night, oh baby, let's go. I'm going to treat you so right, yeah I know that you know.

It's silly. But Germaine has to admit that she feels some kind of a thrill up there, even though her voice is a little creaky and she never blossomed in the spotlight the way Miranda and Sicily did.

The lead singer raises her eyebrows and starts doing a few of the dance steps. Germaine takes the cue and breaks out into the old *Kidz Klub* routine that used to accompany the song. The crowd in the ballroom goes wild. Germaine can't help grinning. She even catches a glimpse of Eddie near the front, managing a smile and taking pictures like an actual supportive boyfriend instead of a pretend one who not so secretly dislikes everything about her.

Germaine and the band nail the ending, and the song finishes to thunderous applause.

"That was incredible!" the lead singer says. "Germaine St. Germaine-Chang, everyone!" She turns and gives Germaine a hug, squeezing her tight and saying just for her to hear, "You did so good! That was awesome!"

For the briefest moment, Germaine doesn't want to let go. The words are something so simple, but no one ever says them to her.

Then she steps back from the embrace and rushes off the stage on a wave of adrenaline.

It crests and dissipates when she sees the expressions on her parents' faces, back at their table.

"Don't you ever embarrass yourself like that again," Céline hisses, looking every bit the furious Wonderland queen.

"You didn't think," her father adds. "You're too old to be pulling stunts like that. You're not young anymore and you're not talented."

"Dad," Germaine starts, crestfallen but not surprised. "I—"

"And you ripped your dress," her mother says, pointing at a tear in the Aphrodite costume that opens to Germaine's calf. "Jumping around up there. It's pathetic."

Germaine says nothing, shaking her head and making her way back to her room. This is as good an excuse as any to bow out of the remainder of the ball. And maybe, if she can distract herself enough by playing the *Kidz Klub* album on her earbuds and watching lights twinkle down on the Champs-Élysées while she gets ready for bed, she'll be able to ignore their criticisms and relive the performance in her dreams.

But it's hard to ignore the unflattering, slightly racy pictures that are posted to social media the next day, and the sarcastic captions and comments that flood beneath. Haz-Beenz Klub. Bouncy Castle Spice: Book her for your next kids' party!

Eddie.

Germaine could break her phone in half. And then hunt him down and break his. *And* his thumbs.

Revenge isn't so bad, after all. Sometimes it's necessary.

One way or another, she'll get it.

SIXTEEN

SICILY

2018

Sicily is sitting on the couch, picking at the split ends in her hair. It's something she does when she's stressed out. Her mother hates it; if she ever catches Sicily at it, she insists on a hair appointment and oil masks to repair it.

"You're only making it worse," she says.

But Sicily can't help it. She's worried about Noah. Ever since the baby shower, he's said he doesn't want to stay at her place anymore. Sicily cringes as she remembers the call from Hugo she got the following day, who was furious about the fight that happened there. He said Noah was traumatized—and apparently so was Jaime.

Sicily had to roll her eyes at that, but she can't argue with Noah's decision—the fight was awful. She cries a little every time he refuses to talk to her on the phone, but she can't blame him. She's been sending little postcards to Hugo and Jaime's house with newsy notes, updating him on her day and asking about school and telling him how much she loves him. Maybe once the baby is born, he'll soften toward her and agree to spend time with his new brother or sister. Then Sicily will get things back to normal.

A knock at the door gets Sicily off the couch and moving, somewhat slowly, due to her growing belly. She welcomes in Oscar, her business manager, who sets up shop at the dining room table for their eleven-o'clock meeting. Sicily likes Oscar. Unlike her relatives, he's no-nonsense and practical, friendly but not overly attached.

But today he looks concerned. He adjusts his rectangular glasses as he spreads papers over the table, too old-school for an iPad or laptop. Sicily sets down coffee for him and tea for herself and sits across from him.

"What's the good news, Oscar?" she says, like she always does.

He furrows his brow. "Well, Sicily, frankly—I wanted to bring up some concerns about expenditure."

"Okay," Sicily says. She was under the impression that they were spending less than usual while she was staying at home and waiting for the baby. But then, they weren't making as much for the very same reason. "Like what?"

"Well." He purses his lips, looking uncomfortable. "Like Squeak and his family, to be very honest."

Sicily frowns. "How so?"

"Sicily, come on." Oscar sighs. "Do his mother and sisters really need three brand-new luxury cars? Does he need his own dance studio, on our dime?"

"Okay—the cars, I see your point. We can talk about that. But the dance studio is an investment," Sicily says. "Squeak wants to become financially independent, and he's always had a dream of starting his own business. And you know what an amazing dancer he is." She smiles, catching herself gushing again. "Teaching was my idea—it's a no-brainer. With my backing, he'll be generating revenue right away."

Oscar scratches his head and makes a note. "Can he rent? Does he need somewhere custom built when he's just starting out?"

"Oscar, I mean . . ." Sicily takes a sip of tea. "I get the nickel-and-diming, and I know we have to be responsible with the money. But I want to be generous toward his family; I really care about them. And what's the point of wealth if you can't spread it around a little? That was the one good thing my parents taught me."

Oscar folds his hands together and leans back in his chair. He hasn't touched his coffee. "Sicily, I hate to be blunt about this, but . . . you're not as rich as you think you are."

Sicily looks at him and sets her tea down. "Okay, I know we're feeling a little bit of a squeeze right now, but—"

"The tour had to be cut because of the bad morning sickness. The single wasn't a big hit. The Vegas residency is on hold indefinitely—where is this money supposed to come from?"

"Oscar, I know," Sicily says with a little more force. She doesn't need him to lay out all her shortcomings for her. "We'll build it back once I can perform again. We have savings, we've planned for this."

Oscar takes his glasses off and rubs the bridge of his nose. "Yes, but we need a *lot* of money to build back up to *making* a lot of money. And you're going to need those savings for the lawsuit, if it happens."

Sicily sits up very straight. "The lawsuit?"

Oscar puts his glasses back on and raises his hands in surrender. "I shouldn't have said anything."

"Oscar, *what* lawsuit?"

"You need to call your lawyer. I can't share anything more than that."

"You work for me. You need to tell me what's going on."

"Call your lawyer." He gathers his papers together, slipping them into his briefcase with a neat *click* and giving her a curt nod before heading toward the door.

~

As early as reasonably possible the next morning, Sicily drives downtown with Chad to meet Deborah at the Corcoran offices.

"What is going on?" Sicily demands to know as they settle down in the leather chairs before Deborah's desk. "Why haven't I heard anything about a lawsuit?"

Deborah raises both hands to calm her. "I only just got official communications myself, although I think this has been brewing for some time. But I didn't want to worry you unnecessarily."

"I don't want another court case of any kind!" Sicily's heart is beginning to race. She was half hoping Deborah would say that Oscar doesn't know what he's talking about and there's no reason to worry. She's still feeling like she has PTSD from Hugo's lawsuit and the conservatorship, not as far in the past as she'd like.

"I know this," Deborah says. "And I think that's what your father and uncle are counting on."

"What? *They're* suing me?" Sicily snaps. "What the hell for?"

Deborah opens a manila folder and examines the papers inside. "For damages and loss of earnings, it looks like—they say they were unfairly penalized when the conservator order was removed."

Sicily puts her head in her hands.

"Would any judge in their right mind go for that?" Chad asks.

"They haven't got the greatest case," Deborah says. She gives a long look at Sicily. "But their timing is very intentional. They've got enough on you to drag this out for a while—I would bet they're expecting you to settle. And for your sake, Sicily, with the baby coming, it's probably a good idea."

Sicily feels panic rising in her throat. This can't be happening.

As Chad drives them back, Sicily calls her mother. "Did you know about this?" she asks.

"No, I mean—not really," Carole says evasively. "I'm not surprised they're pulling it. But they didn't say much about it to me."

"*Much*?"

"Nothing. Nothing, sweetie. You know them—they're just trying to see if they can make a buck. Things haven't been so great for them, financially."

"Things aren't that great for me, either, Mom! They're asking for *millions* of dollars!"

"Maybe they'll settle for a little less." Sicily's mom sighs on the other end of the line. "But, you know, we shouldn't even be talking about this in your state. The stress isn't good for the baby, sweetheart."

"You're telling me!" Sicily cries, then hangs up the phone and calls Emmylou.

"Hey, Sis," Emmylou answers.

"Did *you* know about the lawsuit?" Sicily barks.

"What lawsuit?" Emmylou asks innocently.

"Oh, come on."

"If it's some kind of family lawsuit, I guess that wouldn't surprise me. You know how they are."

"And no one thought to tell me, Emmylou?"

"I'm still not even sure what you're talking about!" Emmylou protests. "But if I *was*, I'd also say that people probably didn't want to worry you when you're literal weeks away from giving birth. Everything's going to be fine."

"It doesn't really sound like it is!"

Chad puts up his hand; she's yelling in the closed car. Sicily heaves a sigh of exasperation and hangs up on Emmylou.

"You need a burger?" Chad asks. "You sound like you need a burger."

He takes her through the In-N-Out drive-through, and she wolfs down the food, unsure whether it's stress eating, sudden hunger brought on by the pregnancy, or both. She keeps her sunglasses on, unwilling to risk anyone taking pictures of her in this state.

"It's going to be okay, kid." Chad takes a sip of his milkshake. He calls her *kid* even though they're closer in age than not, but Sicily doesn't mind.

"What are we supposed to do?" she says quietly. She knows she's always been the meal ticket for her family. She just had no idea that the feast would go on for the rest of her life, no matter how much distance she tries to put between herself and them, no matter how big she gets or how far she tries to run.

Chad shakes his head. "I wish I knew. But I think it should be whatever is healthiest for you and your child."

"You mean settle?" she asks. He shrugs.

"We don't have enough money, Chad." Sicily dips a fry in her little plastic cup of sauce. "They'll sort of be cleaning us out if we settle."

"More money will come. Your career isn't over, I promise."

Sicily slumps down in the passenger seat. "I wish it wasn't so hard to believe that."

∼

Chad drives her home and waves from the window, giving what she thinks is meant to be an encouraging smile. But Sicily can tell he's worried, too. She wouldn't blame him if he started putting out feelers for new job opportunities.

The driveway is flooded with cars, and there's bass thumping from inside the house. When Sicily walks through the door and drops her purse on the side table, she can hardly hear herself think.

"Squeak?" she yells, wandering through the living room. There are people milling about, though most look to be outside hanging around the pool. Squeak jogs through the back door in swim trunks with a towel around his neck, hair wet.

"Hey, babe." He kisses her on the cheek. "How did your meeting go?"

"It went—" She stops, shakes her head. "I didn't know we were having a party today."

He shrugs. "Just a few friends. And they brought their friends, and . . . you know. Social snowball."

Normally his turns of phrase would make her laugh, but she is not in the mood today. These gatherings of Squeak's always tend to go past midnight. "Okay, well . . . I'm sorry I can't join in. I'm just . . ."

She sighs, pressing her hands to her forehead.

"Hey, hey, it's okay." Squeak takes her in his arms. "I'm sorry I didn't run it by you first. Listen, you just go lie down. I'll make you some tea, okay? That prenatal stuff?"

Sicily closes her eyes and nods. "Okay."

She climbs the stairs, lugging the weight that her body has put on. In bed, she can't get comfortable around her belly. Her back aches. Her head aches. And Squeak never comes with the tea.

She puts pillows over her ears, but the whole house is pounding.

And as everything overwhelms her at once, Sicily hits her fist into the mattress and begins to sob. Is there no one to look out for her? No one to look *after* her?

She reaches for her phone and texts Miranda. Hey, you make it out yet?

But she already knows the answer. *Crashed and Burned* is still filming, and Miranda probably can't access her phone.

She dials Germaine and waits, clutching at a pillow as she listens to the ringtone, but there's no answer. It's the middle of the night in Europe.

Sicily is alone.

SEVENTEEN

MIRANDA

2018

It's the last week of filming *Crashed and Burned*, thank god. Miranda has somehow found it in herself to stick it out, but Dora had enough. Yesterday, one of the guys—some himbo who used to play a jock on *Boy Meets World*—peed in the hot tub after his two allotted drinks. When Dora realized that the warm water was coming from somewhere other than the jets, she shrieked and kicked him right in the nuts.

Miranda saw it happen from the tiki bar. When he squealed in protest, Dora threw her head back and cackled. "That'll teach ya!"

In a few moments, security had arrived, grasping Dora's arm and saying *Let's go* in serious voices. Bullying and messy gossip were one thing, but violence was a liability.

"Yeah, all right." Dora adjusted her sagging black bikini and climbed out of the tub. "Old Dora Sanchez doesn't need this bullshit anyway." She raised her arms and flipped the bird with both hands as the security guys escorted her off the premises. "You can all kiss my ass!"

"I'm going to miss her," Miranda says to Desi Jacobs, shaking her head as she sips a mai tai.

"She's my hero," says Desi, the former teen host of a game show on the same channel that ran *Kidz Klub*. She took a hard left turn into insurance fraud at the same time Miranda's auditions dried up. "You think Dustin's okay?"

Miranda eyes the bag of ice that the paramedics have given Dustin to put on his crotch. He's nearly in tears.

"I was hoping to get with that before we wrapped up here," Desi says.

Miranda makes a face. "Isn't he married?"

"Yeah. With kids." Desi frowns when she sees Miranda's judgmental expression. "What? I never pretended to be a good person."

So this morning there is one less chair in the group-therapy circle, leaving eight of them who have made it to the final meeting. Brandon is still looking as chipper as ever, but there's something about his energy that's beginning to fray—he's been just as cooped up here on set as everyone else. Miranda is sure he'll be jumping on the next flight to Cabo the first chance he gets.

"Contestants," he says earnestly, therapists flanking him on either side, "I'm so proud of your progress. You've taken the initiative to go on this journey together, experiencing many ups and downs along the way. I know we've had some tough conversations and even tougher group challenges. But being honest with yourselves is the first step to walking back the crash."

Walking back the crash—Miranda guesses they're making that the tagline of the show, because Brandon and the therapists keep saying it very pointedly. Even Dustin and Tyler started incorporating it into their language, and Dora said it once tongue in cheek. But Miranda still doesn't understand it. Crashes happen, and they're devastating, irrevocable—you can't just make them unhappen by demonstrating team spirit and telling yourself that you're a winner.

"It's been really hard," Desi is saying, shaking her head. She's looking very intently at a spot on the floor, and Miranda can tell she's trying to make herself cry. If anyone's going to make a final bid for that million-dollar prize, now is the time. "We've had to be away from our families and all the people we love. But, really—that distance has made me realize how important they are to me. How much I've—I've hurt them in the past, with my behavior. And I don't want to be that person anymore."

Tears spill prettily from her eyes, and the therapists nod with approval. Tyler sighs. Miranda puts her arm around Desi as she takes a steadying breath, placing a hand to her cheek as if she's embarrassed. Miranda's impressed with the performance.

"Thank you for sharing, Desi." Brandon nods. "That's very brave. Now let's—"

Tyler sighs again, even louder. His eyebrows are furrowed, and his face is screwed up like something is weighing on him.

"Tyler," Brandon says. It's as though Miranda can see the gears turning in his head. "You haven't shared yet. Is there anything you'd like to say to the group?"

Tyler pulls at his chin with his hand and sits up straighter. "Yeah, actually. I—I have a heavy heart about something, something that happened in the past. And unless I address it, I just—I'm not sure if I'll ever be able to move on. I'll never be able to walk back the crash."

Brandon signals for the boom guy to come around, but the audio technician is already moving the crew closer. The anticipation in the air is palpable, like sharks smelling blood. The producers know that Tyler is about to offer them a big revelation, and they're letting him know he'll be rewarded for it.

Miranda does not feel so eager to hear it. In fact, she has an uneasy feeling in her stomach.

Tyler keeps his eyes trained on the floor as though he doesn't even see the cast and crew.

"About ten years ago," he begins, "I did a Holiday Heartwarmers movie. You might know it—*The Bennington Bookshop*? Anyway. My costar was . . . well, Miranda. And I've been holding this in for years, but I have to admit that, at the time . . . she and I were sleeping together."

There's an audible gasp from both the contestants and crew. Brandon's eyes are practically glittering. A reveal that implicates another member of the cast? It's the jackpot.

But Miranda is seeing red. She can feel all the blood somehow draining from her face and flooding to her fists at the same time. How *dare* he. How can he say all this on camera when he threatened her not to breathe a word? How can he frame *her* as desperate? They were in the same shitty movie together. Tyler might have gone on to do bigger and better things for a few more years than she did, but now they're here together again, in the same boat—crashed, burned, humiliating themselves on a TV show.

She cannot believe his gall.

"It was so unprofessional, and it wasn't the right thing to do. I don't know, I just"—Tyler runs his hands through his hair, seemingly unable to stop talking—"I kept silent all these years because Miranda had a rough reputation. I was worried my own career might be jeopardized by association, you know? I realized pretty quickly that I had made a mistake. And then she wound up in jail, and everyone was saying she was basically a prostitute . . . that made me feel pretty awful about myself, that I had been with her."

"Tyler," Miranda says through a clenched jaw. Brandon holds up a finger, as if to say, *Oh, we'll get to you next. Don't you worry.*

"But now," Tyler says, opening his hands and raising his eyebrows. "Now I realize how judgmental that was. How I was being kind of a jerk. And I've learned here, on *Crashed and Burned*, that you have to forgive yourself before asking for forgiveness from others; I have to be tolerant of others' mistakes, because I've made plenty of my own. And over the past few weeks, I've been coming to terms with that."

He finally looks Miranda in the eyes. She can almost hear the sentimental music with which they'll underscore this touching scene.

"So, Miranda," he says.

"No," Miranda shoots back. "No, no—"

Tyler makes his eyes wide and hopeful. "Is there any way you can find it in your heart to forgive the way I treated you?"

"NO!" she shouts, staggering to her feet. "You don't give a shit about me—you didn't back then, you didn't when you found out I was on this show, and you absolutely do not now."

The cameras and microphones have all pivoted to face her. Miranda registers that she's shouting, she's screaming so loud that her voice will go hoarse, but she doesn't care.

"Miranda—" Tyler starts.

"Shut UP! You don't get to come on here and give me some fake-ass apology to trick the world into thinking you're a good person, when you're actually an *enormous* dick! I will *never* forgive you. You wrote 'washed up bitch' in the men's bathroom; I know it was you. You dropped me like a piece of garbage the *second* you thought I might have feelings for you. You made fun of me on set behind my back. And now you come on here, in front of everyone, and throw something we did in private ten years ago in my *face*?"

Her throat is on fire. She's hyperventilating.

But Tyler is unmoved, watching her outburst with little change in expression. "Miranda, you know that we were together on that film set. Everyone knew. Then the producers told me to keep away from you. I'm sorry, but that's the truth."

"Everything he is saying is a crock of *shit*!" Miranda roars.

The last time she was this angry, some bitch was coming at her in the prison showers, shiv in hand. All Miranda could do that day was scream and try to roll out of the way. But not this time. Because luckily, before Dora got kicked off the show, she taught Miranda how to punch.

That's how Miranda lands her fist into Tyler's face. And lands back at the police station, under arrest for assault.

The only people who are happy about the situation are the production team, who got everyone to sign cast-iron contracts so they couldn't sue afterward. And they know one thing for certain: the ratings for this episode will be huge.

Between fingerprinting and the Breathalyzer, the executive producer tells Miranda they definitely want her for their next series.

It's for former stars who've had a major public humiliation: *Rock Bottom*.

EIGHTEEN

GERMAINE

2018

Germaine is back in her bedroom in New York, flipping through *Rolling Stone*. Her Beats headphones, connected to her phone, are blasting Bad Society's newest release. She feels almost like a teenager again as she lies on her bed and pores over an article about a pop star who turned the experience of her divorce into a killer album.

Well—not Germaine as a teenager. She'd been running around on *Kidz Klub* and becoming America's shopping icon back then. But maybe she feels like the teenager she wishes she could have been.

She needs to be back in or around music in some way. Not the old Blast Off! way—she doesn't exactly want to perform, and if she did, it would be as a dancer. But up onstage with Bad Society, it felt like there was something there. She needs to work with bands again. Good ones this time. She needs to immerse herself in that energy, the way she felt at the party in Paris, without being the center of attention. She isn't sure exactly how to do it, but she knows she needs to take some sort of step back in her life—it may be the only way she can move forward.

Germaine looks up, startled. The housekeeper has poked her head in and is trying to say something.

Germaine pulls off her headphones. "Sorry. What?"

"Miss St. Germaine-Chang, your parents have requested you in the library."

Germaine frowns. The library? They go there to have only their most sensitive discussions about business or public relations, ones they can't risk being overheard by visitors or staff. She wanders to the room and finds Terence and Céline in the fireside chairs at the center, surrounded by books that no one ever reads.

Giles and Greg are there, too, luckily without their simpering and passive-aggressive wives in tow. The four of them are murmuring intently and stop when they see Germaine approach.

"What is this?" she says suspiciously, taking a seat. "Why the secrecy?"

"We needed to call a family meeting about Eddie," her father begins.

"*Thank* you," Germaine says. "Has it gotten through to you that he was the one who embarrassed me after Paris?"

"What, do you mean posting the pictures?" her mother asks. "Whatever. It was you in those pictures, not him."

"He's immature." Giles shrugs his shoulders. "So what? He'll grow up once he has a wife and kids. I did."

"You did not." Germaine glares at him.

"And that's what we need to talk about," Céline cuts in. She looks intently at Germaine, as though she knows she's up against a fight. "We've had enough of the stalling. You and Eddie need to get engaged this spring; you'll have the wedding exactly ten months later to avoid any unsavory rumors that you . . . forced his hand."

"Mom . . . ," Germaine starts. She expected this conversation, but not so soon. She thought she still had time.

"I have a call out to Michael Cinco's studio in Dubai. We'll go with Michelle, and we'll fly in your cousins Yun and Leah from Taiwan and Vietnam, and there's a few more in Singapore I'd like to bring along—I thought it was just a good central meeting point, anyway."

Germaine doesn't even bother to ask about Sicily and Miranda. The cousins are varying breeds of models and fashion industry people and will serve as a suitably photogenic bridal party. It's been clear to Germaine for a long time that, should she ever get married, Sicily and Miranda will not be welcome at her bachelorette festivities, and maybe not even at the wedding.

"We're already considering which of our properties will make the best venue," Terence adds. "You're welcome to help with that. The venue, the catering, the decor and so forth. And music, within reason. I guess you like that sort of thing."

Germaine sits very still and calm, nodding along with their plans, fingers laced together in her lap. But inside, her mind is whirling, ticking through all the different paths that might lead her away from this crash course. She has to put a stop to this immediately.

"That would all be well and good," she says, putting her hand up when her parents pause for a breath. "And the plans sound lovely, they really do. But . . . there's a problem."

"What?" Germaine's mother says suspiciously. Both she and Terence had to expect Germaine to put up some sort of resistance, but she hopes her relaxed posture is throwing them off.

"I didn't want to say anything, but—Eddie is impotent," Germaine continues. "That's why he does these mean things to shame me in public. Sorry to be crude, but he just can't get it up. We won't be able to have children."

Greg narrows his eyes at her, but their father looks stunned to silence. Giles seems embarrassed. Céline's mouth has fallen open a little. She glances at Terence, questioning.

Germaine has them on the hook; she can feel it. So she decides to step it up, shifting in her chair like the whole thing is very awkward. "Listen, I don't want to humiliate him—this is a big secret. I've known since we were teenagers. But his family is totally in the dark." She tucks her hair behind her ear and shrugs. "Now maybe you understand why he feels the need to overcompensate in other ways, always talking so big and trying to make me—and our family—look small. I know you want to make it work. But I'm not sure if this is a good alliance for us."

It seems to be working; the expressions on the faces of Germaine's parents fall somewhere between aghast and disappointed.

Terence turns back to Céline. "Michelle never mentioned anything to you about . . . ?"

"Of course not." Her lip curls. "Why would she?"

Germaine's father presses his forefinger to the bridge of his nose. "Well, then, Germaine, if this is true . . ."

Greg clears his throat and shifts in his seat. "Yeah, *if* this is true."

Germaine regards him coolly. "Do you have something for the class, Greg?"

"Well . . ." Greg opens his hands, palms up, in a shrug. "If you've known since you were teenagers, then how do you explain the sex tape?"

Germaine's fingernails curl hard enough into a fist to make welts in her palm.

"The *what*?" Céline asks.

"Yep." Greg raises his eyebrows. "Sweet, spoiled little Germaine made a sex tape. With Eddie."

"What are you saying?" Germaine says through gritted teeth.

"Yes, Gregoire, explain yourself," their father demands.

Greg leans back in his chair, happy to be the center of attention again. "Eddie showed it to me last year—he wanted me to set him up with Germaine, but I gave him the brush-off at first, so he brought up the video. Turned my stomach. I said fine, he could tag along to Bali with the rest of you as long as he never showed me that again."

Germaine could burst into tears. She could spit. She could rip off all her fingernails with her teeth.

"I didn't know he was filming us that night," she says, her voice still calm. But she's shaking. "It was done without my consent. He held it over my head."

Greg rolls his eyes. "Don't get all #MeToo on me. That's just how Eddie is. If you didn't want to be part of his weird kinky hijinks, you shouldn't have had sex with him."

"He blackmailed me with it, and blackmailed you, too!" Germaine's voice is steadily growing in volume. "He *used* you, Greg, as a stepping stone to me, to marry into a richer family. Are you completely blind?"

Greg makes a face like he smells something bad. "No—I don't think that's how it was. It's guy stuff, you don't get it."

"Did he say he'd release the footage if you didn't set us up?" Germaine presses.

"Yeah, he joked about it, but—"

"He *played* you, Greg!" It nearly comes out as a wail, and Germaine struggles to control herself. She needs to be very careful about the next moves she makes. "Do we want someone to have power like that over our family?"

"*You* gave him that power, Germaine," Greg shoots back, red in the face. "That's what happens when you slut around. And now you have to make things right and marry him."

Germaine looks to the others for help, expecting them to be as horrified as she is. But her father is staring vacantly into the middle distance. Giles has the balls to laugh.

"God, that is so like Eddie." He chuckles. "That's one dirty tape you probably *didn't* want to rewind, huh, Greg?"

Greg seems to relax at his brother's words and shakes his head as if that will get the memory out. "Never again. Anyway. Eddie may be a dickhead, but he's certainly not impotent. Or at least, he wasn't when that footage was taken."

"And if he is, oh well," says Giles. "You two can adopt kids."

"We can get beautiful ones in Vietnam," Céline says, her voice crisp and very level. Then she turns to Germaine, and the look in her eyes is frightening. "Gregoire is right, Germaine. You brought this on yourself. A sex tape! How tawdry. That's something I would expect from your trailer-trash friends, not you."

Germaine feels, simultaneously, like she could combust on the spot and like she could take two swift steps from where she sits and snap Greg's neck with her bare hands. None of them will take her side. None of them will even have the grace to show her sympathy. Her own brother saw her naked.

"And what if I refuse to marry Eddie?" she asks very quietly.

Greg shrugs. "Then he'll publish it online, I guess. And all your disgusting moaning and writhing will be on a million websites in the span of one minute."

"Don't be like this, Germaine," Giles whines, still not taking it seriously. "Our kids will see it, and I don't want to have to explain that to them."

"And if he does publish it." Germaine looks from her father to her mother. She will at least give them the chance. "Will you stand by me? Say it was from fifteen years ago and I was just a kid who thought she was in love? That he's in the wrong for filming me without my knowledge?"

Her father looks at her as though she just asked him to make it snow in July.

"Of course not," her mother snaps. "You'll bring shame to us. We'll have to cut you off."

In all her life, being criticized and cut down and denigrated by her family—being cut off from her credit cards and shamed and punished—Germaine has never felt this bad. She feels completely empty, as though each of them has taken turns scooping her insides out and throwing them on the library floor. Perhaps she has always known this moment would come, or perhaps an outside force is taking control of her; but whatever it is, Germaine cannot believe the words that come out of her mouth next.

"Consider me cut off, then."

There is no reaction. They look at her, unblinking, not understanding.

Germaine stands and leaves the room. She doesn't pack. She doesn't kiss her dogs goodbye—her nephews will take good care of them, Germaine knows. They've been begging for a puppy.

The only one she'll miss is Marie.

Germaine walks calmly to the foyer and picks up her purse and coat, putting them on. After Paris, she researched how to put some money in an account of her own and open her own line of credit. She's been saving for a while; she'll check into a hotel for the next few nights and has enough to spend on toiletries, underwear, and a little food, at least. Her parents can cut her off and she won't be destitute.

She'll just have to start over, without the giant safety net of her family's money that comes with so many strings attached. Germaine has been caught in that net for far, far too long.

It's time to cut herself free—no matter the consequences.

PART III

NINETEEN

GERMAINE

2028

Yes, linen for the cabanas is fine." Germaine shifts her phone to the other ear as she works the Keurig in her hotel suite. "I mean, if they have—only Egyptian cotton? I don't know . . . you will? God, Susan, you're the best. Yes. Thanks."

She hangs up and stirs cream and sugar into the coffee, carefully wiping off a fleck that lands on her enormous diamond engagement ring.

Today is the day before Germaine's wedding. She never thought she'd say those words, but here she is, a glam fortysomething getting married. The location is an idyllic all-villa hotel in Santa Barbara with a view of the ocean, in a state close to Germaine's heart. It isn't one of her family's hotels. They're allowed to attend the wedding, but they're guests, not owners—not of the property, and not of Germaine.

Germaine is blissfully unaware of who owns this hotel, in fact, and it's a beautiful feeling. Although she does happen to be marrying a real estate mogul—but it's not Eddie Chou. He married someone else years ago, the sister of Germaine's sister-in-law, so he's still part of the family, sort of. He'll be attending the wedding, too, and will witness her walk down the aisle to meet Justin Yuen, one of the biggest stars of LA real estate.

But unlike Eddie and Germaine, Justin grew up poor as a kid in Koreatown. He knows the value of money and isn't entitled or holier than thou, like many people Germaine could name. He's also into meditation and self-care, and with him her life has become about seeking balance, not chasing after the next big thing. Even if Justin does live in a $20 million house in the Pacific Palisades and drives a Porsche Panamera as his "everyday" car.

Germaine loves him. Aside from the money, aside from the prestige, aside from everything.

She takes quick sips of her coffee, a bit of an indulgence after a very careful probiotic diet for skin health, checks her phone for any updates from Susan the wedding planner, and hurries down to the guest villas to make sure everything is set for the guests' arrival. It's so *Mamma Mia!*, truly. Sicily and Miranda are at the top of the list—Germaine hasn't seen them in forever. Not since they gleefully attended her first wedding-dress appointment last year. It's ridiculous. Everyone is so busy lately, running around with families and careers, but Germaine wanted some time to catch up. She asked the two of them to come this morning, before everyone else, so they could get a jump start on a weekend that will feel just like old times.

Or something close, at least. She's not sure she could redo the all-nighters the 3AM Girls pulled. Plus, she has a few things she wants to talk to them about.

As Germaine exits the villa on the outermost end of the seaside terrace, finding it imperfect but tolerable, she glimpses her first guest arriving with Louis Vuitton luggage in tow.

"*M&M!*" Germaine shrieks, running across the terrace. Miranda throws out her arms and closes the distance quickly, bubbling with laughter as Germaine scoops her up in her arms.

"Look at you!" Miranda exclaims. "Who is this blushing young bride?"

"Oh *stahp*." Germaine pulls a face and throws her hair exaggeratedly over her shoulder. She goes in for another hug. "Aw, Mir, I can't believe you made it. How was the flight? You look just fantastic."

Miranda looks relaxed and tanned, her face plump and freckled and her long hair in perpetual beachy waves. She runs a beach club in Cyprus these days, and Germaine purposely scheduled her wedding in September just for Miranda, when the season is ending and it's easier to get away. The summer seems like it treated her well—she's more boho than she used to be and still as gorgeous as ever.

"Long!" she says. "And I can never manage to get to sleep. But I wouldn't dare be jet-lagged for your wedding."

"We'll just have to see," Germaine teases. "It sounds like you could use some refreshment."

Miranda stretches her arms as they reach her villa, and she sets down her bag. "Time for shots!" she says. When Germaine raises her eyebrows, she takes off her oversize sunglasses and winks. "Just kidding. I'm mostly a wine spritzer girl these days."

Germaine laughs. "I'd have thought that running your own club would have made you wilder."

"Can you believe it's sort of tamed me?" Miranda says, tossing her sun hat on the bed and looking not a little bewildered. "It's hard work. You gotta sober up if you want to keep everyone else partying."

"You should embroider that on a pillow."

"I'd make millions." Miranda pulls back the shoulder of her sundress to reveal that she's already wearing her bathing suit underneath. "Look, I came prepared. I was hoping we could get out there so I can keep up my tan in the offseason."

"As soon as Sicily gets here," Germaine promises.

"Did you know topless sunbathing is legal in Cyprus? But I don't have the nerve for it. I really have changed." Miranda shakes her head.

"No doubt you've still got the body for it." Germaine winks.

"Well, that's a given."

Germaine smiles, hands on hips. "The days of the 3AM Girls are truly over, huh?"

Miranda laughs.

They stroll toward the pool, watching seagulls down on the beach dive for the surf. It's a beautiful day, sunny and warm but not sweltering, and Germaine feels a sense of calm that's eluded her for some time. Soon the three of them will be together again—in just a matter of minutes.

"Hey, you should play a show in Cyprus," Miranda says, leaning over the railing of the veranda.

After Germaine walked out of her parents' penthouse ten years ago, she floated around on her savings for a few weeks before finally taking a risk and DM-ing Bad Society on Instagram. She was able to get in touch with the lead singer, Charlie, who was kind enough to listen to Germaine's story. Germaine was flying blind; she didn't really know what she was asking of the band, but it felt good to say—out loud— how tight of a leash her parents had her on, how much Bad Society's invitation to sing onstage had meant to Germaine, and how she wanted to make an honest living now. And music was where she wanted to be.

Charlie didn't have any openings for jobs with Bad Society, but she promised to call around, and soon sent Germaine some personal contacts for music producers and clubs around New York.

Germaine gratefully accepted a job at the only place that would take her: a midsize Eurobeat club in Chelsea. The manager was a *Kidz Klub* fan, too, and took Germaine on as ticketing staff.

It was the most regular-person job Germaine had ever had, sitting in a tiny booth and taking phone calls and scanning wristbands as the crowds rolled in every night. But she felt like she had come home. The bass in her chest, the adrenaline in the air, the people who dressed as they pleased and danced without a care in the world—all of it made something come alive in Germaine. She became friendly with the talent. She was interested in the DJs' world, and they were interested in her, identifying her as someone they recognized, but they couldn't say from where. Germaine didn't mind. She didn't want the St. Germaine-Chang name to do any heavy lifting for her anymore.

She worked at the club every night, often seeing the same DJs come through. And finally, after a few weeks, one of them invited her to come up and spin records with him.

To her surprise and his, she killed it.

She was a natural at finding the beat and rhythm, just like she did when she used to dance, and the crowd loved her. She allowed herself to become totally absorbed by the music, pushing it to merge with the energy of the crowd.

The manager liked it, too, and allowed her to play one night a week. Germaine created a stage name—G-Force—and one night a week turned into two. After establishing herself as a house favorite at the Eurobeat club, it was a short leap to other hot spots in Manhattan, and in just under two years, Germaine found herself going viral. It was her stage presence, her gender, her age, the way she was oblivious to and in tune with the crowd at the same time—all of it worked together to skyrocket Germaine out of DJ obscurity.

Since then she's built up a career that's rendered her one of the most sought-after DJs in the world, booking for huge gigs in Ibiza, Abu Dhabi, Rio, Marrakesh, and many more. She's played for a royal wedding in Sweden, a superyacht regatta in Dubai, gigs in castles and palaces and mega-clubs. *Rolling Stone* did a think piece on her about reinventing yourself in your forties.

She's never been happier.

Cyprus is small fry in comparison. But Germaine promises she'll do it for Miranda. She'd love to.

"Excuse me?" a voice calls from behind them. "Someone told me I could find a bombshell bride out here?"

They turn to find Sicily strolling up, decked out in a caftan and shades. Germaine shrieks again, and they laugh and hug, even getting a little teary eyed.

"And hello to *you!*" Germaine says, looking behind Sicily—she's brought Liberty, her daughter, who is her total mini-me. At ten years old, Liberty is all smiles and down-home American sweetness, her blond hair a little mussed by the wind and her confidence still in preadolescence, certain that she can do anything.

"She wanted to see the hotel." Sicily smiles indulgently, and Germaine knows that the real reason is because Sicily wants to show her daughter off to her and Miranda. "She wanted to spend the weekend with her big brother, so Hugo and Jaime will pick her up soon—they're all going to their beach house, right, chickadee?"

"Noah promised to show me how to throw a football," Liberty adds.

"His summer hasn't ended yet?" Miranda asks.

"Not yet, but soon," Sicily says. "Northwestern starts late."

"I can't believe he's in college." Germaine shakes her head. "I remember when he was born! I remember when *you* were born, Liberty!"

"He's a good big brother, huh, Lib?" Sicily smooths back Liberty's hair as she nods. "They're all so sweet to her. One big, strange extended family these days."

"I'm going to be a singer soon," Liberty announces.

"Maybe," Sicily says, pulling the girl a little closer as the others laugh. "But no auditions until you're eighteen, remember?"

Liberty frowns. "You said sixteen last week."

"Did I? Now why would I say that?"

"Because I started with thirteen and that's where we landed."

Sicily shakes her head. "Oh, you are killing me, kiddo."

"Tell you what," Miranda says. "Once you're nineteen years old, you can come sing at my club, how's that?"

Liberty narrows her eyes. "Is it a *cool* club?"

Miranda leans down and narrows her eyes back. "The *coolest.*"

"Okay, enough of that," Sicily says. "I bet that poolside snack bar has some ice cream, huh? Why don't you go put it on my tab?"

"You're just trying to distract me." Liberty wrinkles her nose, and Sicily taps her finger on it.

"Yes, I am," Sicily says. "Now shoo!"

Liberty rolls her eyes but giggles and runs away.

"Oh, girl . . . you are not going to be able to restrain that one for long," Germaine says once she's out of earshot.

Sicily presses a hand to her chest and gives them both a look. "I'd like to send her away to an Amish farm for her teens. Reverse Rumspringa."

"You won't be able to. She's got that star power," Miranda says, shaking her head. "How's Squeak?"

"He's good. He spoils our little Liberty all the way from New York, but he has his hands full now."

Miranda nods knowingly. Squeak has both a new wife—an up-and-coming hip-hop singer—and new twins, whom they've named Sound and Furie. "It's a good thing you didn't marry him," she says. "He was a nice enough guy, but not the kind who's going to take care of you long term."

Germaine shoots Miranda a look, but Sicily sighs and nods in agreement, a little downcast.

"I know," she says, sounding rueful. "But I always wanted a big white wedding." Sicily seems to remember herself, recovers, and squeals, "Like *yours*, G! Can you believe you're getting *married*? You were always so against it!"

"I really can't. It's very surreal." Germaine shakes her head. "But love changes you! Or maybe I just got old and decided to settle."

The three of them laugh, the ocean wind blowing breezy and warm through their hair. It's a perfect day, Germaine thinks, and the perfect company.

But there are, in fact, some things Germaine needs to settle, things she doesn't want to take with her into her blissful new life with Justin, so she's going to set the record straight. She's going to come clean.

But who would Germaine be if she wasn't at least a little vengeful? She still has some tricks up her sleeve.

TWENTY

SICILY

2028

Sicily walks over to check on Liberty at the snack bar. As it turns out, Sicily has a bit of a secret herself: she's in love again. *Really* in love this time, and she knows it, because she's older and wiser— mostly older. Though the last tour took a toll on her joints and her voice, the opportunities are only picking up. Her power-ballad hits and lavish stage productions combined with her difficult family background have made her a gay icon and comeback character who's in hot demand the world over. The tide of public opinion seemed to turn a few years ago, with a slew of headlines like How the Media Let Sicily Bell Down and We Owe Pop Icons like Sicily Bell an Apology popping up far and wide.

But two kids and three decades of rigorous performing do a number on you, and Sicily has to be much more selective about what she does onstage—and off. Kent, her new man, works at a major talent agency; her own talent introduced them. He's a little older than she is, divorced, with college-age kids and an ex-wife who spends most of her money (and the alimony) on saving baby rhinos in Kenya.

But he's aging like fine wine—still youthful, with a megawatt smile and kind eyes. He takes a great interest in Noah and Liberty as well as Sicily's life offstage and who she really is behind the scenes. Working in talent himself, he views her work as any nine-to-five job rather than a superstar lifestyle and encourages Sicily to keep some separation and balance within her personal life. It's a perspective she really appreciates.

Germaine hasn't met him but was happy for Kent to join Sicily at the villa later that night and attend as her plus-one at the wedding. Sicily hasn't told Miranda much about him yet, though—just that she met someone and is seeing where it goes. Miranda's not very sympathetic these days. The last time Sicily told her she was dating, Miranda begged her to get her tubes tied. Rude!

"Why can't you just be happy for me?" she'd asked when they'd FaceTimed from across oceans last year. "Why is that always so hard?"

"I can't be the enabling one anymore," Miranda shot back. "I hate seeing you get hurt and set back by unplanned pregnancy. So, like, good for you—but I hope you're being careful."

"I am *forty-three*. You don't have to talk to me like I'm a teenager sneaking out at night."

"Well, you didn't learn your lesson after Noah, so . . ."

Sicily had not taken that well. "And is Liberty another 'lesson'? No. She's my daughter, Miranda. Butt out."

They'd moved past it, but their friendship had been a bit lukewarm since then. Sicily definitely didn't tell Miranda when her last relationship ended, and she isn't in a rush to reveal her new love now.

Had she made some mistakes in her relationships? Sure. But who hadn't? And Noah and Liberty might have been unexpected surprises, but now they were the two people in her life who brought her the most joy. There are a lot of things that Sicily wishes she'd done differently, but for the most part she doesn't have regrets. She'd like to see Miranda say the same.

"You're not cleaning me out, are you, chickadee?" Sicily says, teasing Liberty but making sure that her daughter has not taken more than one ice-cream bar.

"I'm only getting started," Liberty says.

～

They join Miranda and Germaine at one of the large glass tables with rattan chairs and thick navy-blue cushions, enjoying the shade provided by billowing canopies fastened to a pergola. Liberty has retrieved her Hello Kitty wheelie bag from the luggage cart and is chattering happily about Hugo and Jaime.

"Why do you call him 'Hugs'?" Miranda asks.

Liberty sighs like it's so obvious. "Because that's who he *is*, Miranda. He's Poppa Hugs."

Sicily smiles. "That's what she's called him since she was young, and we thought it was too cute. Hugo loves it too."

"So Hugo is what—just, like, around all the time? Why?"

Sicily shifts in her seat. "He's a good man, Miranda. It's been a halfway-decent experience, actually, coparenting with him and Jaime, and they're kind of built-in babysitters when I'm on tour."

"That's really nice to hear, Sicily," Germaine says. She's lacing her fingers together and looking at her thumbs. "I'm glad you were able to patch things up with him."

But Miranda makes a face, glancing suspiciously at Germaine and then at Liberty. "You know he's not your poppa, though, right? Your dad is the dancer, not the singer."

Liberty looks confused. "So? I can have two."

Sicily, sensing tension, shoots Miranda a look. Germaine throws a cushion at her. "Play nice," she says.

Miranda opens her mouth to say something else, but just then Germaine looks over Sicily's shoulder and waves. "Hugo! Jaime!"

"Hugs!" Liberty says, running over and throwing her arms around them both.

"Hey," Sicily says. "Thanks so much for taking her."

"It'll be nice hot weather for the beach house," Jaime says. "You picked a good weekend, Germaine!"

Germaine beams and Sicily relaxes. It's nice that they can all be civil—she's worked hard to repair her relationship with Hugo and Jaime for the sake of the kids, and she can respect the fact that they've done the same. Even if Miranda doesn't. It's not the arrangement Sicily would have picked for herself, but they work well together.

"You're going to have quite the superstar when this one grows up," Germaine says, nodding at Liberty.

"I think Sicily is already bracing herself," Hugo says with a laugh.

"She'll bring the crowds," Jaime agrees. "Whatever she does. Maybe she'll be a painter or join the circus instead?" she says half-hopefully, casting an expectant glance at the girl. But Liberty is already dragging her suitcase toward the exit.

"Let's *go*!" she says.

"Okay, hold up!" Sicily crouches down, not without some difficulty. "Come give Momma a kiss. You be good, okay? You listen to Hugs and Jaime, and tell Noah I'll see him after the weekend."

Liberty runs over and gives her a loud smack on the cheek. "Okay, okay." She points a finger at Miranda. "I won't forget," she says.

Miranda lifts her mojito in a toast. "Nineteenth birthday or bust."

"Do I even want to know?" Hugo says.

"No, Hugo." Miranda manages to keep the edge out of her voice. "You do not."

Sicily waves goodbye to the three of them, heart full. But she's struck by the oddly serious look on Germaine's face when she returns to her seat.

"Everything okay?" Sicily asks, settling back with her Moscato.

"Your family is lovely, Sicily," Germaine starts. "You've all managed to create a little community together despite—everything."

"Thanks," Sicily says uncertainly. She glances at Miranda, who seems just as in the dark.

"And . . . I've been wanting to tell you about something related to that."

"Okay," Sicily says slowly. She's beginning to feel a little uneasy, the wine making her mouth dry.

"Getting engaged to Justin has made me reflect on a lot of things. I want to be more open; I want to tie up some loose ends I've left trailing around and make a fresh start tomorrow. Sicily, when you came dress shopping with us, I was sorry to hear how long it had been since you talked to Kendra."

Sicily snorts, hoping Germaine doesn't intend to have some come-to-Jesus moment about forgiveness. "Don't be sorry. What does she have to do with any of this?"

"Well." Germaine wraps her hands around her glass. "It confirmed for me that I finally have to set the record straight. A long time ago—I think it was 2008. I booked No Exit for one of my parents' hotel openings in Singapore because . . . I wanted to sabotage his career. I don't know; it was stupid. I was angry at how much better the press was treating him than you."

"Very on brand, G," Miranda says. "So far so good. I would've helped you with the sabotage if you'd let me in on it."

"Miranda, come on," Sicily snaps. She's feeling irritated, confused. "Germaine, whatever it is, I don't care, okay? I don't know if I want to hear it."

"Sicily, I'm sorry." Germaine is speaking very calmly, but she looks nervous. "But the night didn't go as planned. He came up to thank me for helping him get the gig, and we were drinking and talking—and he seemed so heartbroken about not being able to see Noah . . ." She shakes her head. "I gave him the ammunition for the court case. It was my fault that he went after you the way he did."

Sicily closes her eyes, opens them again. This doesn't make any sense. "Germaine, no. Kendra got with one of his bandmates. She must have been acting as a direct pipeline for every little sordid detail he needed."

"Maybe. I don't know," Germaine says. "But I was the one who told him about the adoption joke. I gave him way too many details about our 3AM Girl stuff, and that's how he decided to go with the 'toxic family environment' angle. That was me."

Germaine's words sift through Sicily's ears very slowly. The moment is stretching long and thin between them, but Germaine does not break Sicily's gaze.

Miranda is the one to snap the silence in half, sucking air through her teeth. "Yikes."

"Why?" Sicily lets the syllable fall, a single heavy question.

"I don't know." Germaine seems to resume breathing. She talks quickly now. "It just came out. I was at an awful place in my life, depressed, jealous—I mean, I wouldn't have admitted that to myself, but when Hugo started talking about how he never got to see Noah and you had him all the time, it all reared its head. You and Miranda were both having such success. What was I doing with my life? Jack shit. I was bitter, and it was ugly."

"I wasn't successful," Miranda says flatly. "I was sleeping with the director to keep my role."

"What?" Germaine gasps, stricken.

"Tyler destroyed my reputation. And then I got drinking again, and—"

"SHUT UP about Tyler!" Sicily shouts, startling both of them. The ringing in her ears has reached a fever pitch. "You sold me out, Germaine? You got my son taken away?"

"Sicily," Germaine says. "I never meant for that to happen. I was sick about it. I wanted to tell you—I wanted to help—"

"Then you *should* have helped!" Sicily shoots back. She's yelling now, her volume grating against the tranquil luxury of the resort. But she doesn't care. "All those years. You and your billions, traipsing around the world, while I was a prisoner in my own home. Ripped away from my *child*, forced to be my family's puppet—"

"I know. You're right. Sicily—" Germaine tries.

But Sicily puts up her hands and stands, hurrying away from them. She flees back to her villa and shuts the door behind her, sliding down to the floor and leaning against it. She's been so happy lately, but the tears come easily now.

The familiar mistrust of the world hits her at full force again.

TWENTY-ONE

MIRANDA

2028

Well, that went well. They haven't spent time together in over a year, and already Sicily is upset, Germaine has gone from hero to zero, and the ghosts of Baby Daddies Past are haunting the festivities.

Miranda sighs as she walks back across the veranda to her villa, by herself. Germaine seemed to need a moment alone after Sicily ran off.

She admires the natural wood and wide windows of her lodgings that look out over the ocean; at least these suites are gorgeous. Every villa has a king-size bed and fresh gardenias on the tables. Germaine has even sent a bottle of complimentary champagne to each room.

Miranda looks around, taking note of the red fire-exit sign, the English, the prices on the room-service menu in American dollars. It feels strange to be back in the US and around people who Knew Her Then: she's reinvented herself in Europe. And even though Germaine has revealed an ugly side of herself, Miranda owes all this success to her. Five years ago, Germaine used her music-industry connections to get Miranda a job at a beachside club in Mykonos, and Miranda decided that she would absorb everything she could. She worked her ass off to learn how to manage employees, how to plan events, how to deal with customers and rentals and contracts. Finally, she invested everything she had—everything she had *left*, to be accurate—into a fixer-upper property in Cyprus that she turned into her own beach club.

She's extremely proud of it. Miranda always used to roll her eyes when people would say something was their "baby," but it really does feel that way; she put a lot of labor in, and now she gets to nurture it and watch it grow. She named it, simply, Miranda's, going for Old Hollywood *Casablanca* vibes mixed with contemporary Euro-Greco flair. It's hip but not too crazy busy, TikTok chic and understated, and it's become a destination for in-the-know travelers around the world. It's the cosmopolitan, hard-won success that she never knew she needed.

There's only one problem: Miranda is lonely.

She has great friends at the club, top-notch employees, fantastic patrons—but no one she can truly call a partner. She's happy that Germaine has at last let her guard down enough to get married. Miranda didn't know—but probably should have, she reflects guiltily—how burned Germaine had been by a shitty relationship in her teens that went all revenge porn on her. And aside from this afternoon's unfortunate revelation, Sicily seems happy and has hinted at being in a grown-up relationship with someone who's more than a fling. Miranda will believe it when she sees it, but she's trying to be less judgmental these days.

She won't be alone when she goes back to Cyprus. But now that she's over forty, is it too late for love?

She eyes the champagne but goes for the mineral water in the mini fridge instead, deciding to pace her celebrating. Like she told Germaine, running the club has been a surprising step toward sobering up. She doesn't want to do *anything* that could jeopardize it.

Maybe she's too used to her independence now. In the past, relationships with men just made her life more complicated, leaving her feeling used and discarded; Miranda is in no rush to experience that again. She's much pickier these days, more cautious. She's got a good handle on her dignity and worth now, and refuses to be hurt again.

She sits near the window, idly watching other guests arrive and make their way along the veranda to their villas. She recognizes Giles and his wife in tow and ducks away from the glass—she definitely wants to steer clear of Germaine's snooty family. Maybe it would be a good idea to check in on Sicily and make sure she's okay.

The villas have a back door, and Miranda slips out of it, wandering through the lush hotel gardens that act as a courtyard behind all the suites, and enjoying the break in the heat as evening comes on. The foliage reminds her of Cyprus, and she suddenly feels an odd homesickness, split equally between her new life and the life she once built here.

She finds Sicily's villa and knocks on the wooden door.

Sicily opens it carefully, peeking around and looking relieved to find Miranda standing there.

"Hey," she says.

"Hey. You doing okay?"

Sicily nods. She looks red eyed, like she's been crying, but better in general. "Yeah. It's stupid anyway—ancient history."

"Tell someone in Cyprus that ancient history isn't important and they'll slap you," Miranda says. "Our whole tourism industry is built on it."

Sicily laughs. "Yeah, I guess. I'm working through it. It's not as though it really changes anything now, and . . . I guess I *am* glad she told me. But"—tears swim in her eyes again—"I still don't understand why she would do that to me."

"It was wrong of her," Miranda agrees. "It wasn't the 3AM era, but we were all still pretty stupid back then."

Sicily smiles sadly. "Yeah. Miranda, I'm sorry I brushed past the thing you said. That was *not* stupid of you. That's horrible—coerced into sleeping with your director? What the hell was that all about?"

Miranda shrugs, shifts her weight. "Show business, I guess."

"Can I do anything? Get him fired? I've got money to throw around now," Sicily says, and Miranda smiles at the fierceness in her expression.

"Nah," Miranda says. "I've made my peace with it, and he's probably retired. Just a sad old man with a milquetoast career and no legacy to speak of. The best revenge is living well."

Sicily nods, sets her jaw, and then rushes forward to give Miranda a hug.

"Hey." Miranda laughs, muffled against her shoulder. "I'm okay. It's all right."

When Sicily steps back, she has a small smile on her face. "Um . . ." She casts a glance behind her. "Kent is here, actually. Would you want to meet him?"

Miranda hesitates, but she is trying to be less judgmental. "Of course I would, Sis."

She can tell she's made Sicily happy. Sicily opens the door wider and welcomes Miranda in, seeming even a little giddy. "Come on in, then! Kent," she calls. "Come meet Miranda!"

An older man in shorts and a linen button-up emerges from the kitchenette, a pair of aviators stuck in his shirt pocket. He's been around the block but is nice-looking enough.

Except something in Miranda's gut twists when she sees him. He looks familiar, in a bad way—but Miranda can't for the life of her understand why.

"Hi, Kent," she says, pushing the feeling aside. It's her knee-jerk instinct flaring up again, suspicious of any man Sicily gets involved with. "It's nice to meet you."

"Hi there, Miranda," Kent says, shaking her hand.

Miranda reaches forward, watching her hand move as if underwater. At the sound of his voice, she instantly remembers him.

The only ship that's sailing for her now are those Arab yachts where she's a whore for hire . . . honestly, she should just jump to porn now and stop wasting everyone's time. Including her own.

Miranda could never forget that voice. It's him, the man in Sam's office from all those years ago who degraded her minutes before she got her DUI.

As she grasps his hand, she's flooded with a wave of nausea.

Kent smiles, but the warmth does not meet his eyes. He knows her, too. "Miranda," he says carefully. "It's good to see you."

"Kent," is all she says. Sicily hasn't noticed the recognition that's passed between them, but Miranda's mind is racing. Is he going to ruin the weekend by muttering snide things about her to the other guests? Will he drive a wedge between her and Sicily?

Sicily chatters on about the weekend, and Miranda responds as she's able, but her stomach is churning. She should have never come back to California—the waters here are way too muddy for her. And she feels herself starting to sink.

TWENTY-TWO

GERMAINE

2028

Germaine yanks her hand away from her mouth and balls it into a fist when she realizes she's chewing on her nails again. Not this weekend. She is going to keep it together. If she can slip away, she'll go and see how Sicily is doing. But now she has to get the most unpleasant task over with—greeting her family.

She's allowed them to come to the wedding and even designated a small amount of time tonight so they could say hello in the hotel bar, because she's trying to be the bigger person. She really is. At arm's length, though.

Germaine adjusts her martini on the high-top before her as though it will serve as a protective barrier.

But, luckily, the first person to come into the bar is Justin, not her parents. She relaxes at the sight of him—his quiet confidence and easy smile when he sees her. He's incredibly handsome in a starched cotton shirt and twill chinos, a casual dark brown; his black hair, thin at the back, is just beginning to take on a salt-and-pepper tinge. But he's full of energy and aging well.

"Hey," he says, slipping an arm around her waist and kissing her cheek. "You okay? You ready for this?"

"It's been a long day already. But of course." Germaine shakes her head like it's nothing. But Justin squeezes her hand—he knows this is hard on her.

Germaine shifts her weight to both feet, standing up straighter as she sees her father approach, her mother on his arm, expressions just as disdainful as Germaine expected. They join Germaine and Justin at the table and nod a greeting.

"Hi," Germaine says. "Thanks for coming."

"We wouldn't miss it," Terence says, trying to be civil.

"It's good to see you both." Justin smiles wide, shaking Terence's hand and reaching out for a hug from Céline, but she ignores him. So he pats her on the shoulder instead and tries to play it off like he was signaling a waiter.

At least this isn't the first time he's meeting her family. Germaine had the foresight to plan a get-together several months ago, after their engagement, so all that tension would be out of the way before the wedding. Justin had handled it all beautifully—the gibes about Germaine's career as a DJ (not a real job), the disregard for Justin's work (tacky), the *many* not-so-subtle digs about the childhood he spent in the back of his parents' dry-cleaning business in Buena Park while Germaine had been riding horses in Switzerland.

But he bore it all with grace, not taking her parents' bait *or* lying down as their punching bag, but turning each jab around into a self-deprecating joke about how he has a knack for getting any stain out of his Dolce & Gabbana suit coats.

It made Germaine even more excited to marry him.

"Looks like some of your old Hollywood friends are here," Céline says, casting a glance at a few of the other guests who have gathered over at the bar, cutting right to the chase. "We thought we smelled hair spray and Kohl's perfume."

"It's going to be a good crowd," Justin says, agreeing as though she's said something insightful. "We were going to keep the guest list small, but we thought, hey—the more the merrier!"

"Over three hundred." Germaine nods, hoping the great expense of that size is not lost on her parents.

Greg arrives with his new, much younger wife, Imogen, who makes a face as they reach the table.

"Is this the kind of place where they only serve tiki drinks?" she asks. "They better have Aperol spritz."

"Yes, it's a regular bar, Imogen," Germaine says with exaggerated politeness. Imogen is just as snooty as Aalia, Greg's ex-wife. "So I'm sure they can make whatever you want. It's an open bar tonight, so go wild."

"Obviously it's open," Greg says. "What you should've done is pay the tab for the whole weekend, like I did for my weddings. It's just a nice courtesy, you know, for the guests. But whatever."

"Oh, we did," Justin says. "Don't worry. Meals and board, too—didn't we mention? This is an all-expenses-paid experience for the special guests staying in the villas. We didn't want anyone to have to worry about budgeting."

Like Greg would ever need to worry about budgeting, but Germaine loves Justin for saying it. Because of his background, he's much more comfortable talking openly about money than anyone in Germaine's family—she's certainly never heard her parents or brothers use the word "budget." She finds it refreshing.

"Oh." Greg seems to be trying to figure out whether he should be offended. "Well—good."

"You know, Chloé was disappointed to be left out of the wedding party," Germaine's mother says in a low voice, speaking of one of her cousins. "I can't believe you chose those Midwest hicks over your own family."

"Well, Chloé called me 'pancake tits' the last time I saw her—twenty years ago—and Miranda and Sicily are my best friends," Germaine says. "So, yes, it was a difficult decision. She was a close fourteenth choice."

Justin laughs, and so does Greg. "Yeah, Chloé sucks," he snorts.

But their father and mother look unimpressed. "I just hope you're ready to handle their Girls Gone Wild antics tomorrow," Terence says.

"I still don't understand why you didn't book at our Casa Castillo," Céline says, not for the first—or, Germaine suspects, the last—time since the date was announced. "It's only down the road from here."

Germaine has prepared herself for all their snide comments and disdain. Now she gets to sling one back. "Well, Casa Castillo didn't have the option of private villas. We really wanted to give our guests a premium experience, and the Cove had the best options for everyone arriving tonight."

"Villas can be gimmicky," her father mutters into his drink, but everyone here knows that these ones are not.

"They look like actual *houses*, not just guest suites," Imogen says, and Germaine is surprised and vindicated to see how impressed she looks. "And the gardens behind? It's all very European. Doesn't feel like California at all."

Germaine takes a sip of her martini to hide her great pleasure as Giles and his wife, Elizabeth, arrive, followed by Elizabeth's sister Corrine and her husband, none other than Eddie Chou. Germaine stands up even straighter and greets them warmly, drawing herself up to the height they all teased her for.

"Giles, Elizabeth, hello!" she says. "And Eddie, how are you? This must be Corrine. Oh, you look even more beautiful than your photos."

"I've paid enough for implants to make sure she does!" Eddie says with an obnoxious laugh, mismatching the demure—and slightly uncomfortable—chuckles around the table. Elizabeth glares at him, but Corrine waves it off.

"So who's this hotshot who thinks he's good enough for you?" Eddie asks, putting his hands in his pockets and sizing Justin up.

There's no comparison. Eddie, who's grown a beer belly in the passing years and is somehow more arrogant than ever, doesn't hold a candle to Justin. Germaine can't help feeling proud—smug, even?—about introducing him.

"Eddie," Justin says coolly, nodding rather than extending his hand. He knows what Eddie put Germaine through, and had given Germaine the tempting offer of tanking Eddie's real estate prospects. But she declined—she has a plan of her own.

She holds back a smile, knowing Eddie senses just a hint of contempt. The man Germaine is marrying is kind, supportive, generous, and adoring, everything Eddie could never be. Taller and more handsome, with better hair. Oh, and more successful.

"Thank you for having us," Corrine cuts in with what seems to be an apologetic smile. "You're very generous to put us up in the villas tonight."

"I wouldn't have it otherwise." Germaine smiles. "You're an extension of the family."

When the time is just right, Germaine is going to tell Corrine about the sex tape. She'll be smiling and earnest, saying she knows Eddie must have told her all about it, and how it ruined Germaine's life for a long time. But, she'll say with great self-possession, she's healed from it and used the experience to become a stronger person, not the vulnerable teenage girl who thought she was in love.

The truth bomb will explode in Eddie's face, sending killer shrapnel flying into his relationship with Corrine. It can't be a great relationship anyway, Germaine is sure.

She spins the stem of her martini glass and beams up at Justin as he tells the story of a property deal in Barcelona gone awry. That's not the only revenge Germaine has planned this weekend. She's invited two other guys who both need to get their just deserts. One is not really *invited*, per se, but merely hired as a driver to shuttle guests to and from the airport. His name is Zane, and it's time for him to get some comeuppance for how he dumped Miranda when she was in rehab. Germaine was shocked to stumble across his name when she was reviewing limo companies with Susan and knew she had to request him specially. She wants him to see Miranda flourishing and successful, doing her own thing on her own terms. It was him who turned out to be a nobody, while Miranda got her act together in every way.

The other guy is a guest, though only for tomorrow—Tyler X is not villa worthy. In fact, Germaine has invited the entire *Kidz Klub* cast. And while most of them still have modest careers as minor celebrities, influencers, or podcast hosts, Tyler is clinging to the entertainment industry by the skin of his teeth, if you count working as an emcee at a casino in the Ozarks. He can watch Miranda walk down the aisle in a cloud of sea green, looking serene and tanned, and know that he was never, ever better than she was.

And Germaine's parents: let's not forget them. Germaine has finally summited to the point in her life where she doesn't crave their approval. Let them say what they will about the hotel and wedding; they've been locked out of every aspect of the planning. Germaine took no money from them, no advice. When she went dress shopping, it was with Sicily, Miranda, and Justin's mom—in Paris! If her own parents are going to spend the entire time looking annoyed anyway, why try to please them?

As the cocktail party winds down and the guests begin to retreat to their villas, Germaine bids good night to her family and heads with Justin toward their suite.

She doesn't know why she casts one glance backward at the end of the veranda, watching them retreat. Why should she wish they could be happy for her? She has worked hard to overcome this feeling she's had all her life—the desire, the need for their love. She's punishing them by making them mere guests at her wedding, so why is she the one who feels pain?

Whatever the reason, as Germaine looks back, she catches her mother doing the same.

TWENTY-THREE

SICILY

2028

Sicily has slept well in the lush villa bed, draped in linens with a thread count in the thousands and cooled by the sea breeze coming through an open window. She and Kent woke to blue skies and flowers in full bloom in the courtyard gardens.

Sicily completes the morning meditation that has become routine for her and prepares for a run along the hotel's grounds.

"Do you want to come?" she asks Kent. They're trying to make a habit of being active together.

"Sorry." He rubs his face. "Still waking up. I'll join you in a bit if I manage not to be a slowpoke."

She nods and kisses him on the cheek, trying to brush it off as she puts on her shoes. Maybe it was too early in their relationship to bring him to a major event like this; he seemed strangely quiet last night after Miranda dropped by.

"I forgot you were on *Kidz Klub*," Kent had said. "It was so long ago."

It felt like a different life, she had agreed, and it was true. These days she just tries to remember the fun of it, especially when she tells

Liberty stories about the unhinged antics back then of Auntie Germaine and Auntie Miranda.

Remembering those days makes it feel all the more important to put the Hugo/Germaine awkwardness behind her and sort out her feelings later. It was right of Germaine to tell her the truth. Despite all the grief Sicily suffered as a consequence of those actions, if she's honest with herself, she knows Germaine never intended to hurt her. And they're good now—Sicily and Hugo and Noah—they've made their peace with the past. Hearing the truth doesn't really change anything now.

Except for one thing.

Just before heading out the door, Sicily scrolls through her contacts and unblocks Kendra's number.

Hey, Sicily texts. Are you free next week? Do you think we could talk?

Then she zips her phone in her pocket and walks into the sunshine.

Sicily is determined to have a great time today, which is why she's following her endorphin-boosting routine even though it makes her knees ache. The only thing the Cove doesn't have is a gym—or, at least, one that she can locate on its enormous property—otherwise she'd opt for an elliptical trainer. The best kind of exercise is low impact.

Sicily laughs to herself as she heads through the gardens and makes her way to a path along the beach. She's lived a high-impact life since childhood, in every sense, and bears the physical and psychic scars to prove it. Still, this is a new chapter for her: her forties. She can still sing; she can still slink sensually around a stage and hear audiences roaring along to her lyrics. In fact, she performed at the Grammys this year— one of the select few artists who's been invited to appear in their teens, twenties, thirties, and forties. Sicily fully intends to be performing there in her fifties and sixties, too, living proof that there's a way to mature as an artist—and a woman—in this industry.

The boardwalk path stretches all across the Cove's beachfront property, and by the time Sicily turns for the stairs back up the bluff, she's worked up quite a sweat and is feeling much better. She loops back up around the front of the hotel for a cool-down; she still has about an hour before she and Miranda are due in Germaine's suite for hair and makeup.

And . . . they'll be civil. They'll cross that bridge when they come to it.

There's an enormous stone fountain in the center of the grand, circular hotel drive and several off to the sides, in the paths, overgrown with greenery, that lead back to the villas and gardens. She leans against one of the fountains to stretch her quads and watches with interest as other guests begin to arrive for the prewedding fete. There are people from the most elite tax brackets—guests whom Sicily is sure are multimillionaires, if not billionaires; high-flying colleagues of Justin she recognizes from the covers of *Architectural Digest*; New York–socialite heiresses who used to appear in all Germaine's Insta posts.

But one limo holds a rowdier crowd that's slightly out of place among the refined others. Sicily recognizes a group of Blast Off! Network alum marveling at the surroundings and chattering excitedly. She takes a step back and peers across the drive, curious to see who's all here. It's not like she thinks she's better than the old cast, but they truly feel like her high school classmates—people who knew Sicily when she was very different. It's an odd sort of intimacy, and she'd like to save the reunions for when she's had a bit of liquid courage.

Sicily looks closer. There's something familiar about the driver, but of course she couldn't know him. Her interest is cut short when she sees one final passenger climb from the limo and squint in the bright sunlight.

Tyler X.

Sweat immediately coats Sicily's already-damp palms, and her heart begins to pound sickeningly. She imagines—though of course it's impossible—that she can smell him from here, the abundance of Axe body spray, the cinnamon gum he always chewed, smacking right in her ear as he coaxed her backstage. *Come on, you know you want to.*

She hadn't been at all sure she wanted to. And she had told him so, but he kept going; he said she better get used to the attention as a pretty girl in show business. He said she should feel lucky that her first time could be with a great guy like him.

Sicily realized it was a joke to Tyler the second it was over. Her heart sank at the cocky grin on his face and the way he turned away from her immediately, losing interest and flirting with the other girls at rehearsal the very next day.

She worked up the nerve to ask him about it later on, the question that burrowed in her head: *Why? Why? Why?* Sicily hates herself for acting so casual, trying again to flirt with him, laughing along like she was in on the joke.

He wanted to have sex with every girl in the cast, he said. It was a game to him.

Sicily was just another notch in his belt.

Sicily retreats farther back on the path as Tyler heads toward the main entrance. She's managed to avoid him all these years—almost thirty years, in fact. But now he's here, and she feels just like a scared little kid again who doesn't know what to do.

She doubles back on her route and hurries to Miranda's villa.

TWENTY-FOUR

MIRANDA

2028

He's *what?*" Miranda hollers.

"Yeah, here. In the hotel. With the rest of the *Kidz Klub* people," Sicily says, pacing as Miranda tries to make sense of the news. She had been trying to enjoy a nice green smoothie courtesy of the villa kitchen's astonishingly well-stocked appliance inventory when Sicily burst through the door. For a moment, Miranda was sure that Kent had said something to her. But the real news was even more unsettling.

"But how could he be here?" she says. "As a *guest*? Germaine knows he humiliated me on national television. And there's no way those two are friends, unless he was part of her secret little rendezvous in Singapore, too. Hey, are you okay?"

Sicily has stopped pacing and is wrapping her arms around herself, looking like she's about to cry.

"I don't know. Yes. I'm fine."

"Wait—Sis. Why are *you* so upset about Tyler?"

Sicily puts up her hands and shakes her head. "I just—don't like him. It's something stupid. From when we were kids."

"When we were kids . . ." Miranda shakes her head. "Was he mean to you? I don't remember seeing . . ."

"No." Sicily squeezes her eyes shut. "He was—my first."

"Your—?" Miranda says. "Oh. *Oh.* Seriously? How did this never come up? Was he *that* bad?"

Sicily sighs. "He was . . . fine, it's just. I don't think I was really ready at the time."

"Sicily." Miranda suddenly forgets any bone she has to pick with Tyler, all her focus zeroing in on Sicily. She needs to ask, but it's already plainly written on her friend's face. "Was it consensual?"

Sicily groans. "Yes, I mean I think so—I didn't say no, I think I said okay, I think I sort of wanted it to happen, but I don't know. It felt awful afterward."

"Hey, hey." She reaches out carefully to touch Sicily's shoulder. "If it's not a hell yes, it's a no. He assaulted you. Whatever word you want to use, it's not okay. And I'll fucking kill him."

Sicily half laughs, then begins to cry. Miranda pulls her into her arms. Sicily laughs again, then hiccups into Miranda's shoulder. "That wouldn't be a very good start to a wedding."

"Who gives a shit?" Miranda murmurs. "Aw, Sis. Why didn't you tell us? You keep way too much bottled up all the time. We're your best friends, for god's sake."

"I was so embarrassed," Sicily says, muffled, into Miranda's shoulder. "He said he wanted to do it with all the girls."

"Fucking *hell!* Sorry," Miranda says when she realizes she's shouted in Sicily's ear. "That's what he was doing during goddamn *Bennington Bookshop*. I was next on his list—he was just working his way through the cast."

"He's a scumbag." Sicily pulls back and wipes her nose on her sleeve. Then she takes a big breath.

"Are you glad to have that off your chest?" Miranda asks.

Sicily nods. She looks better.

"Good," Miranda says. "Because we have to confront Germaine about this. We don't have to tell her anything you don't want to—but I need to know why there's a serial misogynist running around her wedding."

"I didn't know she was inviting everyone from *Kidz Klub*," Sicily says. "Even the limo driver looked like an older version of your guy, Miranda."

"What? Zane?"

"Yeah." Sicily shrugs. "I don't see how it could be him, but who knows anymore."

Miranda feels an odd tug somewhere inside her. She pauses, looking at her half-finished green smoothie and the bridesmaid getting-ready outfit she laid out the night before.

Then she marches out the door.

"Where are you going?" Sicily calls, jogging after her.

Miranda heads to the front of the hotel and peeks around the fountain. Sure enough, there are three limos parked on the drive and chauffeurs for each conferring by the front door. One checks his watch and heads in their direction toward the farthest car, getting ready for the next pickup run.

It's Zane.

He's older and his face is drawn, his head bald beneath the driver's cap by choice or by nature, but it's him. He turns to get into the limo, and Miranda swears, hurrying Sicily back down the path so they won't be seen.

"What the hell?" she whispers. Those are all cars Germaine booked. She would have checked the company's references with her wedding planner, run security checks on all the drivers. There's no way she invited Tyler or booked Zane by accident. "What kind of sick game is she playing?"

She and Sicily head back toward the villas but pause where the path forks.

"What are you going to do?" Sicily asks Miranda, who is clearly heading for the path of Germaine's suite.

"I'm going to go demand an explanation, and you're coming!" Miranda says.

"I don't know." Sicily sighs. "I still need to shower. I'm all gross. Maybe it's best to just take a breather before it's time to get ready . . ."

"No." Miranda grabs Sicily by the hand. "Absolutely not. This is weird and we are addressing it. *Now.*"

She ignores Sicily's protests and drags the both of them to Germaine's villa on the other side of the pool. Miranda shoulders past Susan the wedding coordinator and pulls right up to Germaine, who's sitting in front of the mirror with a stylist orbiting around her and a gleeful, then surprised, then bewildered, look on her face as she registers Miranda's furious expression and Sicily's sweaty clothes and puffy eyes.

"Um. Good morning—" Germaine starts.

"We need to talk, G," Miranda says.

"I'm just—" Germaine is completely caught off guard. She looks at the stylist. "Marie, can you maybe . . . give us a minute?"

"Yeah, give us just a minute, Marie," Miranda echoes, and then shepherds the woman out of the bedroom and closes the door.

"So!" Germaine says, looking happy but baffled. Her hair is lopsided and half-curled. "I didn't expect you until eleven o'clock, but—"

"Why is Tyler X here?" Sicily cuts in, and Miranda feels a fierce spark of pride in her for being the first to speak up.

"And Zane?" Miranda adds.

Germaine opens and closes her mouth with deer-in-the-headlights eyes. "Those two were supposed to be . . . sort of a surprise, I guess?" she says with a sheepish smile.

"What the hell kind of surprise is that meant to be?" Miranda snaps. "I'm not prepared to see Zane. And you know how badly Tyler's hurt me—and it turns out, he's hurt Sicily even worse."

"Why are you pulling these stunts, G?" Sicily says. "This was supposed to be a fun reunion weekend for us, not to mention the happiest day of your life."

"Okay, okay," Germaine says. "Listen. I know how these guys have hurt you, and that's the point! I wanted to make them see you triumphant and thriving and gorgeous. You don't even have to talk to them if you don't want to, but I also thought . . . if you wanted any opportunity to air grievances, you could. This could be a fresh start for *all* of us."

"I don't think I even want Tyler to see me." Sicily shakes her head.

Germaine looks at a loss. "But these are guys who thought they were so much better than us, and they're not! Is it so bad I wanted them to face the people they'd hurt?"

But Miranda's heard enough. "Scores can never be settled, G! Nothing can be settled. We just have to accept who we were, the things we did, and the things that happened to us." She shakes her head; something about what Germaine is saying sounds very tired— like something Miranda has heard before. "It's the only way we can move on. Forgive ourselves, forgive the world, whatever. Otherwise we'll be bitter and stuck in the past. I don't want to be stuck the way I used to be—I want to be free from it all. You can't 'walk back the crash,'" she mutters at the end, realizing that it's *Crashed and Burned* she's being reminded of.

Germaine looks close to tears, but unfortunately, Miranda is on a roll and can't stop. "I want to move on from Zane, from my mistakes, from the things people said about me, like Kent—"

"What *about* Kent?" Sicily says. "What went on between you two? You've both been weird since you met last night."

Miranda closes her eyes. "Nothing. I shouldn't have brought—"

"No, what?" Sicily demands. "Did he hurt you, too? Did you sleep together? My mind is jumping to the worst possible places, Miranda."

"He called me a whore, okay?" Miranda doesn't mean to sound as harsh as she does. "He worked at my agent's office over a decade ago, and I overheard him saying that I should just go into porn and stop wasting everyone's time."

"Shit." Sicily rubs her hands over her face.

"Sorry," Miranda says. "I didn't want to tell you like this."

"Well, what are we supposed to do now?" Sicily wails.

The three look at each other, wild eyed. Why are they tormenting themselves? Why does all of this matter, and why does it still hurt so much?

When are they going to grow up?

TWENTY-FIVE

GERMAINE

2028

Germaine peers out the window of the hotel's vestibule. Out on the veranda, everything looks beautiful—the arbor of roses, the view of the ocean, the sachets of lavender tied to the back of every polished cane chair that bloom a light perfume over the guests as they find their seats. She is still a stickler for detail, even if she's no longer in the business of annoying hotel staff and acting the picky princess.

Exactly seventy-two minutes before this, Susan and Marie—the intrepid Marie, whom Germaine had poached from her parents the moment she'd made enough money back to pay the stylist a handsome salary—strong-armed their way into the room to find the three women crying and arguing, and demanded that they get their act together this instant lest this entire event run off track.

So Germaine, Miranda, and Sicily put their feelings aside as Marie and her army of stylists swept in with the rest of the bridal party and got to work. Marie distributed cold compresses for their puffy eyes, and her assistant applied color-correcting primer and concealer where needed.

Germaine's look, though painstakingly done, is effortless; the makeup is like a natural second skin, and her eyes are bright and ever-so-subtly lined to create a lifted look so unlike the thick kohl the 3AM Girls used to be famous for.

Germaine's headdress is interwoven with feathers that crown either side of her head, sewn to a gossamer fingertip veil that's so thin it's nearly invisible. Her gown is Dior, handmade in the Paris atelier; its fitted bodice gives way to yards of lightweight satin that ripple in the wind, overlayed with lucent gossamer that matches the veil. It isn't the dress of a princess, because she is no longer that, but of a queen—like Justin calls her.

She'd swept Marie into a big hug, even as the woman laughed and tried to push her off.

"Arrêt! You'll crease your dress!"

But as Germaine looks out over the sea of guests, she feels a tightness in her chest. She thought she'd moved past needing her parents' approval, but she's replaced them with everyone else. She's still trying too hard to keep up appearances. And she tried to learn her lesson about seeking forgiveness over revenge, she did, but she's overstepped Sicily's and Miranda's boundaries yet again. They didn't need Germaine to do the work for them. She should have told them about the *Kidz Klub* invites—or not invited that group at all.

For a brief moment, a part of her wishes that this was a wedding for thirty rather than three hundred, not about showing anyone up or proving anything. Just about happiness and love—for Justin, for her oldest friends, for her husband's lovely parents, and . . . well, yes. For her family as well.

She sighs and leans against the window casement. You can still love people, she thinks, even if they've let you down. Miranda is right: nothing can be settled, and nothing can be changed. Germaine's childhood is a crash that she can't walk back. God knows her parents can't change who they are; or, at least, she isn't the one who can change them. The only thing she can control is the way she reacts to their moods and internalizes their criticism. She can't change her mother or father, or even Gregoire or Giles, and it follows that she shouldn't try to punish them. She shouldn't try to punish Eddie, either. He was a stupid kid, and so was she, and maybe he has regrets now about how he acted ten years ago, when he should have known better—or maybe not. He's another person she can't change, and being spiteful will only hurt her—it's already hurt Miranda and Sicily.

All of that was then. This is now.

"Don't start," Marie hisses as Germaine's eyes begin to well again. "You'll make a mess of me, too." The stylist uses a Q-tip to dab the moisture away as Germaine fans herself and reapplies powder to Germaine as well as Sicily and Miranda, who stand nearby similarly trying to hold it together. Germaine glances at them, knowing they all look like the stunning women they are: Survivors. Victors. Girls who worked too hard and saw too much, too young, growing up in the public eye. They don't need to prove anything to anyone.

They catch her eye. She gives both a small smile, which they return.

She peers back out into the crowd. Her parents are about to take their seats in the front row. They both look unhappy, but Germaine knows by now that this is their default expression. They've been unhappy about one thing or another for as long as she can remember, and it's not her fault or responsibility.

"Susan," she whispers to the wedding coordinator. "Would you be able to bring my parents back here?"

Susan raises her eyebrows, surprised by the last-minute change in what has otherwise been an airtight itinerary that could only be crafted by a St. Germaine-Chang, but she nods and hurries off. Germaine peeks through the window to watch as she approaches Terence and Céline and speaks low to them, pointing backward. They look confused and slightly suspicious, but follow her back to the entrance of the hotel.

Germaine takes a deep, steadying breath before they walk in. Then she greets them with a big smile.

"Hi," she says to their questioning looks. "Would you two walk me down the aisle?"

They glance at each other. Then her father nods and says, "Of course."

To Germaine's surprise, he seems relieved. Her mother stops frowning, the skin between her eyebrows relaxing and her chin lifting, and straightens up. Céline always did love a catwalk, Germaine thinks.

Susan gives the signal that it's time. A string quartet next to the arbor begins to play Handel's "Air" from *Water Music*, and the bridal party heads up the aisle, beginning with Germaine's cousins and friends from New York and ending with Sicily and Miranda, who both squeeze Germaine's hand and give her a wave.

With a surreal, warm feeling in her chest and her heart racing, Germaine links arms with both her parents and moves into position. Her father coughs; are those tears in his eyes?

Her mother glances down at her dress.

"Couture Dior," she murmurs, and Germaine feels herself instinctively bracing for criticism. But Céline gives the smallest of smiles and says, "I would expect nothing less."

Then they step out, toward a beaming Justin and the next glittering chapter in Germaine's life.

TWENTY-SIX

SICILY

2028

Sicily has always been good at compartments. Her life has been a box made up of separate rooms where she keeps the different parts of herself. Stage Sicily is strong, sexy, audacious—an icon. Media Sicily is sparkling and intelligent; she's relatable enough to appeal to the masses but has learned how to stay one step ahead of the interviewers and magazine editors. She knows they still underestimate her. And Home Sicily likes to nest, to work on craft projects or ride bikes or play pool volleyball with her kids. She makes up gift baskets for local LA charities every Christmas and travels to war zones at Easter and Thanksgiving to perform for the troops. Maybe that's why she's had so much trouble finding a good romantic partner—the men are attracted to Stage Sicily like a magnet and follow Media Sicily's appearances, thinking they know her. But then they wake up with softhearted, real, regular Home Sicily, whose normal human imperfection is hard to reconcile with the others. They can't love her for who she really is.

She thought Kent was different—he seemed to understand the compartments, working as long as he has in the industry. Sicily really likes him; in fact, she's told herself she's in love with him, but in her heart of hearts, she knows that romance doesn't last forever. Relationships need something solid to keep them going and growing. And now that Sicily is a little older and a little wiser, she knows something for sure: no one who's been a dick to one of her dearest friends is a man worthy of her love.

The thoughts circulate in her mind all throughout Germaine's wedding ceremony, but somehow they make her feel even more present and grateful for her friends. They're so important to her. While others have drifted in and out of her life, they have remained constant, loving her and supporting her through all her bad times and missteps. Sure, both Miranda and Germaine have made mistakes of their own. But you're not going to know someone for nearly your entire life without accidentally hurting them at least once.

A coordinated cloud of native butterflies is released as the officiant recites the final line of the ceremony, and everyone cheers as Germaine and Justin share a sweet kiss. Sicily's heart lurches to see the joy and tears in her friend's eyes, and she knows in that instant that they will last a very long time.

Everyone moves to the grand banquet hall with cathedral ceilings and sprays of tea roses, dahlias, gardenias, gladiolas, and sea grasses mixed with rosemary that spill over each carefully set table and perfume the space. Every place card has been written by hand in flourishing calligraphy and set next to a personalized gift box that contains Belgian chocolates, beeswax candles, and signature scents for each guest. The high-arched windows behind the head table look out over the western horizon of the sea, so the wedding party will be bathed in gold light as the sun sets. They will almost be too radiant to see.

Sicily wonders, in the back of her mind, whether this was also part of Germaine's master plan. But perhaps it's just a coincidence.

Sicily and Miranda take seats to the left of the center after their grand entrance and cheer on Germaine and Justin, who have learned a bit of ballroom-salsa choreography and move fluidly, confidently, in front of the crowd before continuing to the head table, performing like stars but somehow wrapped up only in each other at the same time. Germaine has changed into a scarlet qipao with gold hand embroidery for the reception, and she looks positively on fire in the sunset light. Her long hair is secured elegantly in a french twist that would have made Audrey Hepburn envious.

Miranda is in the seat closer to Germaine, but Germaine leans over and squeezes both her and Sicily's hands when she sits. Sicily gives her as big of a smile as she can, trying to communicate that it's okay.

She can't focus on anything else besides how fantastic all the details of this wedding are, anyway, and how much fun it is. The DJ starts with classy swing jazz while they eat—a menu of incredible culinary feats, from oysters with Yukari mignonette with finger lime and chives, to braised Wagyu beef with celery root gratin Dauphinois, to Ōra King salmon with black trumpet mushrooms and beluga lentils—and then moves to nostalgic hits and throwbacks from their teenage years as the dance floor opens. There's a constant stream of champagne as waiters roam about the room, bearing trays of glass flutes and small bites of sturgeon caviar, mini tamagoyaki, and puff pastry filled with baked pear, pomegranate, and brie.

Germaine has decided to eschew speeches; she told Sicily and Miranda earlier that she wanted to keep things light and "casual," as casual as an event with bespoke pyrotechnics outside the banquet hall windows during her and Justin's first dance can be.

Desserts of tarte citron and bittersweet chocolate-custard profiterole are served, along with slices from a towering cake of chocolate tahini and rosemary buttercream.

From his table down on the floor, Kent catches Sicily's eye and raises his brows as if to say, *This is off the charts.* She smiles and nods back. Germaine knows how to throw a party.

"I hear we have some celebrities in this star-studded crowd," the DJ booms. "Let's get all you Kidz Klubbers out on the floor! I *know* y'all want to take a photo for those socials!"

Miranda shoots Sicily a look, but Sicily shrugs. She's feeling a lot better now that everything's out in the open. So Miranda follows her down to the floor, where the others are gathering.

Sicily feels a hand on her arm, and she turns to find Germaine.

"Hey," Germaine whispers. "You don't have to do anything you don't want to."

"It's okay." Sicily smiles. "Really."

And it is. She's gotten everything off her chest, and these people don't have any power over her anymore—not the girls who used to be catty to her at rehearsals, not her family, and not even Tyler X, who's already looking a bit bloated from all the rich food, rubbing his stomach with a grimace as he limps up for the photo.

"Everyone say 'Treat You Right'!" the photographer shouts as the theme song plays in the background. Germaine pulls Miranda and Sicily close and kisses them both on the cheek as the photos snap. Sicily squeezes her once before letting go.

The music swerves into pop and hip-hop as "Treat You Right" fades out and the crowd disperses.

"Hey, Sicily," a voice says behind her. She turns to find Tyler, scratching his five-o'clock shadow. Behind him, Miranda pauses, seeming to ask Sicily whether she should tackle him. But Sicily gives a slight shake of her head.

"Hey, Tyler," she says. "How are you?"

"Not too bad," he says. "I mean, I've been worse. How are you doing? Been a long time."

"It has." Sicily crosses her arms and looks him up and down. He looks tired, and more than a little out of place. He doesn't have the energy of the other *Kidz Klub* people, who are either peacocking around to network or having genuine fun catching up with each other. Tyler looks like someone who gave up on trying to prove himself a long time ago. His suit doesn't fit quite right, and his shoulders are hunched. "I'm good, Tyler. I'm doing well."

"That's good. Congrats on everything, you know. It seems like you've done really well for yourself."

"Yeah." Sicily nods. "It turned out okay in the end."

Tyler nods back. "Some party, huh?"

"A signature Germaine rager."

"It is. I should mix some more throwback hits into my Ozarks emcee playlist." He looks around, craning his neck at the high ceiling and the flowers. Sicily realizes that the awe on his face is mixed with sadness, and in that moment she feels a little sorry for him. Of all of them, he's the one who's fallen the farthest from the glittering life they were promised as kids. And while most of his mistakes were his own, Tyler, Sicily, and the others were all cut from the same exploitive cloth that told them they needed to be entertaining and provocative to have any worth.

"I think people would really like that," she says. Then she pats him on the shoulder and walks away, both from Tyler and all the harm he caused.

∼

The rest of the reception is a blast. Sicily and Miranda dance with Germaine, belting their favorite songs and laughing during the "Macarena." "So Bad, So Good" comes on, and they push Sicily into the spotlight, where the crowd goes wild as she lip-synchs to her own song. And when the music turns to a slow jam, Kent finds her again and asks her for a dance.

"Of course," she says, but she knows the hesitancy is written on her face. He puts his arm around her waist and leads her back onto the dance floor as the lights dim, but she has a hard time looking at him. Even more so when she catches Miranda slipping away from the floor.

"Hey," Kent says. "Is everything okay?"

Sicily sighs and drops his hand. "Actually, no. I'm sorry—could we talk?"

"Of course."

The french doors of the banquet hall have been opened to the gardens beyond, and Sicily leads Kent past the other guests who are milling about. Cozy candlelit nooks have been set up among the palms and hibiscus trees—Germaine has thought of every last detail to ensure her guests' comfort. Everything is in the best possible taste, with cushioned bistro chairs tucked behind curtains of honeysuckle.

Sicily and Kent sit, he with a nervous expression on his face. But Sicily feels calm.

"Miranda mentioned that many years ago," she begins, "she overheard you say something very hurtful about her."

Kent drops his head and gives a deep sigh.

"I know it's been two decades," she continues, lacing her fingers together. "But it caused a lot of damage to her. And, Kent . . ."

He lifts his head and looks her in the eyes, as if he knows what she's going to say.

". . . you know how much I like you. I think things have been going really well. But . . . my loyalty has to be to my friends, first and foremost. We've been through so much together—and too much apart. I've let my relationships come before them in the past. But I've learned that from this point forward, I don't want anything to come between them and me."

Kent is quiet a moment. Then he sighs and says, "I was always worried that she heard. It was one of a million shitty things I said to or about young actresses in those days. I remember, though—she was so excited about the part at the beginning of that meeting, but when she came back after using the bathroom, she seemed upset. None of us addressed it. And when I heard about the DUI later . . ." He rubs his hands over his face. "I felt like a complete asshole. It was her birthday, for god's sake. She was still a kid. It was the first time I saw the direct consequences."

Sicily nods. "She was still a kid, yes."

"Sicily, I want you to know I own this. There's no excuse," Kent says. "I was an awful person back then. Acting like the big man, swaggering around—it's how all the agents behaved. Even hers, when she wasn't in the room. Definitely an old-boys club. It's one of the main reasons my first marriage didn't work out, and also why I ended up leaving that agency—the whole thing needed to be burned down and rebuilt from the ground up."

"That doesn't surprise me," Sicily murmurs.

"When you introduced me to Miranda yesterday, I wanted to apologize to her the second I realized who she was. But I was never sure if she *did* hear, and I thought it might be presumptuous to assume she even remembered me. I didn't want to be the one putting her in an awkward position. But if she does remember . . ."

He trails off, looking pained.

"I understand," Sicily says gently. "But I do think an apology is a good idea."

"Do you think she would forgive me? I don't really feel like I deserve it." Then Kent looks at Sicily, sadness in his eyes. "Could *you* ever forgive me?"

She looks at him carefully. A breeze blows through the garden, carrying with it the music and sounds of the party. She knows what acting is, and she's been played and lied to by so many people in her life, from her romantic partners to her own flesh and blood. But there is real remorse in Kent's face. He seems to have already resigned himself to the fact that he may lose her.

"Miranda says we need to forgive ourselves and each other. Forgive the world for what it's put us through." Sicily takes a deep breath. "So maybe the three of us could talk next week? I think she would appreciate hearing what you just told me."

"I would like that," Kent says.

Sicily feels a weight begin to lift.

TWENTY-SEVEN

MIRANDA

2028

In the banquet hall, Germaine has donned the DJ's headphones and commandeered the turntables to uproarious applause. Miranda cheers along with the crowd as Germaine spins the records, totally engrossed in adjusting the bass and mixing one song then the next, jumping back and forth between tracks with the ease of a concert pianist.

Susan has turned the lights all the way down and the disco ball up, throwing glittering spotlights everywhere and bathing the hall in laser lights. Miranda takes to the floor like a pro, as comfortable here as she is at her club in Cyprus, feeling like a better, relaxed, and somehow more energetic version of her teenage self.

And she's bursting with pride for Germaine—despite the hiccups, this wedding has been so joyful. Even Germaine's irritating brothers are on the dance floor, doing the cancan with each other and bouncing around like goofballs. Her parents do a graceful two-step, and Tyler X taps his foot in the corner, hands in his pockets.

And Sicily—wow. Here she is, coming back through the garden doors, Kent nowhere in sight. Instead of clinging to her latest man like she usually would, she seems comfortable without him, at ease in her own skin.

"Where's Kent?" Miranda asks as Sicily finds her in the crowd.

"I sent him home to LA," Sicily says over the music.

"What? Really?"

Sicily nods. "I talked to him about what happened. He'd like to apologize to you, face-to-face. I told him maybe the three of us could talk sometime—but tonight's not about Kent. We should just be having fun."

Miranda has to admit she's surprised. "Thanks, Sis. That would be really nice."

"It's the least I can do. But for now the past can wait!" She swings Miranda around in a spin.

"The past can wait!" Miranda agrees, laughing. One of Germaine's cousins from the bridal party starts a dance circle, and Sicily hops into it, amazingly carefree.

But Miranda still feels something holding her back. There's a tugging like a loose thread, like an idea she's forgotten. It's not because Germaine and Justin seem so happy. It's something from the past that actually can't wait.

She takes one step backward, then another, making her way back through the hall and past the dessert table and bar before she fully realizes where her feet are taking her. But soon she finds herself outside the hotel, in the grand circular drive, where a driver is leaning against a limo, on call in case any of the guests need chauffeuring.

"Zane," she says.

He looks up, startled at first, and then a little sheepish. "Miranda," he says, straightening up and brushing nonexistent dirt off the sleeve of his driver's uniform. "Hey."

"You should be in there with the rest of us," she says.

Zane rubs the back of his neck and shrugs. "I'm more comfortable out here these days anyway. Sounds like quite the party, though."

Miranda folds her arms across her chest, looks down at her feet, and spits it out: "Germaine hired you to teach you a lesson. To show you how good I'm doing, rub it in your face or whatever. I already gave her a piece of my mind about it. I'm sorry."

"That sounds like her," Zane says with a chuckle. "I was surprised when she contacted my company, and even more so when she specifically requested me to drive. But I thought she was just being nice—reaching out to throw me a bone after all these years. I didn't think about the implications until I started recognizing people I used to do two-hundred-dollar shots with. That really puts your ego in place."

"You don't usually drive?"

"My friend and I finally got our business off the ground." Zane nods. "We co-own the limo service. But I do drive whenever we're shorthanded."

"You did it!" Miranda raises her eyebrows. "Zane. That's pretty impressive."

"Thanks. It's nowhere near the kind of money I used to make doing literally nothing, but it's decent pay by regular-people standards. And it's ours." Zane smiles, then looks down and nudges a piece of gravel with the toe of his shoe. "So . . . *are* you doing good?"

Miranda hesitates, thinking of how short a drive downtown Los Angeles is from here, but how very far her old life in Hollywood feels from the spot where she now stands. "Yeah. I would say that I am." And before she can overthink it, she adds, "I've missed you, though."

"You too," he says. "I hear you're an expat now."

"Yeah. Cyprus has a similar climate to LA, but I like it better, somehow." She laughs. "Have you ever been?"

Zane shakes his head. "I bet they've got great windsurfing, though. That and scuba diving—those are my new things these days. If I could do it all over again, I think I would've gone to school for marine biology."

"The water's the cleanest in the Mediterranean," she says. "Blue and perfect—you'd love it."

"I'm sure I would." He takes his hand out of his pocket to rub his chin, and Miranda catches a band of gold on his finger. She feels a slight pressure in her chest.

"You got married?" she asks.

"What? Oh." He looks at the ring and sighs. "No, it's my dad's. I just like to keep something of him around."

"Oh. I'm sorry." Miranda shakes her head. "He passed? I didn't realize."

"Yeah, it all just caught up with him. He wasn't the healthiest guy. They wrote a little blurb about it in *Rolling Stone*, but it was a small family funeral—he might not have preferred it that way, but I did."

"I'm really sorry, Zane." Miranda wants to reach out and touch him, but she keeps her arms crossed awkwardly, unable for one reason or another to step forward. "I know you were close."

"Thanks, Miranda."

"So peanut butter cup girl didn't work out, huh?" she asks.

"Who?" He frowns for a moment, then laughs. "Wait—Chrissy? I can't believe you remember that. Nah. She wasn't looking for anything serious; I kind of was . . . She wanted to stay in LA; I wanted to travel . . . We were too different. Plus, those organic peanut butter cups got expensive."

Miranda laughs. "Gotta stick to Reese's."

"Isn't that the truth." He fiddles with the ring. "What about you? Got some hot Turkish bouncer waiting for you back in Cyprus?"

"No. Not yet." She chuckles, but there's a quiet tension between them, a kind of sadness. The twenty-odd years they've spent apart create what feels like an impassable space between them. Maybe, Miranda thinks, Zane should have been the love of her life, after all.

"I hope you give yourself enough credit, too," Zane says, breaking the silence. "For building a business, you know. I overhear people raving about it when I'm driving them around Beverly Hills. Classy atmosphere, the best hidden gem, unparalleled views of the sea. It sounds perfect." He seems a little wistful. "You were always capable of anything you set your mind to."

"Oh, come on." It's Miranda's turn to be sheepish. "You know that's not true. I pretty much bombed my own chances of a movie career, I've embarrassed myself in front of the whole world, I'm not famous anymore . . ."

Zane has a small, bemused smile on his face. "You need to be happy," he says. "Being famous again—would that make you happier?"

Miranda shrugs. But she knows it wouldn't.

They both look down the drive, watching the sky sink from indigo to navy blue over the hills in the distance. They've drawn closer to each other, Miranda realizes, though she isn't sure who made the first move.

"Hey," she says. "What are your summers like? You should work at my club in Cyprus."

Zane laughs. "Oh, come on."

"No, really. I've been meaning to expand beyond the kayaking and parasailing we offer. If you have your scuba certification and you're willing to get some teacher training . . . you might just be the man for the job."

"I could do that," he says, thoughtful. "We've been wanting to promote one of our drivers to assistant manager—he's a good guy. He could handle it. And, I mean . . ." He looks her full in the face, eyes bright. "I would *love* that."

"Good. Then it's settled."

"Look at us." Zane shakes his head with a rueful smile. "Two adults with their own businesses, making their way in the world. Now we've both grown up."

Something in Miranda shivers; an old feeling that she thought was long lost begins to come back. She smiles. "I used to think I'd hate getting older. But I'm glad we're not kids anymore—we can be happy on our own terms. Run our own lives. Not care about what other people think."

"Thank god." Zane laughs. Then, in a way that feels sudden and yet perfectly natural, he opens his arms and pulls her in for a hug. Miranda presses her cheek briefly to his shoulder; it feels so good to see him again. Germaine may have invited him here for all the wrong reasons, but Miranda's thankful for it. Without Germaine, she and Zane might never have crossed paths.

Now they can be friends again. Maybe something more.

"Get back to that party," Zane says. "I know you're a guest of honor."

"We'll talk, though, okay?" she says. This time, she means it.

He smiles. "We'll talk."

She practically floats up the steps, feeling a lightness that's been long absent. Music echoes through the warm night and, inside, the dance floor is vibrant and alive. For the first time, Miranda realizes she has made peace not only with Zane but also with the girl she used to be—someone who lived only for the moment. Someone who was afraid of the future, maybe, because she wasn't sure she had one.

Now the future is here, colorful, beautiful, loud. And Miranda knows the best is yet to come.

At the bar she bumps into Tyler X, red faced and sweaty from dancing.

"Hey, Miranda," he shouts over the music. "I was thinking. I've had a lot of event experience, and I was wondering if you need any extra hands on deck at your club?"

Miranda smiles sweetly and shakes her head. "No!" she shouts back.

And then she walks away. Zane is one thing, but Tyler? Come on! Miranda doesn't have *endless* patience. She isn't the Mother Teresa of reformed starlets.

In the ladies' bathroom, high on the heady joy of the party and the promise of all the life she has yet to live, Miranda wriggles out of her underwear and drops them in the trash. Her skirt is so long that no one will notice. Only she will know.

And Sicily and Germaine, when she whispers it to them.

3AM Girls forever!

ACKNOWLEDGMENTS

A huge star-studded glowing-Hollywood-sign venti-size thank-you to my amazing editor, Carmen Johnson at Amazon, and my agent, Richard Abate at 3Arts, for believing in this book! Thank you to everyone at Amazon Publishing. Thank you to my friends and family and my loyal readers. MWAH!

ABOUT THE AUTHOR

Photo © 2019 Maria Cina

Melissa de la Cruz is the #1 *New York Times*, #1 *Publishers Weekly*, and #1 IndieBound bestselling author of many critically acclaimed and award-winning novels for readers of all ages. Many of her more than seventy books have also topped *USA Today*, *Wall Street Journal*, and *Los Angeles Times* bestseller lists and have been published in over twenty countries. She lives in West Hollywood with her husband and daughter. For more information, visit www.melissa-delacruz.com.